P9-DEL-266

DAN UNMASKED

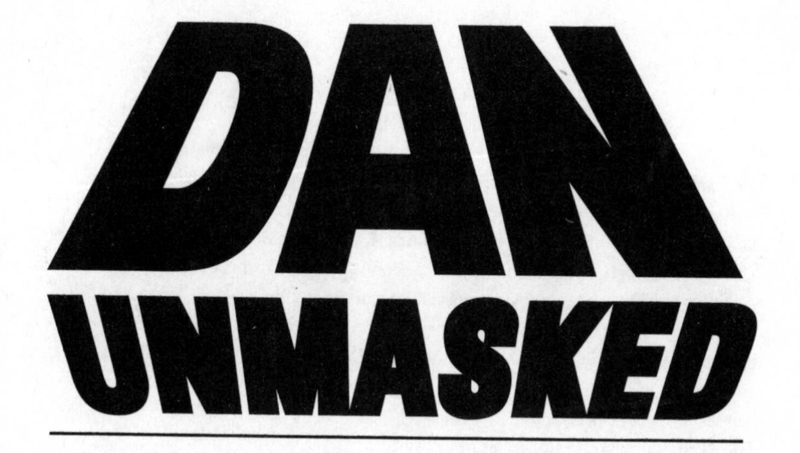

CHRIS NEGRON

HARPER
An Imprint of HarperCollins*Publishers*

Dan Unmasked

For information address HarperCollins Children's Books, a division of HarperCollins Publishers, 195 Broadway, New York, NY 10007.
www.harpercollinschildrens.com

Library of Congress Cataloging-in-Publication Data

Names: Negron, Chris, author.
Title: Dan, unmasked / Chris Negron.
Description: First edition. | New York : HarperCollins, [2020] | Audience: Grades 4–6. | Summary: Thirteen-year-old Dan blames himself when his best friend Nate is hit in the head by a baseball during practice—desperate to help, Dan seizes on the suggestion that even in a coma Nate may be able to hear him, and sets out to read to Nate from the superhero comic books that both boys love.
Identifiers: LCCN 2019026616 | ISBN 978-0-06-294305-7 (hardcover)
Subjects: LCSH: Coma—Patients—Juvenile fiction. | Comic books, strips, etc.—Juvenile fiction. | Guilt in adolescence—Juvenile fiction. | Responsibility—Juvenile fiction. | Best friends—Juvenile fiction. | CYAC: Coma—Fiction. | Cartoons and comics—Fiction. | Guilt—Fiction. | Responsibility—Fiction. | Best friends—Fiction. | Friendship—Fiction.
Classification: LCC PZ7.1.N396 Dan 2020 | DDC 813.6 [Fic]—dc23
LC record available at https://lccn.loc.gov/2019026616

Typography by Chris Kwon
20 21 22 23 24 PC/LSCH 10 9 8 7 6 5 4 3 2 1
❖
First Edition

For Mary

- 1 -

I almost miss it.

I can't stop staring at the base runner in front of me, with his bright white cleats and his too-big batting gloves. He's dancing off second base, clapping dust off those clown hands, shouting out nonsense. Jumping from one foot to the other.

All that fidgeting has drawn me in so deep I almost miss it: my best friend, Nate, sending me a secret message from the pitching mound.

See, me and Nate, we have this sort of superpower, a kind of telepathy, but just with each other. We're always talking. Even when we're not.

Like right now. From shortstop I get ready for Nate's

next pitch. He stares in hard at the catcher's signs. The lefty at the plate gulps. Parents in the stands cheer.

And Nate, he's not even looking my way, but he's talking to me all right.

It's the way he's spinning the ball in his fingers, the way his glove, normally resting on his knee, dangles off his wrist. Nate's telling me he knows all about the kid darting between second and third like his toes are on fire.

Nate starts his motion. He sneaks a peek back at me. My feet twist into the dirt. I run the sleeve of my Mira Giants jersey across my nostrils.

I know Mom must be wincing in the stands. She's been begging me to stop wiping snot on my sleeve since I was five. But today, eight years later, my nose is dry. I only did that to let Nate know I got his message, loud and clear.

When nobody else is looking, Nate and I have a secret signal, proof our telepathy is working. We tap our noses with one finger. Right now, though, half of Mira is here watching this game. Not to mention the fidgety kid's coach over at third. I can't be so obvious.

Nose-on-sleeve it is. Mom can roll her eyes all she wants.

Nate's as cool as ice. He doesn't nod. He doesn't smile. He doesn't even blink. My best friend looks back at the catcher. His shoulders relax.

As soon as the kid leaps toward third again, I take off, straight for second base. Nate steps back off the rubber and whirls around. I catch a hint of panic in the runner's eyes as he realizes he's been caught leaning. His cleats kick up loose dirt. He stumbles.

I twist my body and lower my glove. I reach the base just as the kid starts an off-balance slide. Nate's perfect throw smacks into my glove, right in front of the bag, and all I have to do is squeeze it.

The ump crouches down, peering at my glove. I raise it, proving the ball's in the pocket. I'm already jumping into Nate and heading for the dugout when the ump thrusts his closed fist into the air.

"Out!"

Somehow Nate's little brother, Ollie, beats us to the bench from way up in the bleachers at the end of each game, especially big wins like this one. He always looks the same: goofy grin on his face, giant, binocular-like glasses over his eyes, one arm pressing his prized sketchbook tight to his chest. As usual, his other hand is open and raised. None of us forgets, after reaching up to high-five Coach Wiggins, to bend down to tap Ollie's waiting palm, too.

"Dude, where do you come from?" Jake McReynolds, our third baseman, asks. He uses both hands to mess up Ollie's hair. Nate's little brother frantically tries to put it back into place.

"It's his superpower," catcher Kurt Martinez says. He

unbuckles his chest protector, shakes it off, and stows it under the bench. "Teleportation." This is a game we've been playing since I moved to Mira a few years back and joined the Giants, since I discovered my new teammates were almost as crazy about comics as I am. One of us starts to describe superpowers, and the first one to yell out the matching hero wins. "But where's your brimstone—"

"Nightcrawler!" I shout, and Nate does, too, but just after me. Frustrated, he chucks his glove against the fence. It's pretty hard to beat me in the name—the—superhero game.

I make a game-show-wrong-answer buzzing sound. "So sorry, Templeton."

"Too slow," Kurt and Jake say together.

"You and your thousand comics," Nate complains. "I almost had you."

"Hey, Dan, tomorrow's Wednesday. *Captain Nexus* comes out," Ollie shouts toward me. He reaches between the pages of his sketchbook, and I catch a glimpse of one of his drawings. The kicking leg of a pitcher—who else but his hero Nate?—seems unrealistically high, but Ollie snaps the book shut before I spy any more details. He pulls out #13, the one with Spark on the cover shooting lightning bolts toward the Hollow. His issue's not even bagged.

"What are you doing?!" I ask.

Ollie's eyes go wide. "What?"

"You don't bring a comic to a dugout. There's dirt

everywhere." I swear, Ollie's only a year younger than us but sometimes he acts like he's still in elementary school.

"Look!" Sally, our first baseman and the biggest kid on the team, shouts as he points at me. "Dan's eye is twitching. Have you started vacuum-sealing your comics yet, Summers?"

"Oh, there's an infectious disease lab at the CDC that's vacuum—" Kurt starts.

"Oh my God, Martinez," Sally breaks in. "Give it a rest." Kurt's a huge germophobe. His constant Purell use and crazy trivia about diseases always bother Sally first.

Nate raises his voice above everyone else. "Hey, Ollie's right. Number fourteen tomorrow. Focus." He looks down at his brother, and Ollie beams back at him. "All set for your group read?"

"Mom got the pretzels," Ollie says, nodding.

"Because you can't read a comic without pretzels," I say, then roll my eyes at Nate.

Ollie's talking like I don't know tomorrow's a *Captain Nexus* Wednesday. We've all been on pins and needles for weeks now, wishing #14 could somehow hit the shelves early. All Nate does, though, is shrug. It even takes him a second to tap his nose. I know it's because he doesn't like me picking on Ollie. Wish he would defend me like that when the other Giants mock me for taking care of my comics. Whatever, like it's a crime.

And the truth is, Ollie's the one who told us about *Captain Nexus* in the first place. Even the group read was his idea: Nate always calls it "Ollie's group read" like he doesn't want us to forget his brother invented it. Reading with half the team in Nate's basement is fun, sure, but sometimes I kind of wish Nate and I could just enjoy the new issues on our own.

Coach finishes talking to some parents and swings down into the dugout. He claps his hands to get our attention.

"Okay, Giants!" He points toward the parking lot, where most of our moms and dads are on the way to their cars. "You know the drill. DiNunzio's! We need to talk tournament."

The Giants throw our gloves into the air and hoot. After we collect the rest of our equipment, we rush after our parents. There's no time to lose when pizza's waiting.

- 2 -

Mom takes her phone out of her purse and shows me the alarm screen. "Nine thirty, right?"

"Mom. That alarm isn't even on." I twist in the passenger seat of the minivan, snatch the phone from her hand, and swipe the bar to green.

Mom's really bad with time. When she's in her office working on a report, she thinks ten minutes have gone by when it's really been a couple of hours. Lately she's been letting me set alarms on her phone as reminders. The results have been mixed.

"Your dad'll be here," she says in front of DiNunzio's, her face lit up by the green-and-red flashing neon sign in the restaurant's window. *Hot!!! Pizza!!! Hot!!! Pizza!!!*

We're in the parking lot. The rest of the team's already inside. I hand her phone back and try not to let doubt show on my face. My father's a big-shot architect. Right now he's working on a huge project to restore some old building downtown, in Buffalo. It was his favorite building growing up, the whole reason he studied architecture in the first place. *The chance of a lifetime*, he'd said when his firm landed the job.

It sounded great until I realized what it really meant. Lately Dad's *always* stuck at work, weekends even. This morning I'd asked him to pick me up after pizza and he'd promised he would. Then again, he's been promising to come to our games all summer, too, and he hasn't made it to a single one yet.

"Listen," Mom says, "if Coach orders a spinach—"

I cover my ears and cluck out *I'm not listening* noises. Mom does food inspections for the county. She has all these horror stories about every restaurant in Mira, but she's not allowed to ruin my favorites, like DiNunzio's.

"Don't let Dad forget," I say as I open the door.

Mom grabs my arm before I can escape. "Hey! Congratulations again! The tournament!"

"Thanks, Mom."

As I step out onto the pavement, she blurts out, "Don't eat the spinach!"

I sigh. Really, who eats spinach on pizza, anyway?

• • •

Coach always buys so many pies that probably all twelve of us could each eat a whole one and we'd still end up with leftovers. Nobody would ever go near the disgusting anchovy and pineapple he orders for himself, though. One time Greg Dravecky touched it by accident, and the team gave him the silent treatment the entire next practice, like in the major leagues when a rookie gets his first hit and the bench ignores him on purpose.

"Stand back!" Nate shouts tonight when Coach's weird pizza lands on the table with a heavy thud. He extends his arms, protecting the rest of us from certain death, then smirks at me. "Watch out, Dan, I think it's moving."

"It's the crawling pie!" I shout.

Hands flying across the table, the whole team grabs slices, eager for a pepperoni. Sausage. Anything but anchovy and pineapple. Kurt snags the biggest piece of the meat lovers, then turns his head to dig into his pack for his hand sanitizer. Nate reaches around and steals his slice, grinning at me while the crime is still in progress. I tap my nose.

"Hey!" Kurt cries when he looks back at his empty plate. Nate's already darting around the table with his plate over his head, the grease from the huge slice dripping off the dangling tip.

"All right!" Coach stands up at the head of the table. We quiet down. "Hey, you guys were awesome today! Like the Amazing Super . . . Team . . . Friends!" I swear, of everybody on the planet, Coach could set the record for knowing the absolute least about superheroes and comics. It's so weird that he's *our* coach.

I open my mouth, but Nate leans toward me. "Just let it go, man."

"Listen up, people," Coach continues. "Before I lose you to pizza hangovers, a tiny bit of housekeeping. Next practice is Saturday morning. Tournament starts in two weeks!"

Coach tries to talk some more about the practice schedule, but we're all too busy high-fiving and fist-bumping. Getting into the Western New York Double Elimination tournament used to be just a dream. No team from tiny little Mira had ever done it before.

But today the Giants did it, all thanks to Nate's incredible pitching.

Outside I spend a minute searching for Dad's Volvo before hearing Kurt say, "Hey, Mrs. Summers." That's when I notice it's Mom waiting for me in the minivan instead.

"I'm on time, at least," she says defensively when I open the door.

"Where's Dad?"

"Stuck at work." She watches me buckle in. "He said to tell you congratulations."

I nod. My glove is on the floor where I left it. Feels like

I need to be doing something with my hands, so I pick it up and start to run both thumbs over the stitched decal.

"Hey," Mom says, reaching out to turn my chin toward her. "Your dad's just busy right now. It's a big project."

I force a smile. "Yeah, I know."

"Come on." She thrusts the van into reverse. "I bought ice cream sandwiches. We need to continue this celebration." She slaps her own knee. "The tournament!" Then Mom howls like a wolf, one of her go-to celebrations. I join in, our little pack of two.

- 3 -

Sometimes I wish I'd gone with the short comic boxes instead of the long ones. Okay, you can't fit as many comics in them, but at least they're easier to move around.

"You could help, you know," I grunt at Nate. I'm on my knees, struggling to pull a heavy long box out of my closet. The white cardboard full of bagged and boarded issues drops to the rug with a thump.

"And you could hurry up," Nate says from my desk chair. He lifts his feet and spins around once while flipping a baseball from one hand to the other.

"Don't rush me. If I get agitated, the gamma rays turn me big and—"

"The Hulk!" he shouts.

I shake my head. "Too easy. *Big* and *furry* and *orange*. And those are the only clues you're getting."

He snaps his fingers as I flip up the cardboard lid. "I know this one," Nate murmurs. "What's his name?"

I start to hum the Final Jeopardy tune. I've got the right box. My *Alpha Flight* collection is here, which is what made me think of that particular hero. Some guy in dirty coveralls sold me the first twenty-four issues of the original series for a song—Dad's expression—at the Walden flea market last summer. That was back when Dad and I used to go every Saturday, hunting for bargains. Now it seems like there's never enough time.

These days I spend my Saturdays with Nate instead, except when the Templeton family has to attend some Ollie event. It feels like Ollie enters everything, like he's trying to prove I-don't-know-what to I-don't-know-who. It's like Mira isn't good enough for him. He's always heading out of town for a spelling bee, MATHCOUNTS, Junior Science Fair, whatever.

The worst day was last summer, when Mr. Templeton drove the boys to Toronto for that big comic convention, but I couldn't go because it was my uncle Marty's birthday. That Saturday, like all the other ones without Nate, rolled by in dreamy slow motion, my face buried in the pages of *Captain Nexus and the Nexus Five* back issues, cruising through the Nexus Zone alone.

"Sasquatch!" Nate cries before I get to the end of my tune.

"Bingo." I slide an issue out and show it to him. The orange, furry hero from Canada's greatest super team is front and center on the cover.

"So bring that one," he says. "The guys are gonna be at my house any minute." He sets the baseball back on my desk and leans forward, elbows on his knees. "They don't really care which one you pick, you know. They haven't read any of these old ones. Not like you."

Ollie's group read happens one Wednesday a month. We picked Nate's basement because it was the biggest. We need lots of room to devour the latest issue of the best comic ever, *Captain Nexus and the Nexus Five*, together. I always bring an older comic, too, from my ever-expanding collection of classics. I'm trying to educate the rest of the Giants, slowly but surely, on the greatest heroes and villains ever, though I'm pretty sure Captain Nexus and his enemy, the Hollow, now sit alone at the top of that list.

Whichever issue I bring, I let one of my teammates take it home. When he finishes reading, he passes it to the next guy. My only requirement is that the book comes back in the exact same condition. And I mean *exact*. No wrinkles or bends, no spine stressing. Once Kurt said the words "minor corner wear" together in the same sentence, and I think I might've fainted.

"They . . . don't . . . care?" I clutch at my chest like I'm having a heart attack, then make a big act of falling over backward. A second later, a pillow flies over my bed and drops right onto my face. Of course Nate's arcing toss was perfect.

"These are *comic books*," my muffled voice says through the pillow. I push it off my face. "They're where the *heroes* live. The people you turn to when you're in trouble."

"You're obsessed." I can't see my best friend anymore, but I hear my chair creak all the way around again, then squeak as he lifts his weight from it.

Nate comes around the bed and steps over me. He grabs the top issue of *Captain Nexus*, #14, just out today, off the stack of honor on my nightstand. The entire series is there. I can't bear to box them up yet.

He stares down at the cover. "Do you think it's true? About number sixteen being the last issue?"

I bolt up straight and fling my pillow past him onto the bed. "No way. There's too much story left."

"Yeah, but George Sanderson told Geeker.com—"

"That was so long ago. Besides, I'm not even convinced they really talked to him." I start counting off reasons on my fingers. "No one knows where he lives, how old he is, nothing. He's never given another interview, so who says he really gave that one?"

Nate sits down on my bed. "They wouldn't make it up, would they?"

"Well . . ." I'm about to answer, but I get distracted by #14's cover all over again. Captain Nexus cowers in front of a mysterious bright light. One of his gloves is missing. The curved *N* in the center of his gray shirt, surrounded by five dots like electrons spinning around the nucleus of an atom, is ripped, as if someone's raked their claws straight across the Nexus Five's logo. It's as awesome as it'd been on the counter display at Jackson Comics and Games earlier today, seconds before I paid for it.

Beneath the image, in stark white letters I admit I've traced my finger over more than once already today: *Written and drawn by George Sanderson*. I'm almost as big a fan of Captain Nexus's creator as the actual superhero. I just wish I knew more about him.

"Earth to Summers." Nate has one hand rolled into a fist, like he's speaking through a megaphone. He sets the comic back on my nightstand.

Mom shows up at my door. I didn't even hear the garage open. She's in the plain jeans and golf shirt she wears when she's on inspections—casual, so the restaurants don't see her coming. Her face is pale white, like she's just seen a ghost.

"Whatever you boys do, if you're in Brooksburgh,

never eat at Luigi's Meatball Emporium." She wipes sweat from her brow, leans against my doorframe, stares down at her sneakers.

I catch Nate's eyes and grin. "Right, Mom. You know, next time we're in Brooksburgh."

"On our own," Nate continues.

"Craving meatballs," I finish.

"The things I've seen," Mom mutters, shaking her head. "I need to lie down." She heads for her bedroom.

"Gonna take her a while to write *that* report." Nate laughs. "Now will you please pick a comic?"

"Fine, since you like Sasquatch so much." I slide the issue in my hand back into the box—it wasn't that good anyway—and thumb through the rest of my *Alpha Flights* until I find #10. Sasquatch's grimacing orange face takes up the whole cover. "This one is cool. It has the Super-Skrull in it. We haven't talked about him. He has all the powers of the Fantastic Four at once."

Nate gives me a flat look.

"At the same time!" I insist, shaking the issue in his face. "Strength, invisibility, flames, stretchiness."

"Perfect," Nate says. He pushes off my bed. "Come on, let's go. We're late."

I stand with him, reaching back to snag my copy of *Captain Nexus* #14 for the read.

"Tell me this. What's Green Lantern's greatest power?" he asks me as we start down the stairs.

"Duh. His ring."

"Nope. Willpower. If he didn't have willpower, Hal Jordan would never have been chosen to wear the ring at all."

I feel like I understand almost everything about Nate, but not the heroes he likes. Not all of them, anyway. I mean, he loves Captain Nexus as much as I do, but his other favorites are Batman, Hawkeye, those kinds of guys. Street fighters, a lot of them with no powers at all except for "training." And when he does like other heroes, it's not because of their cool green power rings, the ones that can create any amazing thing they can imagine.

Oh no, it's always because of something like . . . *willpower.*

Bor-ing.

It's like Nate doesn't get that their powers are what make the heroes super in the first place.

- 4 -

"Finally!" Sally cries as we stomp down into Nate's basement. He snaps open the little square of tape on his *Captain Nexus* with eager fingers.

Nate peers around. The ratty old recliner he always reads from sits empty in the middle of the room. Jake and Sally are on the couch, Kurt's at the pool table. That's where I usually stand too. It's hard for me to read *Captain Nexus* sitting down. Too exciting.

"Hold on, Sally," Nate says. "We gotta wait for Ollie."

"Forgot," Sally says. He presses his thumb down hard to reseal the tape. "And for the last time, my name's not—"

"Oh, your name's totally Sally," Jake snorts. Sally's name is actually Bobby Salazar, but Jake started calling him Sally last year and the nickname, which he hates, stuck.

"Where *is* he?" whines Kurt. "My hair's going gray."

I reach the pool table and set my comic on the green felt. I save the *Alpha Flight* underneath for later. No one cares about the old stuff until we finish reading *Captain Nexus.*

Kurt takes his hat off and bends his head toward me. "Give it to me straight, Summers."

"Dude, it's not the waiting turning you gray, it's that hand sanitizer. You're poisoning yourself. Better watch out, you'll turn super villain." I roll the cue ball at him. It runs across his fingers, hopping up and almost leaving the table.

"Ow," he cries, but he's smiling, and he flings it back in my direction. I lift my comics just in time. The white ball rattles in the pocket before popping out again.

"I think Ollie's friend is over," Nate says. "They've been working on some kind of math project. I'm sure he'll be down soon."

Sally's mouth drops open like Nate just suggested the '27 Yankees aren't the greatest team in baseball history. "Who does math in the summer?"

"On the day *Captain Nexus* comes out!" I agree.

"Ollie does," Nate answers, and the edge in his voice shuts us up.

We all know Nate protects Ollie because he's so small, because last year he started sixth and had some trouble adjusting to middle school. We know because, at one time or another, Nate's done the same for each of us. My best friend is big and athletic, and if the way the girls in our grade are starting to stare at him is any proof, good-looking. I mean, we all stalk the halls together trying to look cool, but Nate's the only one who actually pulls it off. He could be friends with just about any of the popular kids in school. But Nate sticks with us, stays loyal to the Giants, saving seats for us at lunch and on the bus. I don't know about the other guys, but it makes me feel almost as awesome as he is, and it's definitely what makes Nate Nate.

Kurt moans and runs his hand over his issue. Our catcher drops his head to the pool table. When he picks it up again, the plastic between his comic and his forehead makes a sticky noise as *Captain Nexus* tumbles away.

"Think fast," Nate says, winging a pretzel at Kurt's head.

Kurt reaches up and snags it. He catches everything. "You'll wear your arm out."

"No way. Nate never gets tired," Jake says. "We should try sending you out to the mound by yourself. You don't really need fielders, the way you strike everybody out."

Nate shifts. "You guys better stay ready. I can't do it by myself."

"I mean," Kurt says, sending the pretzel in a high arc back to Nate, "you already have, though, right?"

Nate's pitched two perfect games this year. In one, he fanned sixteen, leaving just a few grounders for the rest of us. In the other, he actually struck out every single hitter. It was the most amazing thing I'd ever seen. We talked about it nonstop for weeks.

If it were me who'd done that, I'd probably *still* be bragging. But sometimes it almost seems like Nate's embarrassed by how good he is. Like now. He doesn't respond to Kurt. Instead he pops the pretzel into his mouth. His elbow bumps his copy of *Captain Nexus* and it drops off the arm of his recliner. Fluorescent light glints off the plastic covering his issue as he hurries to pick it up again.

That cover. The Captain on his knees, shielding his eyes. I'm dying. What's that light? Why is the Captain afraid? He's never afraid.

"You guys think the Nexus Five might split up this issue?" I ask the group. If we can't read it, we can at least talk about it, and there's nothing I like talking about more than comics. Not even baseball.

"Split up? Why would they do that?" Sally asks. "The Hollow's still out there."

"Yeah, but that's a thing in comics sometimes. Teams break up," I say. "Right when the world needs them the most, too."

Nate grins. "And I bet you can give us the full list."

"Please don't," Sally says. "You're like a human spoiler, Summers."

I tilt the shiny plastic protecting the mysterious cover, trying to predict what might happen with the team next. Sally's right: I've reread every issue so many times, I can recite the entire series from memory.

Originally scientist Bruce Peters, Captain Nexus accidentally discovered the Nexus Zone in issue #1. He was sucked into it and became stranded. While he fought to survive in the harsh, unfamiliar terrain, Bruce's wife, Carol, and his best friend, Hugh, worked frantically to rebuild the Nexus Turbine, the machine responsible for opening the portal in the first place.

But when they finally used it to rescue Bruce, he didn't return alone.

A dark being came back with him. The Hollow emerged wide-eyed and manic, as if it had just been born. It escaped into the world, causing destruction and chaos everywhere it went.

The patched-together turbine exploded as Bruce rode the dark energy waves back to Earth, and he felt ripped in two, so weak he could hardly stand. The Nexus energy helped keep him alive, yes, but it did even more than that. Bruce's young son, Scott, and Bruce's sister Jessie were in the lab with Hugh and Carol the day the scientist came back. They were all exposed, and they each developed strange powers.

They became the Nexus Five.

Bruce, the team's leader, would be called Captain Nexus. Carol, the Blue Witch. Jessie, Spark. Hugh, the Red Flame—and young Scott came to be known as Nexus Boy. The team had spent over a year tracking down the Hollow, hoping to send the creature back to where it belonged.

"The Nexus Five'll never break up," Sally claims. "We'll still be meeting up one Wednesday a month when we're all ancient. Like, *forty*, even."

"Nope," a girl's voice says. Deep in discussion, we hadn't heard the basement door open. Ollie appears in front of us, that same teleportation magic. To his right, a girl I immediately recognize from his class stands straight as an arrow, her dark hair pulled into a tight ponytail, her jaw working a wad of gum so huge it bulges one cheek. She holds a wrinkled copy of *Captain Nexus and the Nexus Five* #14 in her hands, the cover torn. *Torn!*

Jake knocks over his bowl of pretzels and half of them spill across the coffee table. The rest of us totally get why he's so shocked.

A girl. At the read.

Kurt points an accusing finger at Ollie. "Told ya, man. *Nightcrawler.* But no brimstone *at all.*"

The girl keeps her eyes focused on Sally. "Haven't you

heard?" she says between chews. "*Captain Nexus* is only going sixteen issues. George Sanderson said that a long time ago." She tosses her tattered issue on the floor and tumbles down until she's lying flat on her stomach. One of the loose straps of her too-big overalls falls off a shoulder as she shimmies into position on the rug.

"You guys are reading it now, aren't you?" she asks. "I mean, I've already read it three times, but you know. I'll read it again." She flips her copy of #14 open aggressively. Another page tears. I cringe.

My stare transfers from her to Ollie. All of us are glaring at him now. He shifts on his feet. "Um . . . yeah. So, guys, this is Courtney."

- 5 -

Group-read night in the Templetons' basement has rules. *Strict* rules.

Rule One: No one reads before anyone else.
Rule Two: No one talks during the read.
Rule Three: We flip the pages together.
Rule Four: Discussion waits until everyone is finished and has had ten minutes to think about What Just Happened.

Ollie points these rules out to Courtney. They're written on white poster board, propped up in the corner. She cranes her neck. "Did you get that professionally printed?"

"Dan did it," Nate says with a proud smile, jabbing a thumb toward me. My whole body fills up, like I'm being inflated by helium, the extra air lifting my shoulders tall and straight.

The first night of the group read was crazy, everybody talking at once, so we came up with the rules. Most of them were my idea. Kurt's only contribution had been, "Everyone should use Purell before taking a pretzel." And Sally's suggestion to "get DiNunzio's every time" was rejected after I did a seven-minute presentation on the effect of pizza grease on an average comic-book page. I ended with, "Foxing and tanning are bad enough, but self-inflicted smudges? The worst."

"You're so weird, Summers," Sally had said. "What's foxing and tanning, anyway? Some kind of beach sport?"

"Whatever it is," Kurt had said, "it sounds gross." His Purell bottle made a burping sound as he squeezed out another big dose of slime.

Once we agreed on the rules, we decided to preserve them so we wouldn't forget, and Nate, who'd always been jealous of my handwriting, suggested I do the poster board. I worked super hard on it, spent tons of time with colored Sharpies making each letter perfect.

Now, in the basement, Courtney pushes to her feet. The girl clearly can't sit still. I hold my breath as she almost steps on her comic before she half skips over to the rules. She studies my work with her hands on her hips, then glances back at me. "So you do art?"

For some reason my voice sticks in my throat. "I mean, not real art."

"Yeah? And who decides what counts as 'real art'?" She smirks while making air quotes.

I'm not an artist. I know because my dad's a really good one, and I didn't get any of his talent. Still, all I do is shrug.

"Cool." Courtney bounces back to her spot and falls into position once more, nudging Ollie, who seems to be doing his best to avoid our gazes.

Nate shoots me a look, squinted eyes, scrunched face. It says, *Can you believe her?* I tap my nose. He does the same.

"So are we doing this or what?" Sally complains.

For all her admiration of my poster, I guess Courtney didn't actually *read* the rules, because it's not even a minute before she starts disrupting the whole room.

"He's in New Mexico," she says, as if the rest of us are blind. We're on the first page, where Captain Nexus is hard at work on a new Nexus Turbine. He still feels responsible for unleashing the Hollow on the world and spends nearly every moment designing new ways to banish the creature back to the Nexus Zone. There's a window behind him, and George Sanderson's drawn the scene outside in detail, all cactuses and brownish-red dirt.

So yeah, Courtney's probably right. Still, *Rule Two: No one talks during the read.*

Nate and I haven't stopped glancing at each other and tapping our noses. I try to shoot Courtney a look, too, but she's chomping away on her gum with her eyes down, already flipping to page two. I haven't even had the chance to take in George Sanderson's art like I usually do. Examining the intricate details of a *Captain Nexus* issue for the first time is one of the best parts, and she's totally ruining it.

Ollie turns the page with her. Everyone else hears them and hurries to keep up. Now I have to follow or I'll be breaking *Rule Three: We flip the pages together.*

"Captain Nexus better watch out," Courtney says in a singsong voice. "Blue Witch isn't going to be too happy if she finds out what he's been up to in that desert." She's like one of those people who talk during movies to show off. "You might be right," she continues, meeting my eyes. "Maybe the team really will split up. Maybe that's how the series ends."

I can't stand it anymore. I mean, it took about thirty seconds for her to break all four rules. I cough into my hand. "Rule two."

I'm not sure if Courtney hears it or not, but Ollie definitely does. "We're not supposed to talk," he half whispers to her, nodding toward the rules in the corner.

Courtney shrugs and turns her eyes back to page two,

which shows Captain Nexus lowering his head in concentration and drawing a circle in the air. A dark portal opens. He steps through it, and for a moment our hero is in the space between spaces. Then he takes another step and he's back in the team's Manhattan headquarters.

Sanderson's drawn it so that the portal divides the page in half, with the Captain walking from one panel into the next. In the lower corner, a circular overlay shows the Blue Witch waiting for him as he exits his lab. Captain Nexus's wife has her impatient arms folded across her chest.

"See? Told you she'd be mad," Courtney says as, on the page, the Blue Witch scolds her husband for being so wrapped up in his work he didn't realize his own son was injured.

Captain Nexus and Blue Witch head into the living area of the Nexus Five's headquarters, where they find their teammate Spark, Captain Nexus's sister, bandaging Nexus Boy's head. The team's youngest member lost his hearing and ability to speak in the explosion that gave the team their powers. He's thirteen, our age, and I know that he's Kurt's favorite (besides the Captain, of course). The rest of us are torn, though, because sometimes he seems a little bit like one of those corny kid sidekicks. You know, Robin to Batman. Or Bucky to Captain America, before they made him cool by turning him into the Winter Soldier.

Our rhythm back, we start flipping the pages together. The only sounds are Courtney chewing her gum and an occasional hand sifting through a bowl of pretzels. I want to examine the panels more closely, all those awesome details, but the story's too exciting. Blue Witch explains how Nexus Boy was trying to use his black energy powers to fly when suddenly he fell, banging his head on the corner of a coffee table.

Captain Nexus picks up one of the writing pads they use to communicate with Nexus Boy. Everyone's still working on learning sign language—in #4, the American Sign Language school they tried to attend together got blown up when the Hollow attacked it. In an exchange of notes that lasts several panels, Nexus Boy explains that his power abruptly disappeared, like a faucet being shut off.

The team's super confused. Only Captain Nexus's expression shows a glimmer of understanding. What does he think happened?

I hold my breath. Together, we flip to a foldout ad for another comic. A break from the tension. The room sighs.

"Didn't something like that happen a couple of issues back?" Sally asks. At this point, our rules are basically out the window. "Number eleven, right? The one with the mob guys? They never explained why the Red Flame's powers disappeared that day either. He just went off on his own, and then he was powerless."

"Isn't it obvious?" Courtney says. "Captain Nexus is like a battery of Nexus energy. Without him close by, the rest of them are nothing." She scoots up to her knees. "Sort of like you guys trying to win a game if Nate wasn't pitching."

The really annoying thing is she might be right. On both counts.

- 6 -

Saturday morning it's raining outside, so Coach moves Giants practice into the high school gym. We're setting up four corners, the drill we always run when we're stuck inside. The team splits into four even groups, each heading for a different corner of the gym, where we shuffle into diagonal, single-file lines.

The Miller twins head for the batting cage, and one of them—Nate swears he can tell them apart, but honestly I never know which one is Phil and which one is Bill—trips over the pile of helmets outside it. Coach reminds them both to find one that fits before stepping into the cage with him. He's been helping the Miller twins with their batting stances every indoor practice, but that's okay. We don't need him, or those sweaty helmets. We've run four corners a thousand times before.

"Hey, did you end up with the *Alpha Flight*?" I ask Nate. Somehow I lost track of it, probably because I was so stunned by the way #14 ended.

"Ollie did," Nate says, bending his glove into shape. "But I think he let Courtney take it home first."

My heart skips a beat. I remember Ollie's friend almost stepping on her own comic, tearing a page as she read. "But—"

"How do you think Captain Nexus will escape the Zone?" Nate asks. He seems completely unaware of the blinking-red, Courtney-has-my-*Alpha-Flight* emergency lights I'm seeing everywhere—up on the scoreboard, across my best friend's forehead, inside my glove.

But there's nothing I can do about it right now. Besides, I've been asking myself that same question for three days. "I don't know. A portal, maybe? Like the one he used to get to New Mexico in the first place?"

"I'm not sure," Nate says, sounding as worried as I feel. Frowning, he heads for the front of our line and crouches into a fielding stance.

Man, I wish #15 could come out tomorrow. Instead we have to spend a whole month guessing. I know I should be concentrating on the drill, but the last few panels of #14 repeat in my mind all over again.

The Hollow crashed in on the Five in New Mexico, attacking them after Captain Nexus revealed his secret lab to his family. While the rest of the team fought their dark enemy, their leader hurried to complete his new machine.

The turbine was working at first, dragging the Hollow toward the portal it had opened, driving the creature back to where it belonged. But the monster lashed out, striking the Captain with a dark blast, causing that tear across the front of his uniform. He lost first one glove, then his balance, stumbling backward.

Captain Nexus fell through the open portal.

Into the Nexus Zone.

From the other side, the Captain could still see his team, his family, continuing to wage a war against the Hollow. He rushed forward to rejoin them.

The creature cast more beams out, in all directions, scattershot. One struck the turbine. It exploded in a bright flash, and the Captain cowered before the light, just as he had on the cover.

The portal winked shut before he could leap back through it.

Captain Nexus was trapped again.

In the final panel, another full-pager with shocking, jagged edges, the Hollow loomed over the rest of the team, their powers already sputtering and dying. The creature took a menacing step forward, and then the issue ended.

Half of us turned it over and back again in frantic disbelief.

Coach blows his whistle. From the opposite corner, Kurt slings a hard ground ball at Nate, who bends at his knees to field it cleanly. He spins, throwing to Jake, then immediately looks to the right, waiting for a throw from that corner. After the second ball pops into his glove, Nate swipes a tag—"Dead meat!" Greg Dravecky cries—then slings a grounder toward Sally. His turn complete, he heads to the back of our line.

This is four corners. Two balls flying around the gym from side to side and corner to corner. The idea is for everyone to get a chance to practice all the infield skills: fielding grounders, throwing to first, manning a base, tagging out a runner. Super fast, it's all about quick reactions and accurate throws.

As Nate retreats, I step forward and lean into the same fielding position. I've done this dozens of times before, but my heart still pounds.

The dimpled yellow practice ball bounds along the hard gym floor toward me. At the last second, it takes a big hop and shifts to the side, and I have to dart that way to snatch it. I do, then wing it to the left. The second ball almost smacks me dead center in the chest, but I get my glove up just in time.

Both balls are flying at blinding speed now. I turn out from the front of my line, falling in behind Nate at the back. "I don't think he can make a portal from *inside* the Nexus Zone," he tells me. "The portals let him go from one point on Earth *through* the Nexus Zone to another point on Earth. How's he going to cut through the Zone if he's already there?"

"He just needs more . . ." I raise my fist. "Something."

"More what?" Nate shakes his head. "See? Even you don't know how he'll get out of this."

On the other side of the gym, Kurt makes a sliding stop of an errant grounder, and the whole team cheers.

"Maybe Nexus Boy can open the portal," I shout. Everyone's cheering so loudly, though, Nate can't hear me.

I grab his arm, turning him toward me. "Nate, maybe—"

I see the ball in the corner of my eye. It's coming from the right, and it's wide. Greg reaches out. Too late. The throw grazes the end of his glove, changing direction.

It flies straight into the back of Nate's turned head.

My best friend goes limp, one arm flopping loosely in the air as he crumples to the floor.

I slide down to my knees. "Nate!" I screech, but he doesn't move. His eyes are shut, his expression slack. I touch his shoulder, but he doesn't respond. He's out cold.

Nate and me, we're always talking. Until suddenly, we're not.

- 7 -

Mom and Dad drive me to the hospital first thing the next morning. Even on a Sunday, I hadn't expected Dad to take the time off. Work is his life; he actually missed Grandma's seventieth birthday earlier this summer because some updated plans were due.

"How long will it take?" My voice quavers from the backseat. "For Nate to wake up?" I'm gripping the door handle so hard my fingers are turning white. I'm thinking of all the things I could've done. Paid more attention. Kept my hand off Nate's arm. Jumped in front of him so the ball hit me instead.

Mom twists against her seat belt. "No one knows, honey. I'm sure the doctors are doing their best."

When we get to the waiting area, I see Ollie and Mr. Templeton right away. They're just sitting there, heads bowed, examining their hands. It's strange to see Ollie without his sketchbook, but neither of them are reading, not even magazines.

Mr. Templeton is built like Nate, big and athletic. Ollie looks even smaller than usual next to his father. In fact, I'm not sure I've ever seen them side by side before. Seems like Nate's always been in between them.

Ollie's dad looks up. His eyes are weird, like they want to close and he's fighting to keep them open. He just keeps blinking.

"Rob," my dad says, and Mr. Templeton stands. "How is he?"

"They put him in a coma." Mr. Templeton steps forward to hug both my parents. His voice breaks when he talks again. "His brain. The swelling."

I feel myself gawking up at him. All Mrs. Templeton had told Mom last night was that the doctors had to figure out what was wrong with Nate. There'd been nothing about swelling brains or comas.

Nate's asleep. He's just asleep.

I stare at Mr. Templeton's big, shaking hands, thinking about my own hand on his son's arm, turning him. I remember I'm supposed to move, say something, but when I look up to find him staring hard at me, all I can do is gulp. He crouches down and grips my shoulders. "It was an accident, Danny. That's all, just an accident. He'll pull through. Nathan is tough." His words are confident, but there's a wild panic in his reddening eyes.

He's wrong. It wasn't an accident. It happened because of me.

I should tell him, but I can't.

Mr. Templeton nods toward the corner. "Maybe we should . . ."

"Sit with Ollie, Dan," Mom tells me before moving off with Dad and Mr. Templeton. They start to whisper.

I climb into the chair Mr. Templeton had been sitting in. For a few seconds I watch Ollie twisting his fingers together without saying anything. My mouth is dry. My words feel stuck in my throat, like I tried to swallow a pill that didn't get down the whole way.

Mom's sending me that eye-widening stare that means I'm supposed to be doing something I'm not. Taking the garbage out. Turning off the TV, doing homework.

Talking to Ollie.

It should be easy. I've known him forever. Or maybe I've known Nate forever, and Ollie's just sort of been . . . there. In the background. Behind Nate. As close to invisible as you can get.

"Hey," I finally manage to say.

"Hey," he answers in a low voice. He doesn't look up.

I keep seeing that ball in my mind. Flying through the air, my hand reaching out to grab Nate's arm at the same moment. Its fingers looked like someone else's, made of rubber, fake, as they spun him toward me.

It couldn't have been my hand. Not mine.

But it was. All this—the accident, Nate in a coma, sitting here in this strange-smelling hospital, his brother on the edge of tears—it's real. Something catches in my chest and I have to cough to shake it loose.

Ollie finally stops twisting his fingers and breathes out. He meets my eyes. For a second it looks like he's going to say something more, but then he doesn't.

The rest of the Giants come and go. Jake first, then Sally. Kurt and Craig next. Greg and Mark aren't far behind, then all the rest, one by one with their parents. Sometimes the waiting room is nearly empty; other times it's teeming with visitors.

Dad leaves to get some work done. Mom asks if I want to go with him.

"No," I say, and she doesn't press me.

Hours pass. For about the tenth time, Kurt heads to the corner, where there's an automatic dispenser for hand sanitizer. He holds his palm underneath, and it spits out another plop of foam. He's rubbing his hands together as he walks back toward us.

"Dude," Sally says. *"Enough."*

Kurt stops in his tracks. "Dude," he mocks Sally back. "Have you never heard of MRSA? We are in a hospital, you know."

"NASA? You mean, like, space?"

"MRSA!" Kurt shouts. "It's an infection that—"

"Shut up!" Sally, Greg, and Mark yell at the same time. Some nurses turn their heads our way. We get quiet, but it doesn't last long.

"You think Nate'll be back for the tournament?" Jake whispers.

"Who cares?" I say, meaner than I mean to. Everyone goes quiet again.

The rest of the Giants are gone by the time Coach Wiggins arrives. He takes his cap off when he steps through the automated doors. They whoosh shut behind him. His eyes are distant, lost, and he doesn't see me at first. When he finally does, he tries to smile, but it comes out thin. He looks like Kurt when a pitch sneaks under his mitt and ends up catching him in the wrong spot.

Another hour passes before the doctors let Mom and me go back to see Nate. His room's super cold, full of machines that beep, lights that blink. Tubes run out of his nose and mouth. An IV drips into his arm. He's covered in blue-and-white blankets.

Mom squeezes me tight. We don't talk. Nate's eyes are closed, and I close mine too. I reach out to him with my mind. Telepathy, like I'm Professor X or something.

Nate?

Nothing. No response at all.

Of course not, because I don't have stupid telepathy. I can't send my astral self out on some heroic quest to find my friend. I don't even have an astral self, because they don't exist. I know that comic books are just paper and ink.

Still, I find myself closing my eyes again. Reaching out again.

Nate? Where are you? Come back.

My eyes search his hands and feet for movement, trying to notice the flick of a finger, the kick of a leg, anything that might be a response.

Nate doesn't tap his nose. He doesn't move at all.

But he's right there! I see him, and my eyes can't lie, can they? Except, even while I'm seeing him right in front of me, my best friend is so frozen it feels like the Nate I'm looking at is empty. How can he be here but not here at the same time? It's so confusing.

"Mom?"

She squeezes me again. "Yes, honey?"

"Where do people go? In comas, I mean."

"I don't think anyone really knows, Dan," Mom answers. "I read once that some people dream. And some say they knew what was going on around them the whole time. But not everyone. It's kind of a mystery."

"Why don't they just wake him up?" It's what I say, but it's not really what I mean. *They can bring him back, right?* That's what I mean. They can bring him back from wherever he is, because it doesn't matter what my eyes are telling me, my heart says that's not Nate in front of me at all.

"It's . . . complicated. The doctors are really smart, and they're going to work awfully hard. But Nate has to get a lot better first. Otherwise it might be dangerous to try to revive him."

"But he'll get better if they just wake him up." *Bring him back.*

Mom puts her hand on my head and pulls me toward her. Leaning against her, I watch the small signs of Nate's breathing, keep my eyes fixed on the rhythm of the flashing lights around him. They track his pulse, his heartbeat. Nate *is* alive. And if he's not here in this room, he's got to be somewhere. He needs to come back. Why won't he come back?

I've seen Nate when Ollie's upset. He gets this lost look on his face, like someone's ripping his heart straight out of his chest. I shouldn't cry in front of him. He'd hate it. I don't want him to feel that lost because of me.

But it doesn't matter, because I can't stop myself from sobbing softly into Mom's shirt as she hugs me closer and closer. And because Nate's not really here to watch me crying anyway. He's not here to talk without talking again. To pitch again. If he doesn't get back soon, he's going to miss the next *Captain Nexus*.

Hold on.

A puzzle clicks into place in my head. Nate *is* somewhere else. And if he's still there and not here, he must be trapped.

I know Nate. He'd be doing all he could to get back. I know he won't give up—but what if he can't do it by himself?

He might need help. Because maybe the somewhere else he's stuck in . . . *no, it's dumb; it's just a comic book*, but . . . but what if it's true?

What if Nate is trapped in the Nexus Zone?

- 8 -

I wake up late Monday morning. Normally Mom—she's always awake first—would've forced me out of bed, made sure I saw the list of chores attached by magnet to the fridge, but today she lets me sleep. Both my parents have left for work by the time I stagger downstairs. And for the first time all summer, there's no list.

I keep thinking about Nate. I want to call him, or FaceTime with him like we usually do, but then I remember I can't. It's so stupid. All they have to do is wake him up. Mom said they could. Why are they waiting?

Maybe it's because they actually can't. Maybe the real truth is that those doctors don't know any more than I do. And what do I know?

Exactly nothing.

Google's already open on my laptop, so I search what I hadn't been able to last night: *Where do people go in comas?* A ton of results come back, so many my eyes blur. One woman blogged about everything she could remember. She heard the people in her room, recalled the dreams she had. One thing stuck out to me, though, when she tried to explain where she went.

"I had no weight," she said. "I flew through the air. I could go anywhere I wanted to. So I did."

I could go anywhere, so I did.

If I had any doubt before, it fades away now. Maybe no one knows where people go in comas because everyone goes to a different place, wherever they always wanted to be. So where would Nate go? Easy, same place I would. The dimension that had fascinated us both since we saw that first double-page spread of it a year ago.

The Nexus Zone.

I'm sure now: by causing the accident, I trapped him there without a way back.

I slam my laptop shut, lean back against my headboard, and eye the stack of *Captain Nexus*es on my nightstand. I grab the first few, glancing at #1's cover before tossing it aside. It's #2 I'm looking for. I've never been nervous to reread *Captain Nexus* before, but as I slide the comic from the bag, I almost can't breathe.

On the first page, as he searched for a way out of the Nexus Zone, Captain Nexus grew worried he might be stuck there forever. He spent his time mapping out the strange land, discovering Lake Carol, which he named for his wife, and Scott River, after his son. He ended that first day by hiking and naming the Nexus Mountains. The landscape was all crazy colors, yellows and blues and bright greens. The water in the lake shimmered white. The Zone had been such an incredible, beautiful place, but Captain Nexus, separated from his family, had been miserable and desperate there.

I remember mocking him a little bit to Nate. It was early in the series. I had no idea I'd end up thinking he was the greatest hero ever. "Man, if that was me," I'd said, "I'd be running around that entire place. Imagine it! A whole new dimension. I'd need to see every inch. I definitely wouldn't waste time worrying about my family. You?"

Nate shrugged. "I don't know. I think I'd probably miss Ollie."

I laughed. I thought he was joking.

Now I turn to the next page in issue #2. Eventually night fell and in the pitch-blackness, Captain Nexus felt even more alone. He found a rock outcropping and camped underneath it. There were storms with bursts of lightning so bright that, for moments, they made the night seem like day. He shivered and thought of his family and friends. He knew they would never stop searching for him, but that only made him feel more isolated.

Is Nate that lonely? How will he know I won't quit on him either? How will he know I'm coming for him?

Maybe he doesn't. Maybe I can't.

The doorbell rings. Nate has rung that same bell so many times I almost think it could be him. I scramble to my window and peer down. The person who steps back from my porch and looks up isn't Nate, though. It's that girl Courtney. She sees me and waves. Great, now I have to go down.

"Hi," she says when I open the door.

"What?" Too mean, but I can't help it. What's she doing here?

"So." Courtney glances over her shoulder, like someone might be eavesdropping. She lowers her voice. "We need to talk about Ollie."

"What about him?"

"We were working on a project. He quit."

I'm not sure what to say. The last thing I want to think about is math, so I don't say anything. Courtney bites her lip. "Would you talk to him for me?"

"His brother's in the hospital. They don't know when he's going to wake up. I think your math stuff can wait."

Courtney looks down at her feet, teeters in place. "I know about Nate," she says. "And I'm really sorry. But there's nothing we can do about that."

I tighten my fist before realizing I'm still gripping *Captain Nexus* #2. I almost ruined it. It makes me think of my *Alpha Flight*. "Hey, do you have my comic?"

She wrinkles her nose. "What comic?"

I huff out air. "*Alpha Flight*? Number ten? Na— He—" I panic, like I'm drowning and can't reach the surface. Will I ever be able to say my best friend's name again? "I heard Ollie gave it to you."

Her face brightens. "Oh, yeah. He gave me a bunch of books I never read before."

"Well, that one's mine. I need it back."

"Okay," she says slowly. For a second that constant light in her expression fades, but it comes back almost immediately. "I'll get it to you. Promise. It's just . . . I don't have it right now."

"Fine. Come back when you do. Until then . . ." I move to close the door.

"Listen," she starts, her voice high and her eyes wide as she watches the door swinging toward her. "I know you want to help Nate. But only the doctors can do that." I've shut the door now, but she's still talking, loud enough that I can hear her through it. I imagine her standing up on her toes as she calls out to me. "You can still help Ollie, though. Nate would want you to."

I think I'd miss Ollie.

Does Nate miss me like that? The rest of the Giants?

Does my best friend miss me as much as I miss him?

I press my back against the door, slide #2 onto the little table in our foyer where Dad always dumps his keys, and wait, hoping to hear Courtney leaving. Right when I think she might be gone, she shouts again. "It's not a math project, you know. It's a comic book."

Her words echo in my ears. *Comic book.* Comic book?

I fling the door open again. "A what?"

"It was supposed to be a surprise. A present for Nate. That's why Ollie lied and told him we were working on math. He wanted to keep it a secret." She squints at me. "Who works on math in the summer?"

I blink. "What kind of comic book?"

"Captain Nexus."

"George Sanderson does *Captain Nexus.*"

"We're doing our own version. Like a . . . like a fan fiction. Ollie's drawing it."

My mind spins. That sketchbook. Does it have more than baseball drawings in it? "You're doing it together?"

Courtney stands a little taller. "I'm the writer."

"Okay," I say, forcing myself to sound bored. Sure, it sounds kind of cool. That doesn't mean I care. More important things are going on. "But I'm not surprised he doesn't want to work on it right now. Give him a break."

She stamps one foot. "A break is the last thing he needs. We have to convince him to keep it going."

"We?"

"He's just sitting up there in his room, thinking about his brother. He needs a distraction." I resist glancing over my shoulder at the stairs leading to my own room, where I was just doing the exact same thing.

"You can't just let him wallow," Courtney says. "He should stay busy. Working on his art'll keep his mind off things until Nate comes back. I'm sure of it."

She waits for me. I still don't know what to say.

"Okay, how about this?" she continues. "Come check out what we've done so far. Ollie left all his work with me this morning, when he told me he didn't want to draw anymore."

She pauses. I'm trying not to stare at her. I focus on her yellow bike instead, lying in the grass behind her. I don't know. I really would like to see this comic of theirs. And maybe I could get my *Alpha Flight* back while I'm over there.

"I live in Creekwood Heights," Courtney says. "Number 351. The green house with the long driveway. I need Ollie if we're going to finish by our deadline. Just come look. Deal?"

"I'll think about it."

"You'll come." She nods at me, as if she can see the future. Maybe that's her superpower. I try to think of a single hero who can see the future, and it's a tough one. Too much power, I guess, as if there is such a thing.

Snowbird? Not exactly. Spider-Woman? Sort of.

Those are big time reaches, Summers, I hear Nate's voice say, and I feel a tiny bit better because he's still talking to me, even if it's only in my head.

Courtney starts backing down the steps toward her bike. She lifts it off the grass and climbs on. Her black ponytail swings from one shoulder to the other.

"What's your deadline?" I call out.

She looks back at me. "Oh, right. Next Wednesday. It's—"

"Nate's birthday."

Courtney smiles. "Remember: 351. Green house." She stands as she pedals, picking up speed toward the street, before shouting back over her shoulder one last time. "Long driveway."

- 9 -

Mom's been gone kind of a long time. She followed Mrs. Templeton down the hallway to ask the doctors some questions and hasn't come back yet.

The hospital seems quiet for a Wednesday night. Besides a woman sleeping across three chairs, I'm the only one in the waiting room. I'm glad I brought the latest *Captain Nexus*. I raise #14 in front of my face, hoping the nurses behind the desk will stop staring at me. Over the top of my comic, a doctor materializes, her short, dark hair cropped tight around her face like Magneto's helmet. Her coat wavers when she turns, and for a second it almost looks like a white cape. *Moon Knight!* my brain shouts.

Nate's not here to echo the same answer a half second too late.

The doctor whispers something to one of the nurses, then catches sight of me. I lift *Captain Nexus* higher, hiding my face. It doesn't work. I hear footsteps, then feel a presence looming over me.

"He's pretty awesome, isn't he?" a bright voice says. I lower my comic and, as I suspected, it's the doctor. "I'm kind of obsessed with Captain Nexus myself."

I study her—the stethoscope around her neck, the *Dr. Tori Loretta* name tag pinned to her white cape-coat. "You read *Captain Nexus*?"

She frowns. "Sure, doesn't everybody?"

I shrug. Not my parents. Or any parents I know, come to think of it.

Dr. Loretta bends at the waist, resting her hands on her knees. "Number fourteen, right? You're all caught up, then?"

It's like she's challenged my fandom. I mean, really . . . am I all caught up? I throw her own words back at her. "Isn't everybody?"

The doctor straightens. She glances at the empty chairs around me. "What's your name?"

"Dan."

"I'm Dr. Tori. You here all by yourself, Dan?"

So that's why she came over. "No, my mom brought me. I'm waiting to visit my friend."

"What's your friend's name?"

"It's—" Nate's name sticks in my throat again. I swallow hard. "N-Nate. He's in a coma."

Dr. Tori's smile fades. "I'm so sorry to hear that." She sits next to me. "You wanna talk about it?"

At first I shake my head. But then, before I can stop them, words tumble out of my mouth. "I don't get why the doctors don't just wake him up."

"Mmm," she says, nodding. "Well, sometimes they have to wait for whatever's wrong to get fixed. The body's pretty amazing. If you give it a chance to rest, it does a whole bunch of healing on its own."

"You mean, like . . . brain swelling?"

"That's exactly what I mean."

"How long does it take for that to get fixed?"

"It depends on each patient. Everybody gets better at a different speed." We both grow quiet for a few seconds, until she reaches out and taps my comic. "You might be able to help, though."

I turn my face toward her so fast my neck cracks. "How?"

"Stories. They make your brain light up."

An announcement comes over the loudspeakers, and the doctor jerks her head up. "Sorry, that's me." She stands, tucking her hands into the pockets of her coat.

"When you get into your friend's room, tell him stories." She points at my comic. "Like *Captain Nexus*. They'll help him stay connected."

She turns to walk away but after a few steps, stops and looks at me again. "You have a computer at home?"

I nod. My head is spinning.

"Look up a study called FAST."

"Fast?"

"Familiar Auditory Sensory Training. F-A-S-T. If I remember right, it's most effective in the first few weeks."

Nate is flat on his back, with a tube taped to his upper lip. Across the room, a sign written in big red letters hangs from the mirror.

SPEAK ONLY POSITIVE THOUGHTS IN THIS ROOM

The nurse had given me this same instruction before she left me alone. "It's best to assume he can hear you," she'd said before pointing out the sign.

Yeah. That's the idea.

It's still really cold in here. The nurse said something about that, too, that the temperature helps with the swelling. I'm alone, sitting in a chair at Nate's bedside, watching him breathe. Listening to the steady beeps and whirs of the machinery around him. Trying to think of the right story to light up his brain with, picking through my memories. But every one that comes to me is about baseball, catch in his backyard, smashing home runs over the fence, diving to stop grounders. And they all end in that gym, the four corners drill.

The accident. At least, that's what everyone else calls it.

All those baseball memories keep getting stopped up inside me. Blocked by a pressure in my chest. I can't force them out. I can't turn them into words.

Comic books it is, then. *Captain Nexus.* I flip to the last panel of #14, opening it in front of me so that Nate—if his eyes were open—could wonder at Sanderson's drawing of the Hollow with me all over again.

"Dude looks so angry," I tell Nate. "Like someone stole his Halloween candy. Or made him eat an anchovy-and-pineapple slice." I start to laugh, but it fades. "Do you remember this?"

Of course he does, dummy. It wasn't even a week ago.

I wait anyway, but Nate still doesn't move. He hardly breathes. The machines make the only sounds. I remember I'm here with him, but I can't be sure he's with me.

"I'm sure Captain Nexus'll find a way home next issue. Don't worry."

No response. Nate's somewhere else, alone.

I squeeze my eyes shut, try to reach out to him again. Use our special telepathy. But there's nothing there except the dark insides of my lids. My eyes start to tear up again, and I fight hard against it this time. Seeing me cry will only make Nate feel more lost. Trap him deeper.

Think. I have to do something. I stare down at my hands, then run my fingers along the glossy pages of *Captain Nexus.* My thumb stops on a panel of the whole team fighting the Hollow together.

The team.

"I won't give up, Nate." I swipe at my eyes with one angry sleeve. "Promise."

I almost collide with the nurse coming down the hallway as I tear out of the room.

- 10 -

I barely sleep that night, I'm so eager to get to Courtney's the next day. The green house with the long driveway isn't hard to find, even amid the web of streets that make up the huge Creekwood Heights subdivision, biggest one in Mira. I kick my stand down, hop up the steps, and ring the bell.

A tall woman answers. She looks like a blown-up version of Courtney, black ponytail and everything.

I smile at her. "Is Courtney home?"

Courtney's mom hesitates at first, then says, "Sure. One moment." She calls for her daughter and waits, keeping one suspicious eye trained on me.

A few seconds later, Courtney thunders down the stairs and jump-stops into the foyer. "You're here." She steps to one side and gestures over her shoulder. "Come on. My dad lets us use his office."

Courtney's mother clears her throat.

"Oh, sorry. This is my mom."

"Nice to meet you, Mrs.—" I don't even know Courtney's last name.

"Hoffman," Courtney helps. "Mom, this is Dan Summers. He's going to work on the comic."

"Is Ollie coming over, too?" Mrs. Hoffman asks hopefully.

"Um, not today."

"Such a sweet boy," she says, frowning. "And so talented. Do you know how his brother's doing?"

I don't mean to, but I whisper it. "Still in a coma."

Courtney grabs my arm and starts to pull me. "This way. All our stuff's in the office."

We wind deeper into the house, through the kitchen, past a laundry room, and finally into an office with a big, old-fashioned wooden desk at its center. There's a gleaming whiteboard attached to the far wall. The desk faces a picture window with a view of the thick woods behind the Hoffmans' house.

Courtney runs to the desk and slaps her hands down

on some big pages scattered across it. My eyes, though, are drawn to the fancy credenza behind her. Must be a dozen baseballs there, all signed and sealed in square plastic display cases.

"Holy . . . ," I say. "Daryl Strawberry? Ron Darling? Mike Piazza? Are these real?"

"Yeah, my dad's a huge Mets fan. Whatever." Courtney points at the big white sheets, each maybe two or three times as big as a regular comic page. "Are you going to look at these or what?"

I allow myself a final glance at the autographed balls, then turn my attention to the overlapping black-and-white panels filled with pencil drawings. Captain Nexus, Spark, Blue Witch, the whole team. Maybe not the same as George Sanderson's work, a little looser and without color, but super close.

"These are amazing."

"Told you. Ollie's awesome." She shuffles through the stack of pages—there must be a dozen, twenty maybe—and pulls one from the middle. "Look. Full-page battle scene."

The Nexus Five surround the Hollow in the Nexus Zone, attacking the creature from a series of hillsides. It's a fight that never happened in the real comic, but it's . . . familiar, like it definitely could've.

"This is perfect."

Courtney shrugs. "It's totally not. But it's getting there. See here? Captain Nexus saves the rest of the team." Her finger taps the partially finished image. "The story's kinda whacked. Needs a lot of smoothing out. Ollie was just so excited to give his brother his own *Captain Nexus* as a birthday present."

She pulls open a drawer, removing a T square, some pencils, a triangle, and another curved, ruler-looking thing. Underneath these are several typed pages. She slides them out and hands them to me.

"My script," she says, thrusting her shoulders back. "Our story."

Story.

I want to tell her my idea, but I'm still not ready. It seems like they have all this figured out. What if she says no? "Why do you think I can help?"

She holds up two fingers. "Two reasons. First, Ollie admires you almost as much as his own brother."

"Me?" I know what Ollie thinks of Nate, how much he worships his big brother. Mostly because I feel pretty much the same way. I mean, how could you not? Dude is as perfect as those no-hit, no-walk games he'd pitched earlier this summer.

But me? I assumed Ollie never thought much of me at all.

"Didn't you do some double play where you flipped in the air, threw the ball, and did a somersault when you landed?"

"That was last year, against Shale." Before Nate got so good we stopped needing to make plays like that.

"Have you never seen his drawings of it? In that giant sketchbook he carries around?"

I shake my head. I thought Ollie only had drawings of Nate in that book. He definitely tried to show it to me a few times, but I was always in the middle of some conversation with Nate. It just seems crazy that he would have drawn me, too. *Me.* But then again, I had no idea he was working on a comic for Nate either. Guess I don't know as much about Nate's little brother as I think I do.

"Well, I have," she says, making an exhausted face. "A thousand times." She lowers her voice. "I think Ollie's always wished he could do the things you guys do. That he was bigger and . . . you know, stronger. The way I wish I could be Spark. The way you and Nate probably want to be Captain Nexus."

She pauses. "Ollie—" She shakes her head. "He's so smart, and his hands create the most wonderful drawings." Courtney runs light fingers over more of Ollie's work. "But I think sometimes he feels invisible around you guys."

Invisible. When Nate's paying so much attention to his brother, and Dad's off busy at work, it's sometimes how I feel, too. Memories of chasing after Nate when Ollie was trying to tell me something, show me something, flash through my brain like those wild lightning storms in the Nexus Zone. I never thought about how that must've made him feel. I only cared about having Nate to myself, not letting anybody wedge into the tiny world we'd made.

Slowly, I trade out the pages for the T square and triangle, tools I recognize from art class. "So Ollie draws with these?"

"Yep. We're just doing the pencils right now. Someday he'd like to try inking." She bites her lip. "Or he did. Before."

I slide the curved ruler-thing to me. "What's this?"

"French curve. You use it to help with certain lines." Courtney moves it to one of the pages, lining it up with the curve that starts under Blue Witch's arm and continues to her waist. It matches up exactly. "Some lines are easier with this. Mostly he works freehand, though. He's that good."

I tear my eyes from the drawings and stare instead at the empty speech bubbles that dot most of the pages. "Why aren't they saying anything?"

Courtney grins at me. "Reason two why we need you. I haven't lettered them yet. I've been waiting."

"Why?"

"Because I suck at it." She finds a completed page. "See for yourself."

The page is lettered, if you want to call it that. The *w*'s slant hard to the left. The *t*'s and *i*'s and *j*'s and *l*'s all look the same. In some bubbles, the dialogue runs out of room, the letters either leaking out of the lines or bumping into each other in a rush to finish. It looks like the line at a GameStop when a new *Halo* comes out, everybody in the back pushing so the people in the front get smushed up against the door.

I groan. I can't help it.

"That bad?" she asks.

"Sorry, but . . . yeah. How can your handwriting be this terrible? I thought girls—"

"What? That we all dot our *i*'s with cute little hearts?"

"No, I—"

"It's okay. My penmanship does stink. Totally not breaking news. And look, I'm ruining Ollie's work with it." She thrusts a pencil toward me. "You try. Do it like that poster in the basement. The one with the rules."

I take a step back. "No, I . . . I can't."

She narrows her eyes. "Sure you can. Your work is awesome."

When I still don't reach out for the pencil, Courtney takes my hand and force-folds my fingers around it. "Just one." She gestures toward the silent image of the Red Flame on the top page, then points at a page of her script.

I take a deep breath and concentrate on each letter as

I fill in the empty speech bubble. Courtney watches my hand, then glances at my face and grins. I try to ignore her and concentrate.

"That's it," she says, like she's Coach Wiggins watching me execute a flawless bunt. "Do the whole bubble."

When I finish, *HOW WILL WE GET OUT OF HERE?* leaps off the paper, and suddenly the Red Flame comes alive. It was me. I brought him to life with words Courtney wrote but *I* put on the page.

She slaps me on the back so hard I lurch forward. "Told you! Awesome!"

"Really?"

But she's already flipping through more pages, all of them waiting to be lettered. "People use computers to do this stuff now," she says. "But we're old-school. Like here"—she points at one of Ollie's pages again—"normally you'd ink and color the pages first, before you letter them, but—"

"You're not inking yet."

She shakes her head. "Nope. I think Sanderson does *some* computer stuff. We just don't have the money for that."

"How do you guys know how to do all this?"

Courtney shrugs. "Anybody can learn it, if you do the research. There's a how-to on Geeker. Don't you have Google?" She releases a satisfied exhale. "So what do you think?"

What do I think? After using her words to bring the Red Flame to life, I don't dare spell out the possibilities running through my head. It's exactly what I was hoping for. "We need to do this."

She hops up and down. "Yes!" Her smile flattens and her tone grows serious. "But we need Ollie."

"Definitely."

She heads for the door. "Let's go get him, then."

"Wait. I need to say one thing."

Courtney stops and turns, her eyes scrunched up.

I try to stand straight and appear confident. "It has to have Nate in it."

"What does? The comic?"

I nod.

"That . . . I don't get it. How would Nate be in *Captain Nexus*?"

"I'm not sure. That's what we have to figure out."

"But why?"

Stories, Dr. Tori said. *They make your brain light up.* Something else, too.

It's most effective in the first few weeks.

We're already running out of time. I tap a finger onto my dialogue bubble, the Red Flame alive with speech. "Because we're going to use this comic to wake Nate up."

- 11 -

"So, what do you love about comics?"

We're barely two houses up from Courtney's. She looks back long enough to ask her question, then pedals away, like she wants me to chase her to answer.

My bike had barely bumped out of her driveway when I realized I forgot to ask for my *Alpha Flight* back. It's too late now. I look ahead at her bouncing ponytail, annoyed she didn't offer it to me herself. I put all those angry thoughts into pedaling harder, until I pull even with her. "I like the art."

"This way," she says, darting down a dirt track I wouldn't have noticed, into the woods between two houses. "We can cut to Pinewood, then take that up to Mercer."

The Templetons live on Mercer. If she's right, this shortcut'll save us fifteen minutes at least. Feels kind of like I'm cutting through the Nexus Zone. No, actually, it feels like the bike trail. This narrow dirt track definitely reminds me of the course Nate and I built in the woods behind my house last summer. It must be a mess now. We haven't been out there since maybe October, when the first snow covered up the jumps.

"You like the art," Courtney says. "Okay. But I didn't ask what you *like* about comics. I asked what you *love* about them."

"Is this some kind of test?"

She grins over her shoulder and pedals harder. "Absolutely."

I can't fail. I need them to agree to make a comic with Nate in it. So far Courtney has only said, "Let's see what Ollie thinks. Nate's his brother."

Yeah, but he's *my* best friend.

I feel myself biting down on my lip.

"Take your time," she says before surging ahead again. I kind of want to hip-check her into the trees.

We pop out of the woods onto Pinewood. Courtney slows. I catch up again.

"I love the way the paper smells."

Her eyes shift down to her hands. "Me, too." She says it like a confession.

"I love the way some artists draw so many details," I add. "How they make it so I have to go over the issue again and again to notice them all. I love the way it feels like I'm the only one who sees them."

"Yes!"

"I love the way they're not movies, and they're not books. They're both." I can't stop. "I love it when I reach the middle of an issue, where the staples are, some epic battle scene with a thousand characters that I can lay open on my bed and spend hours staring at until I figure out who every single one is."

Courtney stands up and leans, turning right onto Mercer. "Yes!" she repeats. "What else?"

"I love the way I find something new every time I reread an issue, especially *Captain Nexus*. I love it when I stumble on some dialogue that makes me wonder if I understand what it's really saying, so that I have to read it over and over to be sure. I love—"

I stop myself, out of breath from talking so fast while pedaling. I never realized all that stuff, never actually thought about the particular things I loved about comics. I just loved them. But it's so cool to say why, out loud. "What about you?"

We swing into the driveway leading to the Templetons' blue-and-white house and start to coast toward the garage. Courtney takes a deep breath. "I love the way, when I'm feeling down or having a bad day, the heroes give me hope that tomorrow will be better, even if I'm not sure how."

The only thing I wanted to do after Nate got hurt was reread *Captain Nexus*. Not play Xbox, not watch YouTube. Not even toss a ball against the pitch-back net out back. Just find some secret way to help my friend, hoping it would be buried in the comic pages.

We park our bikes next to each other outside Nate's house. Ollie's house. "So did I pass?" I ask her. "Right answers, I mean?"

"The only wrong answer would've been if you couldn't come up with any answer at all."

A few minutes later, Mrs. Templeton knocks softly on Ollie's door. "Ollie? Honey, Courtney's here again. She brought Dan Summers this time."

There's a long beat of silence. Mrs. Templeton chews on one nail. Finally the lock clicks, the knob turns, and Ollie's door swings open. Courtney's so excited she chucks me in the arm and I almost fall over again. "Cut it out," I hiss, but she's already squeezed past me into his room.

I've always ignored Ollie's bedroom on my way to Nate's; usually he has his door closed. Now I see it's a shrine to comic art—posters of famous covers framed on every wall. There's a Spider-Man figure curved around his window, as if the hero is actually swinging across his wall, but that's not all. Pages upon pages of sketches and drawings are taped to the walls, flutter from the back of the door, cover the floor some like some kind of paper carpet. It's like I've stumbled onto his hidden lair, Ollie's secret identity suddenly revealed.

I wander over to a black-and-white drawing, from the X-Men. The framed page is signed by Jim Lee. *The* Jim Lee. "Is this real?" I ask.

"Yeah, should be," Ollie mutters. "Bought it at Comic-Con. Me and Nate went with Dad. Came with a certificate and everything."

That Toronto trip I couldn't go on. I'm examining the framed details with a little pang of jealousy when Courtney speaks up from across the room. "It's almost as great as Ollie's pages. Right, Dan?"

Ollie's head snaps around to me. "Saw them at Courtney's," I explain. "Awesome, man."

His eyes widen for just a second; then he turns his attention back to his computer, shaking his mouse to wake it up. "Thanks," he mumbles.

I notice his sketchbook on the floor—in the corner, propped up on its side, pages fanned open like he threw it there. I kind of want to go over and find his drawing of me making that play against Shale, but my feet refuse to move in that direction.

"I'm serious," I say. "You should enter the fan contest.

The deadline's coming up, isn't it?" Tall Ship Comics, *Captain Nexus*'s publisher, was running a competition for fan art inspired by their bestselling comic. The top ten submissions were going to get published in a special annual. The grand prize winner got to meet George Sanderson himself. I remember reading about it and wishing I could draw. Why hadn't I thought of Ollie?

"All sorts of adults are going for that. Don't you read Geeker?"

"Kids can enter, too." I turn to Courtney. "Right?"

"I'm sure," she agrees.

Ollie shakes his head. "My stuff's not good enough."

"I don't know," I say. "I think—"

Courtney cuts in. "Dan thinks we should finish the project. We both do." I catch her hint. She's right, we need to focus.

I straighten my shoulders. "Definitely."

Ollie hangs his head. "What's the point? It was for Nate. Now . . ."

"Now," I say, "it's going to be even more for him."

It's going to show him the way home.

Ollie frowns. "I tried to draw it. I couldn't concentrate."

The room is quiet. I'm not sure how I can help him. It's so weird, talking to Ollie like this, without Nate here to translate, to help us understand each other. I never realized he was doing it before.

"Dan has an idea," Courtney says after a few seconds. "He wants to change the story."

"Change it how?" Ollie asks.

"Well . . ." I stall, because saying it in front of Nate's little brother is harder somehow, as if he'll know Nate is trapped because of me. "I want to put Nate in it."

Ollie's squint at me is full of doubt. "What are you talking about?"

"A doctor told me reading a story with Nate inside it would help wake him up." Okay, not exactly what Dr. Tori said, I know, but close enough.

"I don't get it," Ollie says. "How could a comic wake Nate up?"

"Stories, they . . . they light up your brain."

"What?" Ollie and Courtney say it at the same time.

I feel my cheeks warming up. "I . . . there's a study." I rack my brain for the name. Dr. Tori told me to look it up, but I never got the chance. "FAST. I think that's it. F-A-S-T."

"It was a real experiment?" Courtney asks.

"I don't know. How can you tell?"

"Were there scientists and stuff?"

"I wasn't there or anything. Like I said, a doctor told me about it. At the hospital when I visited Nate." I huff, annoyed at their doubtful expressions. "Listen, somebody has to do something. If the doctors aren't going to wake Nate up, then . . ."

Ollie spins in his chair and starts googling away. He finds FAST, a Northwestern coma study, quickly. We read the first article together. It talks about families recording stories about major events—weddings, vacations—then playing them for coma patients. The research claims their brains showed increased activity. They recovered sooner.

"See?" I say, pointing. "It can work. We can help. With stories."

Ollie crinkles his nose like my idea smells funny. "But I think the stories they're talking about are supposed to be memories, not comics."

The hospital. Sitting at Nate's bedside, words stuck in my throat, tears filling my eyes.

Memories are too hard.

I gulp. "Nate would want a comic. That's the kind of story he would hear."

Ollie thinks a minute. I hold my breath. "Sorry, I just don't think I could do it," he finally says. "Drawing Nate over and over again? No way."

"Why not?" Courtney asks. Her eyes scan the room for Ollie's sketchbook, finding it in the corner. She purses her lips at him, then heads over to it. She picks it up, flips through the pages. "You've done it before."

"That was," Ollie sighs heavily, "different. He isn't here anymore."

"He's not gone," I yell, surprising even myself.

"No, he's not," Courtney agrees at normal volume. "If we do this, it'll be like Nate's with us again." She glances at Ollie. "With you. Moving around."

"Talking," I add. "And . . . and being a hero."

"We have to try it," Courtney insists. "Don't we?"

Ollie repositions his thick glasses on his face. His frown softens. "Do you think we can still finish by Nate's birthday?"

"Not without you," I say.

He looks back over his shoulder at the article on his screen, then turns toward Courtney. "Can you write that? A whole new story?"

Courtney sets her feet and folds her arms over her chest. "I can write anything."

The room is quiet for what seems about the same amount of time the Watcher has studied the Marvel Universe. Eons.

"What do you think?" I ask Ollie when I can't stand it anymore.

Ollie bites his bottom lip. He nods. "What I think is that we need to get to work."

- 12 -

I sprint toward the grounder speeding at me, lowering my glove so I can scoop it off the ground. My cleats kick up dirt as the ball and I close in on each other. We meet and I immediately crow hop toward Sally, stretching from first. I reach into my glove, but the ball isn't there. I glance back over my shoulder, watching the grounder I just overran roll slowly into the left field grass until it stops, lifeless.

Craig Hawkins trots over from center, where the outfielders stand huddled together. He snatches my error up. "Nice boot, Summers. Does it come in my size?"

"All out of extra tiny," I spit back.

Booting an easy grounder like that is about the worst

thing ever for a shortstop. *Coach'll be on me in a second for that error,* I think as I squeeze Craig's throw-in, but nothing comes. What gives? I just did everything wrong. Didn't stay in front of the ball, tried to one-hand it, took my eyes off it. But Coach stays silent.

"Two hands, Summers," Kurt calls out to me from the side, where he's crouching down, waiting for Jake's next warm-up pitch.

"Thanks, Captain Obvious." I'm embarrassed enough to mess up an easy play like that without the double dose of Craig's mocking and Kurt pretending he's Coach.

And here's what makes it all worse: I don't even want to be here. I should be working on the comic. There's still no word from the doctors, no plan to wake Nate up. More and more it's looking like it's going to be up to us.

"Maybe I should quit the Giants," I suggested to Mom last night.

"You'll do no such thing," she said. "That team needs you."

"Nate needs me."

Mom came forward and hugged me. "Of course he does," she said, brushing my hair back from my eyes. "But trust me on this: baseball's good for you right now. Nate got you guys this far. You don't think he'd want you to stop now, do you?"

"Let him stay home if he wants," Dad countered from the kitchen doorframe. He quieted, though, when Mom shot him a sharp look.

It was settled: I wasn't quitting the Giants. Because Mom didn't want me to, but also because she was right about Nate. If he were in my shoes—man, how I wish he was, so I could take his place in that hospital bed—Nate would never quit on his team. Never.

Coach Wiggins tosses another ball into the air. He swings at it, only eking out a weak foul down the line. He slumps his shoulders and mutters something I can't hear.

"Keep swinging, Coach," Sally cries. "The breeze out here feels great."

It's the kind of joke that would normally get the rest of us rolling, but his words sort of die on the air. We shift our feet uncomfortably. Coach stares out at the useless ball.

Then Mark Lefferts, our new third baseman, charges Coach's dead foul like it's the last out of the tournament. He jumps to a stop where it came to rest, barehanding it and firing it off to first. He's so gung ho all the time now, like he's afraid of making the tiniest mistake.

Mark had been the one who threw the ball that glanced off Greg's glove in four corners. He hasn't said a word about it since. Sometimes he can't even look me in the eye, and I'm pretty sure I know why.

When something bad happens in a comic book, there's

usually a way to reverse it. It was a dream or a clone or a different Earth altogether. The hero's not really gone, he's just been frozen in ice or she's lost her memory. Like a rubber band, things eventually snap right back into place. The hero returns, the team reunites, the villain goes back to his evil ways.

I'm still waiting for that rubber band. I'm still waiting for Nate to wake up, any day now. We all are. Until then, we hold our breath.

Mark's throw smacks into Sally's glove, but our big first baseman doesn't squeeze it. The ball pops out, dropping down onto the infield dirt at his feet.

I haven't seen him flub an easy catch like that all year.

"Spend a little less time enjoying the breeze and a little more time squeezing the throw, Sally," Mark yells across the diamond.

Our first tournament game is Monday night, only two days away, and this has been our worst practice ever. Everyone's jabbing at each other about dropping the ball, missing cutoff men, forgetting to cover the right bag, swinging and missing. On top of that, we're down two more players.

When we got to the field, Coach had given us the news that the Miller twins weren't on the team anymore. Rumor was their mother blamed Coach for Nate's accident. I wish I'd known. Maybe I could've told her the truth—whose fault it really was. Her sons could've stayed on the team.

They could've kicked me off instead.

No Miller twins meant our roster of twelve was down to nine since Nate's accident. One little injury and we wouldn't have enough players for a real game. Plus, two guys normally riding the bench became starting outfielders, and, on top of all that, Jake had forgotten he was our backup pitcher. When Coach popped a brand-new ball into Jake's glove and told him to start warming up on the side with Kurt, the look on his face couldn't have been any closer to Captain Nexus's expression when he'd found himself trapped in the Nexus Zone. Wide eyes, open mouth, no way out.

Jake's pitches have been sailing over Kurt's head or bouncing under his glove all afternoon, each time clanging into the chain-link backstop. Another ping sounds out now, as a ball hops once and catches the end pole of the fence.

I check on Sally. Normally he'd be mocking Jake something awful for all those crazy off-target pitches. *Call the zoo, he's getting wild!* Or, *I've seen better curves on a square!* even though none of us has the faintest idea how to throw a curveball, least of all Jake. But after the way that breeze joke went over, he keeps his lips clamped shut.

Jake's pitching arm hangs from his shoulder. His head droops. Two years ago he pitched a lot, but he hasn't had to take the mound all season, not with Nate always out there. He's struggling big-time.

"Huddle up," Coach says when practice comes to an end a half hour later. He reads off the schedule for the upcoming game: what time we need to be at the field, who's responsible for bringing which equipment. He doesn't mention how terrible we've been playing all morning. He doesn't talk about winning, or losing.

He doesn't talk about Nate.

"You sure your dad doesn't mind us working in here?" I ask Courtney that afternoon. We're settling into our usual spots around the office.

"He doesn't care." Courtney turns from the window to face us, leaning back on the sill. "So how are we going to do this?"

"Brainstorm," Ollie says. "Make a list of possible story ideas first, pick one, then figure out the details later."

"Nate's character should get stuck in the Nexus Zone," I hurry to say. "And the story is how he escapes. If we read that to him, it'll give him a way to wake up, to . . . to come back."

"Maybe," Ollie mutters.

"What do you mean, maybe?" I ask.

"Nothing, it's just . . . nothing."

But Courtney won't let Ollie get away with that. "Stop. What's going on?"

Ollie spends a few seconds organizing his pencils. "I

heard something the other day," he mumbles. "My parents were talking with the doctors. They were picking a date to wake Nate up."

Finally. "That's awesome," I say, taking a few steps closer. "When?"

"I didn't hear the whole thing. Not anytime soon, I don't think. In a month or so, maybe."

"It sounds like good news, though," Courtney says. "As long as they do it sometime, right?"

"There was something else." Ollie does that thing again where he stares at his twisting fingers. "They said . . ." Deep breath. "They said if it doesn't work, Nate might not come back at all. That's why they have to wait for the right time to try it."

It's now or never.

"Well, we'll have to be done before then," I tell them, pounding a fist on the edge of the desk. "We have to show him the way home."

"How?" Courtney asks.

"I don't know. That's the part we have to figure out."

She steps to the whiteboard and grabs a blue marker, reaching up as high as she can, writing *#1* and circling it. "Okay," she says with clenched teeth, "then go."

An hour later all we've done is make a list of suggestions at least one of us thinks is dumb. I've taken over, switched to the red marker.

"He can build another turbine," I say, but Courtney shoots me down right away.

"Where's he going to get the parts?"

I slump into the whiteboard. "Your shirt," Ollie warns, pointing.

I stand straight again. Our red and blue marks have transferred from the board onto my white T-shirt. *Open a portal to* now appears directly above *DiNunzio's Pizza.*

"Hey, that'd be cool," Courtney laughs. "Pizza anytime."

But Ollie doesn't smile. He leans forward in Mr. Hoffman's big office chair and drops his head into his hands. "This isn't working."

Courtney tries something different. "Maybe we should try to figure out how George Sanderson will do it," she says. "For Captain Nexus, I mean."

Ollie lifts his head. "Hopefully we'll find out next issue."

"Agh," she moans. "That's *eighteen* days away." She says it like she's counting down to Christmas. Which is crazy, of course. *Captain Nexus* Wednesdays are way better than Christmas.

"And that's cutting it way too close," I complain. "Besides, Dr. Tori said FAST would be most effective in the first few weeks. It's already been a week." Exactly one week, actually. How did we let it get to Saturday again so fast? "The sooner we do this, the better. We can't leave it up to the doctors."

"Maybe we really should find George Sanderson and ask him about number fifteen," Ollie suggests sarcastically. "Fly off to Britain and steal his ideas, since we obviously don't have enough imagination to come up with our own."

Courtney narrows her eyes. "Why do you assume he's British?"

"All the great writers are British," I say. "There's Gaiman. And Moore. And . . . and Morrison . . ." I know there's a thousand more, but her glare freezes my brain up.

"Just how old are you?" Courtney asks. "Those guys are all from forever ago."

"I'm into the classics." *In fact, I think, you have one of my classics, probably crumpled in a ball right now. It's got Sasquatch front and center on the cover, in case you forgot.* I almost say all that, too, but right now I know it's better to stay focused.

"You're an old man with your old-school names." She rubs her nose. "And they're all dudes. What about Gail Simone or Kelly Sue DeConnick or Marjorie Liu? Or Kelly Thompson or Chelsea Cain or—"

Ollie interrupts by heaving a breath. "Guys, it doesn't matter. Sanderson won't even give interviews to the comic sites. He'd never talk to a bunch of kids like us." He lowers his chin into his hand and stares off into the distance. "Man, I'd love to meet him, though. Some of those pages he draws . . ."

It's almost like they both know as much about comics

and their creators as I do, way more than most of the Giants, even Nate. I wonder why Ollie never challenges me in the name-the-superhero game.

We go back to brainstorming. We need to come up with an idea fast, so we can start working on the comic, but we keep getting stuck, and my mind wanders. I'm thinking about the doctors saying Nate might not come back at all, and I'm thinking of Captain Nexus, too. It really would be cool to meet George Sanderson and hear how to escape the Nexus Zone—early, before the next issue comes out and the rest of the world knows. Maybe we wouldn't have to steal his idea, but we could use, like, a version of it in our book. It's dumb to even fantasize about that, though, because nobody even knows where *Captain Nexus*'s creator is from, never mind how to find him now.

- 13 -

"Keep your head up, man," Kurt says to Jake. Sweat streams down our new pitcher's temple. His cheeks are flushed. We all know he's in trouble; when Kurt called time and trotted out to the mound, the entire infield joined him.

It's Monday night, the first game of the tournament. Shale's coach is conferencing with his gangly hitter halfway up the line, while the runner on third, another lanky Shale player, teeters on the bag. The shrimpy kid on second is sitting on his base, retying his cleats.

This is our third time playing the Shale Braves this year. We crushed them the first two. I couldn't believe they even made the tournament.

Today we're losing 8–1.

"Yeah, man," Sally says. He hitches his belt up. "This kid weighs like thirty-eight pounds. You totally got this."

Jake nods, takes a deep breath.

"You okay out here?" Coach asks Jake when he joins us on the mound.

Jake doesn't answer at first. He kicks at a spot in front of the rubber. Finally he picks up his head and glances around, tugging his cap, using it to scratch the sweat off his forehead. He's walked at least a half-dozen batters today, and now Shale's best hitter, a tall kid who boomed a three-run homer back in the third, is twisting his front foot into the dirt of the batter's box.

"I'm okay," Jake says with another sigh that makes him sound quite a bit less than okay.

"Throw strikes," Coach reminds him. "No more walks."

"I'm trying." Jake sounds like we've already been kicked out of the tournament.

"Hey," Coach says, reaching out and pulling at Jake's cap. "Imagine you're . . . I don't know, Captain Spider . . . Dude."

Sally shakes his head. He can't even muster the energy to make fun of Coach right now. He smacks his glove against Jake's backside before skipping back to first.

Kurt holds his catcher's mitt up. "Just hit the target." He

pulls on his mask and jogs toward home plate.

I hesitate, lingering. Greg Dravecky, second base, stays too. And Mark Lefferts, the new third baseman, toes on the very edge of the grass like there's an impenetrable, invisible force field surrounding the dirt on the pitching mound.

No one talks. Maybe Jake doesn't get it, but I know why we're all standing on the mound when we should be getting back to our positions. Mark, who threw the ball, Greg, who didn't catch it, and me, the one who turned Nate at the wrong moment.

"Don't think about Nate," I say. I'm looking at Jake, but I'm not just talking to him.

Jake sniffs and frowns. "I can't help it. Can you?"

No one has to answer because, no, none of us can help it. Not thinking about Nate, about what happened, what each of us did—or didn't do—would be like taking a break from breathing. And we have to keep breathing, right?

The final score is 12–3, Shale. From the bench, I check for Ollie in his usual spot in the stands. He's right there, middle of the front row, but today Courtney's sitting beside him for the first time. Weird. I assumed she only knew the bare minimum about baseball—what Ollie told her, that he had a super talented brother we all depended on. I figured she didn't care about it otherwise.

I send a short, unenthusiastic wave their way. Ollie

stands, walking down toward the grass and his waiting bike. His mouth pinches in one corner. I hadn't realized how much our losing would affect him, but I see it now, what we're doing.

Killing his brother's dream.

Courtney spreads her hands out in a helpless gesture, then follows him. I think about going after them, as if I can somehow explain what they just witnessed, but I can't. We were terrible.

You guys better stay ready, Nate had told us in the basement. Was that only a couple of weeks ago? *I can't do it by myself.*

Because Nate knew: we're supposed to play like a team. But we didn't today. Not at all.

"You'll get 'em next year," Dad tells me when we arrive home. He's staring at some building plans on his iPad.

"Or next week," I say, tossing my glove and hat on the floor in the foyer.

"Pick those up," Mom says, pointing at my pile. "They have to lose twice, Mike," she informs my father. Mom played softball when she was a kid. She gets it. Matter of fact, she was the one who taught me how to throw and catch and hit. The few times I played catch with Dad, he couldn't figure out which way to turn his glove. Anyway, that was years ago, back when he had time for that sort of thing.

"Double elimination, Dad," I add. "We're in the losers bracket now, but we still have a chance."

"Oh," Dad says. "Well . . . great, then. One more game."

Mom's gaze bores into Dad's eyes.

"At least!" he corrects himself. "At least one more game."

I snatch up my equipment and stomp upstairs. The thing is, if the Giants don't start playing better, Dad'll be right. One more game is all we'll get.

- 14 -

I get to Courtney's house early the next day. She looks surprised to see me an hour before we normally meet, but she recovers quickly and invites me in. As soon as we're alone in the office, I tell her the idea I came up with lying in bed last night, staring at the ceiling. "We should submit for the annual."

She screws up her expression, super confused. "What do you mean?"

"The Tall Ship contest. Ollie's work could win, don't you think?"

Courtney narrows her eyes. "Sure . . . but he said he didn't want to enter, didn't he?"

"So we do it for him. In secret."

"I'm not sure that's a good idea."

"Don't you think it would make him feel better, to win something?"

"Yeah," she says, slowly, "but it could make him feel worse if he loses."

I spread my arms out in a *duh* motion. "That's why we submit for him. Secret. If he loses, he never has to know about it."

Courtney taps one finger against her lips. I hold my breath. I want Ollie to win, definitely. To make him feel better, sure, but also because this is probably our only shot, however slim, at meeting George Sanderson.

I figured it out last night. Ollie'd been kidding, but he was actually kind of right. George Sanderson invented the Nexus Zone. If anybody knows how to escape it, it's got to be him. We just have to find a way to ask the most private guy in the world what's going to happen in the comic he never discusses. Besides, tomorrow's Nate's birthday, and Saturday's his party. No way this comic we're *still* stuck on is going to be ready for either. So if I can't give Nate something he needs, maybe I can do my part to give his little brother something he wants.

"Don't try to tell me you're not into secrets," I prod Courtney. "You guys were the ones making a secret comic for Nate." Her finger stops moving. Still, she doesn't answer.

I try one more time. "I don't think there's any way he loses. You?"

Her grin matches mine. "No," she says. "I don't."

When Ollie joins us a few minutes later, Courtney's setting up the desk and I'm erasing the whiteboard. I wipe out the word *after* and, as the *af* disappears last, think of *Alpha Flight.* My comic's probably upstairs, in Courtney's room. "Hey—" I start, turning toward her.

But Ollie, who usually comes in all quiet, storms into Mr. Hoffman's office, a manila folder stacked with pages raised high over his head. "I got it!" he cries.

Courtney's hand freezes inside the desk's top drawer. My half-started sentence hangs in the air. "We'll all be in it," Ollie explains, leaning on the edge of the big desk. He heaves a few deep breaths.

"In what?" I ask.

"The comic. Me and you and Courtney and Nate get added to the team, sort of like . . . like a sub-team."

"You mean the West Coast Avengers?" Back in the eighties, the Avengers got so big they split into two teams, with Hawkeye setting up the new squad's headquarters in California.

"No," Ollie says, "not corny like that. It'd still be one

team, with four new heroes. They would just change their name. They wouldn't be the Nexus Five anymore. They'd be—"

"The Nexus Nine," Courtney finishes.

Ollie's breathing normally again, but he's still talking way fast. "Exactly. And Nate could be this hero called Somnus, who controls sleep, but his power backfires. He falls into a deep slumber—like a coma—and his new teammates, us, we have to wake him up."

"No," I say. "His name can't change. It has to be Nate. We have to say his name a lot when we read the story. That's what those FAST articles said, remember?"

"Okay, well, then . . ." Ollie looks like he's trying to let go of his idea but can't.

"And it's not about Nate falling asleep. It's about him escaping the Nexus Zone."

"You keep saying that," Courtney says. "I thought waking Nate up was the point."

"It is," I say, "but . . ." I can't explain to them how I know. I just know. "Escaping the Nexus Zone is the way to show him *how* to wake up."

"You know," Ollie says, his voice scratchy with emotion, "some of us have good ideas, too. They can't all be yours. Nate's not all yours."

"Somnus? That's your good idea? What's that even mean?"

"It's—" he starts. "It's the Roman god of sleep, okay? I spent all this time looking it up, but I guess that's not good enough for you." He throws his folder down. It bursts open as it crashes to the floor. Papers spill out, notes and sketches and lists. There's a character in a black uniform that looks just like Nate, and another with a dark ponytail that's longer than Courtney's, but not by much. I see the head of a third hero wearing goggles instead of Ollie's thick glasses.

I wonder if I'm in there, too, what powers he gave me. But I can't get lost in that thrill, because it's not about me. This is about Nate. Waking my best friend up, showing him how to escape the Zone before it's too late, *that's* why we're here. We can't afford to get distracted.

"How about we all just work on our own ideas today?" Courtney suggests. She kneels to reassemble Ollie's folder. "We can pick the best parts."

Ollie retreats into a corner, picking at some chipping paint on the windowsill. I came here thinking submitting to the contest would get us closer to saving Nate, but I feel farther away from him than ever.

After an hour or so of our silent working, Courtney's mom pops her head in. "Ollie, how's your brother, dear?"

Ollie examines his own feet. "The same," he mumbles.

I stop and listen. We've been trying hard not to ask Ollie too many questions about Nate.

"They're planning to bring him out of the coma in a few weeks, I think, but they're not sure exactly when. I guess the doctors don't like what they see. His readings, or something like that."

Nobody says anything.

"They're afraid of how long he's been on the ventilator, too," Ollie continues. He looks up at Mrs. Hoffman. "I guess it's not good to be on it so long, but the pressure in his brain still hasn't gone down enough."

Courtney gulps so deeply, I hear it from across the room.

"Oh, I'm so sorry," Mrs. Hoffman says.

Nate's not the same. He's getting worse. A few weeks, that's all we have. I wish those doctors would just pick a date so we'd know for sure what our deadline was. They can't wake him up before we use our comic to show him the way home.

"It's not as bad as it sounds," Ollie, noticing our expressions, says quickly.

Mrs. Hoffman steps toward Ollie and pulls him into a sideways hug. "I hope he gets better real soon. I'll be praying. And please let your mother know I'm here if she needs anything."

Ollie's nodding as he separates from her. He sits at the desk and absently pushes a blank piece of comic paper around it.

Courtney's mom shifts her attention to her daughter.

"Don't forget your father is supposed to call at six. Try to be done by then so you can talk to him."

"Mmm." Courtney focuses on a corner of the whiteboard, paying more attention than seems necessary to eradicating every trace of our black, blue, and red notes.

Mrs. Hoffman switches on her stern mom-voice. "Courtney."

"What?" Courtney half shouts, spinning around and slamming the eraser down.

"Come out here. Right now." Mrs. Hoffman points at the floor.

Head down, Courtney obeys her mother and steps into the hallway. Mrs. Hoffman leads her away from the office and they conduct a low conversation in the kitchen.

"Is her dad out of town?" I ask Ollie.

"He doesn't live here anymore, Sherlock." He stalks to the desk and yanks open the top drawer, retrieving a pencil. "Quit asking her about him."

"Are they getting divorced?"

Ollie sends me an exhausted expression. I can't help it. I've only had one other friend whose parents got divorced, and he ended up moving away the next year. Steve Bochy. I remember Nate and I showed up at his house just as the moving truck pulled up, how he had to tell us he was leaving for California with his mom and her new husband. We ended up helping them load the truck.

I just met Courtney. Sure, she can be kind of annoying, but I don't want her to move. She reappears in the door-frame, and I immediately wonder if she heard me say that word. *Divorced.*

If she did, she doesn't say anything. In fact, none of us say much more the whole afternoon. Not about comas or brothers, divorces or fathers, double eliminations or base-ball. No arguments about whose ideas are best. No more brainstorming. Mostly we just lean over the desk, watching Ollie work. He draws the most amazing full-page panel of the Nexus Zone, featuring Lake Carol and the mountains beyond it, the lightning storms, Scott River.

At the very end, on top of a hill that seems miles off, he adds the tiny figures of three kids. They're using the high vantage point to look out over the landscape. One of them, one of us, has a hand over his eyes, staring out into the vast Nexus Zone.

Searching for a way home.

- 15 -

By the time Nate's thirteenth birthday party comes the next Saturday, he's been in the hospital exactly two weeks, but it feels more like forever.

Mom and I pause outside his room. Ollie and his parents are already there. Jake, too, with his mom and dad. They've lived next door to Nate for a decade.

They're all facing the other way, huddled over an ice cream cake, their murmured voices drowned out by the louder memories blasting out of some laptop speakers. Shouts, screams of delight. The computer's sitting on a card table at the foot of Nate's bed, and a projector next to it sends fast-moving clips onto the white wall. If Nate's eyes were open—could open—they'd be staring straight at the home movies filling his room.

My heart pounds. Beads of sweat dot my forehead. No one's seen me yet. If I leave now, they'll never know I was here. I turn and lower my shoulder into Mom, trying to squeeze past her. She pushes back. We freeze into a stalemate in the hallway.

Mom grips my shoulders. "I know this is hard, Dan."

I pull away from her. I was so sure Nate would be back with the Giants by now, a bump on his head maybe, but otherwise the same old Nate. But he looks like he's trapped deeper than I ever imagined, lying in that hospital bed, eyes closed, not moving.

"Come on, Dan," Mom whispers. "I'm right here with you."

Ollie's approaching the projector. "Hey," he says to me through a mouthful of cake. He reaches out and plays with the focus.

I glance at the screen. A family vacation the Templetons took out to Chautauqua Lake a couple summers ago flashes across it. I've seen this movie. Nate is trying to teach Ollie to water ski, but Ollie keeps biting the dust—er, water—face-first. "What's all this?"

"The doctors told my parents about FAST, too," Ollie says. "So, you know"—he gestures at the screen—"home movies. They figure maybe hearing our voices, old memories, will help."

Jake is laughing so hard he has to set his cake down on Nate's bed. "Dude," he says, smacking Ollie's shoulder. "You are the worst water skier ever."

"Shut up. I was little."

Jake looks up and down his short frame. "Yeah, you're a regular LeBron James now."

Mom has been hovering behind us, but after taking in the first few moments of our conversation, she seems to decide it's okay to join the other adults. We must look normal. I'm trying to get better at that. Maybe it's working.

The scene on the screen shifts. Our bike trail in the woods. Last summer. Nate steams toward a jump, standing up on the pedals as his bike hits the mound and leaps high into the air. He turns his front wheel back and forth like a pro BMX-er, then sticks the landing with a dust-filled skid.

I remember this day; it was me filming him. I even hear my own "Whoop!" as he lands.

"Yeah!" Nate cries on the screen, giving me a thumbs-up.

It's so weird to see him full of life on a wall, feet from where his body remains unchanged—the tubes attached to his nose, his shallow breathing, the thin blanket pulled up to his neck but still leaving his feet exposed. Guess I finally found a reason not to be jealous of him for being so tall.

There's something else, too. Something about the trails we made, the mounds of dirt, our jumps, the pond in the background. Something familiar, but I can't quite put my finger on it.

Jake snatches up his cake, swallows a quick forkful, then puts it down on the bed again, inches from Nate's socked feet, powder-blue ones he'd never wear in the real world.

"Where's that bike trail?" Jake asks. "We gotta do that."

My mind fills with responses.

It was our place, mine and Nate's. You can't come.

How can you eat cake right now?

How can you laugh?

"Your turn, Dan," Nate's projected self yells from the wall.

I've heard him say my name thousands of times before, but this is the first time since the accident. I look back at the real Nate, lying in the bed, then to the laughing, joking, two-dimensional Nate on the wall. Back to the real Nate again. The fake one. The real. The fake.

Real. Fake.

Something rumbles in my head, picking up speed, an onrushing train.

Then everything is quiet, and all I see is the ice-cold cake, inches from Nate's helpless toes. I grab the food off the bed and thrust it toward our new pitcher, Nate's replacement. As if anyone could ever replace Nate.

"That's not a table, man," I tell Jake.

The paper plate starts to fold against his chest as Jake reaches for it. I let go before he has it and it tumbles down, flipping once and landing on the clean floor with a wet thud.

Jake flaps his frustrated hands against his sides. "Aw, come on, Summers!"

I search for an empty corner to hide in. I can't be here anymore. I came to see Nate, but he isn't here, he's somewhere else.

I race for the door and rush into the hallway. Right away I slam into a white coat and stumble back. "Whoa," Dr. Tori says, her eyes flashing with recognition. "Hey, you're—"

I spin away, sprinting down the hall until it veers left. I can still hear voices behind me, Mom's loudest of all. "Dan!"

I take another turn, right this time, no idea where I'm going. The hallway ends. I'm trapped.

Dr. Tori jogs around the bend, a clipboard dangling from one hand. She comes to a stop in front of me, her shoulders rising and falling with each heavy breath. "Hey. Dan, right? The *Captain Nexus* fan. Was that your friend back there?"

"Why did you tell them about FAST?" I yell. "Why?"

"Why did I . . . ?" Her eyes widen. "That wasn't me. I don't even work in neurology. But Dan, it's a common study. His family should know about it, too, don't you think?"

"Home movies aren't going to help. You said a story. He needs *Captain Nexus*."

Superheroes are the only ones with the power to save people. Why can't anyone else see that?

Dr. Tori straightens and pulls her clipboard tight to her chest, regarding me a moment. Mom rounds the corner and skids to a stop right next to the doctor. She glances at her, then glowers at me. "Daniel Summers."

"Dan's mom?" Dr. Tori asks her.

Mom seems surprised that the doctor answers her before I do. She nods, too out of breath and confused to use actual words.

"Can we speak in private a moment?"

Mom nods again, and the two of them move off a few feet, leaving me alone in the corner. I'm sort of afraid to move. Besides, I've got nowhere to go.

They whisper some, and then Dr. Tori steps toward me again. "I think you should come up to my office," she tells me. "And your mom agrees."

I check Mom's face. "I'll be right here when you get back," she assures me.

Two quick steps bring Dr. Tori to the elevator. She presses the button for up, then gestures for me to join her. "Hurry up. I have something important to show you."

Dr. Tori's office is amazing. Compared with the mostly white hospital corridors, the huge room filled with red-and-gold Iron Man memorabilia is like staring into the sun. There are action figures and posters, coffee mugs, pens and pencils. There's even a full-size shell-head helmet on the sill of her window.

"I thought you were a *Captain Nexus* fan," I say.

"Oh, I am." She sets her clipboard on her desk and perches on the front edge of it. "But I'm also a heart surgeon." She taps a finger on her chest, just to the left of center. "So I'll always be a Tony Stark fan first. Did you know in the original armor it wasn't an arc reactor that kept the shrapnel away from his heart, it was—"

"A magnet. And transistors."

"That's right," Dr. Tori says. "You know your stuff."

I shrug and examine the detail on the helmet.

"Dan, I told you about FAST because you looked like you could use some hope that day. I thought knowing about the study would help you. But I'm not your friend's doctor. His real doctors have a responsibility to his family. You understand that, right?"

"I guess."

"Why do you think those home movies won't work? They're memories, aren't they?"

"Yeah, but . . . I know Nate. He's—" How do I tell her I think my friend might be trapped in the Nexus Zone? That only being shown how to escape can really bring him home?

"We're making a comic for him. It was supposed to be ready for his birthday, but . . ." I spread out my hands. "We missed it. I think maybe I'm ruining it. My other friends were doing fine before, but now I'm doing it with them and it's like everything's different. We have no good ideas. I'm not helping. I just stand there with no job. They don't need me."

She twists her mouth to one side and thinks for a few seconds before saying, "So it's like your friend on the baseball field, right?"

"What?"

"I heard one of the other doctors say he was a pitcher on your team. Is that true?"

"Yeah. So?"

"Well, I mean, the pitcher only throws the ball, doesn't he? Once the other team hits it, he just stands there and—"

I shake my head. "No way. That's not how it works. A pitcher has all sorts of jobs. Like if a hit happens and there are base runners coming home, the pitcher has to go in behind the plate and back up the catcher, or else—"

"Oh, I see," Dr. Tori says. "So he's not really doing nothing, watching the rest of you do all the work."

"Of course not. Who ever told you that? Nobody just stands around. Every position has a job on every kind of play." I'm almost yelling at her. "The hitter waiting on deck screams, 'Slide!' when one of us is racing home and the throw is going to make it close. The first-base coach yells, 'Back!' the moment the other team's pitcher starts a pick-off move toward first. The pitcher has to cover first if a grounder is hit that way." I huff. "Nobody stands around. Ever."

Dr. Tori taps her finger against her chin. "Makes sense." She moves around to the other side of her desk and pulls open a drawer. "Can I tell you a secret?"

I nod.

"When I was about your age, my father passed away. A heart attack, totally out of the blue. For a long time, I didn't think I could do anything worthwhile without him around to help me." Her eyes are soft. She catches me staring and redirects her gaze out the window. "Then I found his old comics. Iron Man changed everything. I mean, really, he had an injured heart and look at all the good he was doing. A real hero.

"I decided I should do the same thing. So I went to medical school, studied hearts because I wanted to help people who needed theirs fixed. I love doing it. And you know what?" She looks at me again, smiles and winks. "I'm not half-bad at it, either."

Dr. Tori's hand dives into the drawer, and emerges with a button. She approaches me with it, and as she gets closer, the image on its face comes into focus. Captain Nexus. "I save these for the people who get it," she whispers as she pins it onto my shirt, right over my heart.

She takes a step back from me. "You love *Captain Nexus*, right?"

I nod again.

"Here's the best thing I can suggest, Dan. Keep working on the comic, because I can tell you love doing it. Because it'll light up your brain during a time when other stuff wants to make it dark in there." She taps a knuckle against her temple. "And if you don't feel like you're helping your friends, maybe you're just not seeing the whole picture."

I squint more doubt at her.

"Sometimes you're supposed to be in a spot, even if the ball's not meant to come your way, right? Just in case. So maybe you're supposed to be in that room with your friends. That's your spot, your job, right now. And there won't be a thing in the world you can do to help them if you aren't waiting right where they're expecting you to be."

- 16 -

The Templetons and Jake accept my apology when I return to Nate's room. Mom stays quiet through the whole car ride home. I use the time to continue cooking up a big idea in my head, one Dr. Tori gave me.

The Giants have a practice scheduled for the very next day. I text and call around that night, asking everyone to arrive early, before even Coach gets there.

"What is this?" Sally, who's always been a loud chewer, asks when I reach him. He gulps his dinner down.

I try to seem confident. "Players-only meeting."

"Cool," he says. One of his forty-nine sisters complains about wanting to change the channel. We hang up.

Mom's clicking away on her laptop in the kitchen, zooming in on a photo of a basket of lemons. Some of them have white stuff growing on them, others are green and furry. "They put these in the water," she mumbles.

She's started to type up one of her reports when I finish my last call. "Mom, can you bring me to practice early tomorrow?"

She answers without tearing her eyes from another picture on her screen, this time a dead bug, turned upside down on its back on a stainless-steel counter, five inches from a huge knife on a slimy cutting board. "Sure."

"Thanks." I zip up to my room. I have a lot of planning to do. Tomorrow's not going to be easy. I want to make sure I do it just right.

"Everybody reads *Captain Nexus*, right?"

The whole team, kneeling or sitting cross-legged in front of me along the third base line, nods and murmurs.

Kurt squints at me. "You know this is baseball practice, right, Summers? We have baseball to . . . practice."

"For what?" Jake asks. "The season's almost over."

"No, it's not," I insist. "Do you think the Nexus Five will stop fighting the Hollow, even if they lose their powers?"

The Giants stare at me.

I take a deep breath. I can do this. I have to. Because *Captain Nexus* isn't the only story that might reach Nate.

Winning the championship . . . he'd definitely want to hear that one, too. But we have to actually pull it off first.

"The Five had talents before Captain Nexus came back and gave them their superpowers, right? Spark was a doctor, the Blue Witch was . . . she was an engineer, wasn't she? The Red Flame worked at that aeronautics facility. Advanced machinery. Remember how Scott Peters was in honors everything before he became Nexus Boy and dropped out of school?"

I pause, waiting for more arguments. None come. I take a deep breath and organize the thoughts that first formed in Dr. Tori's office. "Before Nate got so good, we knew how to play, how to field our positions even when the other team was hitting the ball. We're just like the Nexus Five."

"It's not the same," Jake says. "I can't—"

"Yes, you can. I've seen you do it. Didn't you shut out Dromberg two years ago?"

"Yeah, but that wasn't like Nate. I didn't even strike a single guy out."

"Exactly! You moved your pitches in and out of the zone. You let them hit, and you let us field." I look around at the rest of the team. "And we did, just about every chance that day, remember?"

"That was so long ago, man," Sally says. "We were just kids."

"Yeah, *Captain Nexus* didn't even exist yet," Kurt agrees.

"Might as well be a past life."

I'm running out of words. Coach Wiggins pulls his Jeep into the lot and parks.

"That talent's already inside us, guys. It didn't go anywhere. We just have to stay focused on what we do best. Stick together."

"I guess," Jake mutters.

My teammates study their gloves, the grass around them. Coach climbs out of his car. Two bicycles ride up behind it, splitting around the Jeep and coming back together once they're past it. Ollie. Courtney. They've been showing up to every Giants game, and most of our practices, too.

Dr. Tori's voice echoes in my head some more. *Keep working on the comic, because I can tell you love doing it.* Something about lighting up your brain in dark times.

How can I help the Giants understand when suddenly I'm not sure myself?

I think hard, staring at my approaching friends as they race toward the field. Maybe it's because of how hard she's pedaling, her ponytail bouncing, but Courtney's voice from our first bike ride together pops into my head next.

What do you love about comics?

That's it.

I toss my glove at our catcher to force him to look up at

me. "Kurt. What do you love about baseball?"

"I . . . what do you mean?"

"I mean, what do you love about it? Why do you play?"

Kurt hesitates. The field's so quiet, I hear birds chirping in the woods.

"I guess . . . I love digging a pitch out of the dirt, or sliding over to block it." He squeezes some Purell into his hands and rubs them together greedily. I'm not even sure he knows he's doing it. "I love gunning down a runner who's trying to steal second."

Jake raises his hand.

"What is this, Mrs. Estrada's math class?" Sally snorts.

"Oh, man, she was the *worst*," Mark says.

"I love," Jake says really loud, so that everyone else quiets down. "I love catching the corner of the plate so the hitter only gets a piece of it. End of the bat."

"Stealing a homer at the wall," Craig adds.

"Guarding the line, saving a double," Sally says.

Kurt sits up on his knees. "I love how there's no clock. Maybe someday there'll be a game that goes on forever."

"Yeah," Jake agrees, his eyes distant, as if he's in the stands at Kurt's never-ending dream game right now.

"I love—" Kurt hesitates, like he's afraid to say the rest.

"What?" I encourage him.

"I love playing the same game my grandfather played in

Cuba. It's like . . . like it helps me know who he was, even if I never got to meet him."

Sally nods, and his voice is low when he agrees. "Yeah, man. Awesome."

Jake stuffs his face into his mitt and inhales. "I love the way my glove smells," his muffled voice announces. "Like leather and oil and dirt and grass and sweat."

The whole team gawks at him.

"What?" he says, lowering his glove. "Is that weird?"

"It's super weird," Sally says, chucking his mitt at Jake, who ducks. When he looks up again, Sally's in mid-dive on top of him. They start to wrestle. The rest of the team joins in.

For the first time since Nate got hurt, we're ourselves again. The Giants are a team again.

Coach has shouldered his bag. He's craning his neck. It's definitely the first time we've all beaten him to practice like this. And most of us are in a wrestling match better than pay-per-view. He starts marching toward us with a confused look on his face.

"We wanted to play for Nate," I shout at the group, over Sally's cries of "Yield, villain!" I step back to avoid Mark, rolling toward my legs. "But we can't forget to play for ourselves, too. Because we love baseball. We can't forget how we used to play, before we started relying on Nate so much."

Coach creaks open the gate and drops his bag on the bench.

"We have to be more like the Nexus Five, guys."

"There's nine of us," Sally says. He's pushing Jake's face into the grass with one hand as he uses the other to count the Giants. "The Nexus Nine."

The Nexus Nine. Wow, Ollie was kind of right. That does sound good.

I watch everyone nod in agreement. "Even without their powers, when number fifteen comes out, I bet the Five will defeat the Hollow. We can win the tournament the same way." I meet as many eyes as I can. "Together."

Coach Wiggins arrives at our circle. "What's all this?"

The Giants freeze in mid-wrestle. No one says anything. He surveys us, claps his hands loudly. "Okay, break it up. Let's play some ball."

That afternoon, we have the best practice ever.

- 17 -

Tuesday evening Sally and I team up on a perfect hit-and-run against Mason City. It's a risky move by Coach, because even though Sally's one of our best hitters, he's slow as molasses on the base paths. Nate used to call him the Reverse Flash.

But we don't question Coach's signs, and I poke a single through the hole in the infield. Sally races off first, motoring around second and heading for third. As the relay comes in, he starts his slide. It's going to be super close, and at first I think he's out for sure, but the throw from the cutoff man comes in hot and high. The ball gets past their third baseman, heading for the fence. Sally staggers to his feet and charges home, taking one last, big, leaping step across the plate.

We escape Mason City with a 5–4 win, our first of the tournament. We're still alive.

The next day Ollie's visiting Nate, and Courtney's cousin is having a birthday. No choice—our comic has to wait. But I need to be doing *something* for Nate, so I change into shorts and a T-shirt and rush into the backyard. In the woods behind our house, up a short path toward a clearing, the bike trail Nate and I built last year winds its way around a little pond hidden by the trees. It takes me a minute to recognize the first jump, covered over with dead leaves and pine straw. The rest of the trail is nearly as bad, and it reminds me even more how long it's been since I found the time to sneak back here.

Some kind of animal has burrowed deep into one side of the tightly packed mounds. I poke the hole with a stick, hoping for a snake, but there's nothing. I retreat, scrambling up the tall hill we used as a starting gate. I sit, pulling my knees into my chest.

I wait for my best friend. I wait for Nate.

This was our place; we never told any of the other Giants about it. Not that it was something we discussed, some promise we made or blood oath we took. It was just ours, and we both knew it.

Actually, the bike trail started out as Dad's idea. He

used to dump his grass clippings back here, and one day he suggested we build some ramps and a course around the pond. He even drew up a little diagram to show me how it could look.

I didn't need much convincing. We started the next day. But then he landed his dream job, the huge downtown restoration project, and all our work out here just . . . stopped. Maybe this weekend we could start up again, he would tell me. Or maybe next week. But maybe never came. I'd gaze out my back window at the trees, unable to see the half-finished hills and barely dug-out trail through them but knowing they were out here, like ghosts from another time.

Until one day Nate was over, and he caught me staring. "What do you keep looking at? Is the Hollow about to attack us from your backyard or something?"

Nate and I never kept secrets. We couldn't, not when we each knew what the other was thinking all the time. So I told him all about the bike trail project, and he immediately got so gung ho about it, he actually wanted to work on it more than me.

My best friend couldn't stop talking about how awesome the daredevil course filled with death-defying jumps was going to be. And before I knew it, we were dragging shovels and rakes out to the trees, working long summer days for weeks to carve out the curling paths and build up the dirt ramps.

On our work days I would beat Nate back here, of course, since all I had to do was walk out my back door. But I'd always wait for him before starting any work. We were doing it together, and it felt like I shouldn't make a move until he showed up.

I used to sit in this same spot. Unlike our man-made ramps, this hill had been here already, at the edge of the pond, which sometimes froze over hard enough in winter for hockey. It was why Dad had chosen this part of the woods for our course. The mountain made a perfect launching ramp, like the ones Olympic ski jumpers use.

Nate would ride straight through our yard, up the path, crashing through the woods, popping out of the trees, big smile on his face, Pepsi in one hand, the long spade draped over his legs bouncing as he pumped his bike over the brush. I turn that way now and the breeze blows. Leaves rustle, branches waver, but there's no bike. No Pepsi. No shovel.

No Nate.

I stand up and walk the trail, fighting memories as I stagger down the hill, dirt sliding beneath my feet. Over the first mound, where Nate scratched a big *X* on the ground the day we'd first starting working out here.

"Right here," he said. "First jump. Angle of that hill,

it'll be awesome. We'll fly."

"We should wear capes," I said. "We'll be heroes."

"Because we can fly?"

"Sure. Why not? Flying's a cool power."

Nate stabbed his shovel into the center of the *X*. "I guess. But you don't always need a power."

"What else would you need?"

I remember him shrugging, like he knew the answer but didn't want to say. But in my mind, if you had powers, you were either a hero or a villain. I never thought of myself as a villain. Not before four corners, anyway.

"Well, I'm wearing a cape."

Nate shrugged some more. We started digging. I never did wear that cape.

Why didn't we come back this year? We'd gotten so wrapped up in the season, the Giants' winning streak, the *Captain Nexus* reads and rumors, we totally blanked on this place. But now that I'm here again, I'm finding I can remember Nate in a way I wasn't able to in the hospital, sitting right next to him.

I pick up speed. Over the second jump, then around the curve where you had to skid one foot along the dirt for balance if you were going too fast. Down the straightaway toward the third jump, a quick curve past two trees. The final, fourth jump, then up the back side of the hill.

By the time I reach it, I'm sprinting. At the top, the

starting gate, I bend over, hands on my knees, panting.

More memories of Nate spin through my mind, all the times we chased each other out here, all our talks about heroes and teams and comics and baseball as we dug and raked and planned.

When I stand straight again, I see it: what seemed so familiar on the screen in Nate's hospital room. The pond's the same shape as Lake Carol, and this hill that I've stood on so many times before looms over the water just like the highest peak in all of the Nexus Mountains.

We never planned it this way, not on purpose anyway, but standing here now, it's all so clear. The bike trail *is* the Nexus Zone.

Maybe I'm imagining things, maybe my eyes are just seeing the trail this way because I've spent so much time staring at Sanderson's drawings over the past year. The Nexus Zone is ingrained deep into my mind, and here I am, in a place that looks almost exactly like it, except in miniature. A real place, here, on Earth, not just some made-up comic-book drawing.

Did we do it without realizing? Was there some unseen force guiding us?

I stare. Think. Dream.

If . . . if Nate is trapped in the Zone, too, then maybe when he escapes, he might show up here, the way Captain Nexus sometimes ends up in Manhattan, sometimes New

Mexico. Nate could crash right through these woods, just like he always used to, looking for home.

Maybe it's dumb, but what if it's true? What if this is my spot, the place I need to be, just in case?

Everyone's waiting for Nate at the hospital all the time—his parents, the Giants, the doctors—but no one's waiting here. Not a single person is making sure this place—our place—is ready for my best friend to come back to.

In my head, I know these things aren't real. Nate won't suddenly materialize in this clearing. Our comic can't wake him. But every time I think they might be true, even for a second, my heart soars. I feel like a little kid again, back when I would set my head on the pillow with a smile on my face because I still believed in the tooth fairy.

I look around at the downed branches, the overgrown brush, the unkempt dirt. How could I have let it decay so badly? I definitely need to come back, as often as I can, with my shovel and rake next time. To wait for Nate. To take care of what we built together. Our place.

- 18 -

Heroes don't usually seek out a lot of credit. That's part of what makes them heroes.

They have secret identities, after all, so most people have no idea who they really are. And that's how the heroes want it. I mean, they wear masks for a reason, right?

One of the best parts of a comic, though, is when someone close to the hero finds out who she really is, the powers he has, all the great stuff she can do. In that moment they remember the amazing battles, the incredible feats, the rescued people, realizing that all this time the hero has been right next to them, but they never even guessed it.

Sometimes one of the people really close to the hero

already knows his secret. They're desperate to share it with the rest of the world, to show everyone who thinks he's nothing but a billionaire playboy or a kid who's always late for class or a pilot who takes too many risks, who the hero *really* is.

Ever since I found how great Ollie's art is, I've been wanting to tell someone about it. About him. Dad, maybe, if he could spare a few seconds, but he's been working more than ever. The Tall Ship contest will have to do.

"Hurry up," I say. "He'll be here any second."

"Relax." Courtney puts a hand up right in front of my face. "I'm almost done."

It's Saturday morning. Nate's been in the hospital a full three weeks. This whole week had been mostly useless. It had taken us more time than it should've to pull together our submission of Ollie's work—choosing which drawings to send, taking careful photographs under the right light, drafting our cover letter—and the deadline crept up on us. We had to get this email off by five p.m. today or Ollie wouldn't be entered in the Tall Ship *Captain Nexus* Fan Art competition at all.

"Do you think they send a confirmation?" she asks.

"Probably."

"We should use my address and email, then. Otherwise they'll send stuff straight to him."

"Good idea."

Courtney keys in her contact information but keeps Ollie's name. Then she straightens and points at her screen. "Okay. Read it through one more time."

I examine our letter, four or five revisions away from that original draft, looking for typos I know I won't find. We've been over it so many times there isn't even a stray comma.

The doorbell rings. I hear Mrs. Hoffman welcoming Ollie into the house. In a panic, I reach out for the mouse and click send.

"What'd you do?" Courtney asks, grabbing at my hand as if it wasn't already too late.

"He's here! We weren't going to get another chance."

Ollie appears in the office doorway. Courtney closes her mouth and the lid to her laptop at the same time.

Our friend narrows his eyes. "What's going on?"

"I—" My breath catches.

"Just more Geeker rumors," Courtney says smoothly. "Nothing new."

The next few days are some of the most painful of my life. We continue struggling with ideas for our comic, suffering through a bunch of false starts.

The story's not good enough. Start over.

Ollie hates his art. Start over.

Nate doesn't have a big enough role in the plot. Start. Over.

Without the finished comic, I'm afraid to visit Nate in the hospital. What do I have to show as proof we're not giving up? Nothing but half-finished pages, stories going nowhere.

Ollie overheard the doctors talking to his parents again about waking Nate. He still didn't get an exact date, but it sounded like it was getting closer. We need to hurry, or Nate won't be able to find his way back to us when they try it. If it isn't ready in time, if we don't light the right path for him, he might stay lost forever.

We all feel the pressure, but for some reason we can't make progress on any one idea. It's like we're afraid of going down the wrong fork in a road, of not being able to turn around and find our way back in time. In a lot of ways, we're as trapped as Nate is.

Between sessions, I keep heading back to the bike trail, sneaking out first Dad's old shovel, then his rake from the toolshed. I bring something else, too, on my phone—photographs of George Sanderson's Nexus Zone, mostly from the first two issues of *Captain Nexus and the Nexus Five*. Just in case they aren't burned into my brain already, which they totally are.

I check the photos as I work, doing my best to finish

turning our place into my very own version of George Sanderson's invented land. The Nexus Mountains rise, Scott River begins to meander toward Lake Carol. Nate'll recognize it for sure.

My new projects keep me busy. The days blur, from Giants practice to the bike trail and back to Courtney's. One afternoon I finally remember to ask for my *Alpha Flight* back.

"Oh, yeah," Courtney says. She bites her lip. "I have it, definitely, but not here." She lowers her voice. "I left it at my dad's apartment. Sorry."

Ollie shoots me a look of warning. "That's okay," I tell her, fighting back my thumping heart and trying not to imagine the condition my comic must be in by now.

We get back to work. Every time we're stuck, which feels like all the time, I bring up issue #15 of the real comic. "Captain Nexus will escape. We'll see how he does it. Then we'll know what to do. We'll get moving again."

It's Tuesday when Courtney finally shrugs and responds. "You're probably right. Guess we'll find out for sure tomorrow."

That night, I struggle to fall asleep. When I finally do, I dream again and again of fake hands grabbing my best friend's arm, the ball flying toward him . . .

I jolt awake. Wednesday, finally. But not just any Wednesday.

It's a *Captain Nexus* Wednesday. #15, the most anticipated issue yet.

A full month has passed since *Captain Nexus and the Nexus Five* #14 came out, and almost as long since Nate's accident. Geeker's been going wild with rumors of what might happen next. The entire internet's on the edge of their seats. The mods have even had to shut down their boards a few times because the servers got overloaded.

Mrs. Templeton invites us all to the group read, same as always. Kurt and I pedal toward Jackson Comics and Games that afternoon, same as always, except today my hands are super sweaty on my handlebars. And it's not even that hot out.

We park our bikes and dart for the door. Kurt gets to it first. He pulls his sleeve down so it covers his hand and tries to tug the door open that way.

"Will you forget about germs for two seconds?" I cry as I shove him aside.

Some high schooler we don't recognize is sitting behind the counter. He has a nose ring and long, greasy brown hair. "Where's Reggie?" I ask.

"Home sick. Flu or something," the kid says without looking up from his textbook.

Kurt peers around the register, then yanks his Giants cap off. "*Captain Nexus*?"

"Captain what now?"

"*Captain Nexus*," I say. I'm really trying to stay calm. "Number fifteen? It's supposed to be out today. I'm sure Reggie must've mentioned it. It's kind of a big deal."

"Guys, I don't know anything about comics. I'm just filling in. Friend of a friend thing." The kid gestures at the shelves. "What you see is what you get."

Kurt rushes over, scanning the racks. He finds one copy of #14. He picks it up and shows it to me, shaking his head. No #15 in sight.

I turn back to Nose Ring. I'm trying not to have an actual asthma attack. "Reggie always keeps the new *Captain Nexus* up here. One per customer."

The kid pushes against the glass so that his stool leans back on two legs. He peers under the counter. "There's nothing down here."

Kurt darts forward. His fingers are still gripping tight to his hat. He sets it down so he can hoist himself up. "But it has to be," he insists.

"Hands off." Nose Ring pries Kurt's fingers from the glass, and the Giants catcher drops to the floor, immediately scrambling for emergency Purell.

Nose Ring's muffled voice floats up from under the

counter. "I'm telling you, there's no stack of *Captain Neon* anywhere down here."

"Nexus!" Kurt and I yell together.

We search the store. The annoyed kid, eager to be rid of us, lets us go everywhere. But *Captain Nexus* #15 isn't in Reggie's office in back or in the storage closet. It didn't slip behind one of the racks, or get pinned under a long box. It's nowhere.

The issue must be late. But George Sanderson's *never* late.

Dejected, we mount our bikes and start pedaling back home. "Maybe they'll have them at Wegman's," I suggest, even though I know they never carry comics like *Captain Nexus* in the magazine section of our local grocery store.

When Kurt looks up to remind me of that, his eyes widen. He clutches at his hair. "My hat!"

"You left it on the counter."

"I gotta go back."

We hustle back to the shop. When we arrive, a big HurryUP! delivery truck is parked outside, the orange-and-brown logo of a man running with a package under his arm filling one entire side.

Dropping our bikes, we rush back in. Boxes are everywhere—there's even one on the glass counter, and it's currently smashing Kurt's hat. Nose Ring's already cut it open. He reaches inside and pulls out a small stack of crisp new comics: every one another gleaming copy of *Captain Nexus and the Nexus Five* #15.

The kid points at the HurryUP! deliveryman. "Shipment was late," he says, shrugging. "How was I supposed to know?" He turns the cover toward us. The Nexus Five—all of them but the Captain—are battling the Hollow. Nexus Boy looks unconscious, Spark crouching over him. The Blue Witch and Red Flame are still fighting, but they seem overmatched. The Hollow's grin makes it look like the creature believes it's only seconds from victory.

"This what you wanted?" the high schooler asks.

I can't find my voice. My hand stretches out to touch the issue as Kurt's soft mutter speaks for us both.

"Whoa."

- 19 -

As we file down into the Templetons' basement, everyone is careful not to touch Nate's empty recliner. We step around it like it's a minefield. No one wants to think about Nate not being here for the read. First time ever.

The recliner had been Nate's dad's, but he'd upgraded, and one afternoon after I got off at Nate's stop with him, we found his old recliner, faded blue and tattered, parked at the end of the driveway. Nate rushed into the house and asked what it was doing out there.

"That old thing? There's a charity group picking it up," Mr. Templeton said.

"Why can't I have it?" Nate asked. "For the basement."

"You don't want that ratty chair. You've got nice couches down there."

Nate pulled at his dad's arm. "Pleeease."

Mr. Templeton shrugged. "If you boys can get it down there on your own, have at it."

As soon as he turned his back, Nate and I looked at each other, tapping our noses again and again, like we might lose track of where they were on our faces.

We wrestled the bulky chair all the way up the driveway, through the front door, down the long hallway, and around the turn to the basement door. For a minute, it didn't seem like it would fit, but finally we pushed it through, the wooden lever scraping on the doorframe, Mr. Templeton yelling out, "You boys watch out for my walls now!"

At the read, I glance down at that same wooden lever, finding the deep gouges that marked that day's adventure. I can't stop my sigh of relief. There's proof the Nate I remember was really here.

Mrs. Templeton still bought two issues of the comic. She gives one to Ollie. The other she balances on the arm of Nate's recliner, as if there's some chance the waiting book might lure him home. It won't, but this issue *is* going to help us finish *our* story. And when we read that to him, Nate'll hear us. He'll come back.

Kurt and I are at the pool table again, Ollie and Courtney by the stairs, Sally and Jake on the couch. Maybe it's my imagination, but I feel everyone staring at me. I exhale and glance at Nate's empty chair one more time.

Without Nate, we're all breaking *Rule One: No one reads before anyone else.* But finding out what happens next—how Captain Nexus escapes the Zone—is the most important thing right now. More important, even, than the rules.

"Come on," I say to the room. "Let's read."

Captain Nexus staggers to his feet, bringing with him a fistful of yellowish dirt. He tries to open a portal back to New Mexico. The doorway flashes into existence, then sputters. For a few seconds it's wide enough for him to see his team. They're still battling the Hollow.

The dark, void-like creature is turned back by a blast of freezing ice from the Blue Witch. He regains his footing and creates a black shield to fend off her attack. Just as the Captain's wife presses her advantage, however, her powers weaken. The Hollow converts his shield into a floating bubble of grayish energy. It envelops the Blue Witch, her skin already changing from light blue to its natural color as she twists away.

The bubble picks her up and the Hollow uses it to slam her into a wall. The Blue Witch crumples to the ground.

"Carol!" Captain Nexus shouts. In the center of the page, he raises one leg into the portal, which shifts and shimmers. The battle continues in the panels surrounding him, left to right, top to bottom.

Nexus Boy surges forward to face the Hollow. He clenches his fists, raises his hands, but nothing happens. The Hollow shows him a jagged smile. Then he shrugs, summoning all his power, and sends a black beam of solid energy straight at Scott Peters. The youngest member of the team flies backward from one panel into the next, slamming into some machinery and landing in an awkward heap.

"No!" Captain Nexus cries, stepping through the portal completely. We turn the page. When our hero reaches the other side, he finds himself not in New Mexico at all, but still in the Nexus Zone. The portal failed, dumping him back in the same place he started.

The Captain tries again. Nothing. He calms himself with deep breaths. Maybe he just needs to concentrate. He raises his hands, hesitating, then calls forth as much power from deep inside as he can.

The air sparks, but the flickering lights fade out, like embers floating up from a dying fire. He can't get to his team. He can't even see what's happening anymore.

"No . . . ," Captain Nexus moans. "No!"

He blasts a nearby rock with a beam of energy, then drops to his knees in anguish.

I look up for the first time since we started reading. Everyone else still has their noses buried in #15. My gaze passes over them until it falls on Nate's recliner. He was right, that day at practice. Opening a portal that used the Nexus Zone as a byway couldn't work—not reliably—when you were already there.

My mind travels back to that gym, all of us lined up for four corners. How deep in thought he'd looked as he considered ways to escape the Nexus Zone, just seconds before the whole world changed.

I blink hard, then look back down at my comic and turn the page again.

- 20 -

In the New Mexico lab, the Red Flame's powers are fading. He's barely able to sustain the weak bonfire he's surrounded the Hollow with.

The Blue Witch, holding her forehead, groans. She takes in the scene around her. Her husband is missing, her powers gone. The Red Flame's skin is changing, from smooth to blotchy, from pink to orange. Spark is frantically giving CPR to Nexus Boy.

The Five are in trouble. Only Hugh has any powers at all, and those fizzling flames will be gone any second. My stomach's doing loops like I'm on a roller coaster. But man, I love this moment, too, when I start to understand how the cover ties into the story.

"Keep him alive, Jessie," Blue Witch calls out to Spark. She limps toward the smoking turbine, passing the Red Flame along the way. "You got him?" she asks Hugh.

Hugh, the Red Flame, eyes the Hollow. The creature turns this way and that, searching for a path through the flames. "For now," Hugh grunts.

"Buy me some time."

"How much time?" he asks with wide eyes, but the Blue Witch, concentrating on disassembling the turbine, ignores him.

"Do something!" Jake's strained voice comes from across the basement.

"Shhh!" Courtney hisses. Look who's suddenly on board with *Rule Two.*

I used to be an engineer, the Blue Witch thinks on the page. *I've watched Bruce fix this infernal machine a thousand times.*

She examines the turbine, detaching the main power unit. She adjusts it, then fires it back up, aiming the black, diamond-shaped energy at the Hollow. The creature roars in anger.

Used to be? the Blue Witch thinks while smiling and shaking her head. *I* am *an engineer.*

The Red Flame's powers finally sputter and die. The

Hollow is locked up by the unit's Nexus energy now, though, allowing a powerless Hugh to stumble over to the Blue Witch's side.

"Can you modify this?" she asks him, gesturing at the unit. It's working so hard at pushing their enemy away, it looks like it might vibrate into pieces any second.

"To do what?"

"Open another portal. We need Bruce back."

"I'm not sure," he says, staring down into his empty hands. "My powers . . ."

"I'm not talking about powers now, Hugh. I'm talking about *you*. You can build anything. You always could."

He sets his jaw. Carefully, while Carol holds it steady, he detaches the back of the unit and gazes at the mechanical guts inside.

"The circuit board is there," Hugh says, pointing. "But it's clamped down by those wires. If I jostle the red one, the flow will stop altogether." He peeks at the Hollow, straining, staggering closer, arms reaching. "He'll be on top of us before we can do anything else."

"So we need someone with delicate hands who can conduct a sensitive operation without making a mistake?"

Hugh, looking downtrodden, raises his meaty, sausage-like fingers and nods. "I'm sorry. I don't think I can."

"Well," Carol says, glancing at Jessie. "Too bad one of

the best surgeons in the world isn't around to help."

Hugh follows her gaze to where Spark is helping Nexus Boy sit up again. He grins.

Captain Nexus searches his surroundings, eyes eventually falling on a rock formation behind him. A twisting path leads up toward a promising-looking stand of trees at the top.

The Captain hikes the trail. He pushes through the trees only to find himself at the sheer edge of a great cliff. He stands there, overlooking the lush, colorful landscape of the Zone, spread out before him for miles upon miles. Lake Carol. The Nexus Mountains. Scott River.

It's a pristine, gorgeous place, but also undeniably empty. There isn't a single animal. Not a bird, or a deer. Nothing, not even insects.

At the bottom of the page, Sanderson's drawn a stark image of the Captain, his missing glove, torn uniform, and desperate expression set against a stark white background. The panel doesn't need words to show us the truth.

Captain Nexus is completely alone.

When I glance up to check if Nate notices how awesome the Nexus Zone image is, all I see is his empty chair. He's like an echo in my head now. His voice comes to me in spurts, sometimes at the same time as the words on the page. Something the Blue Witch said. *I'm not talking about powers. . . .*

I pull my gaze from the recliner. It falls on Courtney instead. She grins. The emptiness I felt thinking about Nate fills up just a little.

This, I tell her with my mind. *This page. This art. This story.* This *is what I love about comics.* She winks at me, like she actually heard my thoughts. Which is weird, because I never thought I'd have a Nate-like connection with anyone else. Especially not a girl.

Spark pulls the circuit board out without disturbing the wire. She presents it to Hugh and Carol. "I declare this operation a success."

Carol stares at the board. She barks out a laugh filled with realization. "We can open another portal."

"How?" Hugh asks.

"We don't need the turbine, see? We can reverse just this unit, siphon strength off the Hollow through it. We'll use his own power against him. The converted energy will—"

"Generate a mini-portal!" Hugh finishes.

Carol grins. "Exactly."

Hugh scratches his chin. "It just might work."

"It *will* work."

Hugh reconfigures the complicated board. Spark slides it back into the power unit, following Hugh's expert advice but using her own delicate touch.

"Ready?" Hugh asks Carol.

"Ready."

Hugh throws the switch. The flow of energy reverses, pulling black power away from the Hollow, out the back of the unit. It spirals in midair until a dark portal begins to swirl into formation. Soon enough, a new window into the Nexus Zone appears.

Captain Nexus hears the electric sizzle of a portal flashing open. He races back to the clearing.

"Bruce!" It's Carol, calling to him from the Earth side. "Hurry!"

"I'm losing it," Hugh, grimacing, warns. The Hollow twists against the flow of power, pulling at the beam like a rope. Hugh is forced a few staggering steps forward.

"Help him!" Carol cries, grabbing hold of the unit with her teammate. Jessie nods. She boosts Nexus Boy to his feet. All four of them tug at the unit, resisting the Hollow.

Captain Nexus sprints for the portal. The Hollow makes a final lurch, lifting the four powerless heroes off their feet. Linked by the ropelike beam of power, as if they're locked in some sci-fi tug-of-war, the group spins in midair. Nexus Boy loses his grip first, slamming into a wall. Then Carol, tumbling into a nest of cables. Hugh, crashing into a control center. Jessie slides across the floor to the other side of the room.

The Hollow's shriek is victory itself. But he struggles to regain control of his rapid, out-of-control spin. He flies backward, slingshotting across the lab.

Straight through the portal.

The creature slams into Captain Nexus and they both tumble and roll backward.

In New Mexico, the power unit crashes to the floor, bursting into flames. The portal snaps shut.

In the Nexus Zone, Captain Nexus pulls himself to a standing position. The Hollow does the same. They square off, no more than ten feet apart.

And the creature begins to laugh.

- 21 -

Everyone in the Templetons' basement exhales at once. All that's left is the inside of the back cover. Captain Nexus and the Hollow locked in a fight, the Captain gripping the Hollow's wrists as dark energy floats off the evil being's extended hands. They're clearly in the midst of the most epic battle to ever grace the pages of *Captain Nexus and the Nexus Five*. Except for the standard price and issue number in the upper left, the background is stark white again, as if only the two characters exist in that moment.

The cover of the next issue has never appeared on the last page like this before. There's a caption at the bottom.

NEXT: Join us for our FINAL issue . . .
CAPTAIN NEXUS!! THE HOLLOW!! WINNER TAKES ALL!!

"Told you guys," Courtney says. She closes her comic and turns it over roughly, then starts flipping through the pages again.

"It can't be the last issue," Sally moans.

"I don't know why you're so surprised," Courtney says. "George Sanderson always said there would only be sixteen."

"He said that once," Ollie says. "And you sound like you're happy about it."

"I'm not happy." Courtney frowns, wounded. "I just knew."

"*Captain Nexus* can't end," Jake says. He stands, like he's going somewhere, but only turns around once completely and falls back onto the sofa.

"Hey, one of us should read it to Nate," Sally suggests. He reaches out with one hand and pushes Jake so hard he falls over to one side. "Dan, take number fifteen to the hosp—"

"No!" I shout.

Sally's brow furrows.

"I mean . . ." What I mean is that Captain Nexus is still

lost in the Nexus Zone. When we read a comic to Nate, it has to show him the way out. #15 didn't do that. There's no answer in these pages. The Captain is trapped worse than ever. This issue is worthless.

There's a moment of silence, like at the start of a major league game after something really bad has happened and all the players have to take their hats off and bow their heads. *Captain Nexus* is ending. It's right there in black and white: *NEXT: Join us for our FINAL issue . . .*

Maybe Captain Nexus won't escape at all. Maybe he'll be trapped in the Zone forever.

Forever.

I kick at the leg of the pool table.

"Hey, that's Nate's table," Ollie says.

Ignoring him, I lean back over my comic and stare down at the preview of #16's cover. The words underneath—*FINAL issue*—strobe at me. My eyes blur. #16 is another four weeks away. Dr. Tori told me FAST was most effective in the first few weeks. We're already past that.

Jake puts words to the question bouncing around my head. Bouncing around, probably, all our heads. "What are we gonna do now?"

Nobody answers.

The next day the Hoffmans' office feels warmer than usual. Maybe it's the late-afternoon sun slanting in through the big picture window, slicing the room in half with a hot patch of light that travels over the carpet and across the top of the desk. Or maybe it's something else.

"Just draw anything," I tell Ollie, shaking my hands over his blank page. We've gotten off to another slow start. The ending to #15 is still bothering us.

"There's not even a story yet," Ollie complains. "What am I supposed to draw? I'm tired of just sketching out possibilities. I need something real."

I turn to Courtney. "He's right. Where's the story?"

She takes a surprised step back. Her voice is soft. "I thought we were plotting it together. Then I was going to write the script after."

I try to slow down, cool down. It doesn't work. "We can't wait for that anymore." I point at Ollie. "Don't you get that his brother is running out of time?"

Ollie slams his French curve down on the desk. It snaps in half, one piece of the transparent plastic flying across the room and landing at Courtney's feet.

"You broke it," she says.

"So what?" he answers. His voice trembles a little. Tears form in the corners of his eyes before he wills himself to talk again. "They're waking him up. Wednesday. They're waking Nate up on Wednesday."

Courtney steps back toward the desk. "*This* Wednesday? But that's," she counts off on her fingers. "That's six days."

Ollie shakes his head slowly. "Not this Wednesday. The next one."

"Well, that's better," she says, sounding relieved. "That gives us almost two weeks."

"Still. I'm not sure . . . we might not be ready," I whisper.

"We won't be," he says. "Because we haven't even started. Not really. This whole thing is stupid. I'm going home."

"We can't keep taking days off!" I shout.

Courtney sends me a hard look, lips pursed, eyes glowering.

"Fine, then. I'll do it myself." I grab a blank sheet of Ollie's paper and storm out of the room, squeezing past a shocked Mrs. Hoffman halfway down the hall. Outside, I yank my bike off the grass, the awkward white paper bending under my arm.

I head home. But I'm not going to my house.

- 22 -

I pedal around the side of our house, through our yard, and up the narrow path without a thought to slowing down. I hit the clearing with so much speed I have to slam on my brakes to skid to a stop, nearly running over the rake and jerking my handlebars hard to avoid mounds of dirt. The old bike trail looks like a construction site now.

I don't bother uncovering my shovel this time. I'm not here to dig or rake or chop. I just need some time to think. Here, in the place where I feel closest to Nate.

The short ride from Courtney's has already wrinkled and dirtied the paper I grabbed from the office. Leaving it wedged under my bike seat, I pace over to the pond.

After a minute of staring, I start skipping some stones across the water.

Nate and I used to do this all the time. I'm thinking of the hurt look on his little brother's face when he broke one of his favorite art tools a few minutes ago, and suddenly Nate is standing right next to me.

"Ollie was asking where we go," Nate said one day last summer. We were still in our Giants uniforms; we'd just won a close game against the Hampton Pirates.

I remember snapping my head around to him, then trying to steady my voice. "What'd you tell him?"

Nate winged a flat stone onto the surface of the pond. It skipped high once, then low several times before finding its way to the opposite shore. "Nothing, really."

I glanced over my shoulder at our cut-through, thinking if he hadn't already, Ollie would definitely try to follow us out to our project someday.

"We should start changing up the times we come." I wanted to make the time this place was just ours—mine and Nate's—last as long as possible. It seems silly now, trying to protect my time with Nate from his own brother, like we were in some kind of contest. A contest where Nate was the prize. But Nate was never a prize, he was my friend. Scratch that. Nate *is* my friend.

And he's not gone, not yet.

Maybe Nate had wanted me to say it was okay to invite

Ollie. But instead I only flung another stone at the pond. It plunked heavily into the water, hardly skipping at all.

Nate turned to me. "No, not like that. Sidearm. Like this." He skipped another flat rock all the way to the other side.

I tried again. This time my stone crossed the halfway mark.

Nate smiled at me. "Better. You're getting it."

Suddenly I felt like I was a hundred feet tall, but I couldn't say it out loud, so I changed the subject. "You pitched awesome today."

"Nah. My changeup sucked. That's why I gave up those two homers." Nate hadn't become unhittable until this summer. "When Coach came out to the mound, I was so pissed I almost told him to take me out. Put Jake in."

I hadn't even known he'd started throwing changeups. "That's crazy," I'd said. Then, after a thoughtful pause, "Why didn't you?"

Nate shrugged and frowned, like my question was a weird one to ask. "I knew you guys needed me."

Today, my stone skips all the way to the other side, first time ever. I turn to make sure my best friend saw, but Nate fades, then disappears entirely.

The double elimination started with eight teams from all over Western New York—small country towns like Mira, suburbs like Brooksburgh, even city teams from Buffalo. After we'd been dropped into the losers bracket in that first game, we couldn't lose again or we'd be eliminated.

That meant four games stood between the finals and us. We'd won the first, leaving three more to reach the championship round.

On Saturday, the huge, dangerous power hitter from Buffalo West strides to the plate in the last inning. We're winning 8–4. Jake's been pitching awesome and we've all been backing him up with diving plays and miracle catches. Each trip back to the dugout we remind each other to stick together, how we used to play before Nate started striking everyone out.

I'd been wrong about #15 showing us the way out of the Nexus Zone, but I'd been right about something else—or maybe it had been Dr. Tori who was right. The Nexus Five had remembered who they were before they got powers, all the special skills they'd spent years honing before they became superheroes, and they'd outsmarted the Hollow.

If we were really so much like George Sanderson's comic-book team, if we were really the *Nexus Nine*, it was time for us to show it.

We'd heard rumors about this Buffalo West kid—Tim Parker—and if anything, the warnings weren't strong enough. He's already hammered a couple of deep homers to left, plating all four of their team's runs.

Jake's kicking the dirt nervously. I trot in to talk with him. The bases are loaded; another home run would tie the game. I cover my mouth with my glove. "Paint the corners, man," I tell him, not sure he has enough control to pitch with that much accuracy. "Trust your fielders."

He sniffs and gestures at Parker. "Have you seen this kid? Two homers off me already."

"Don't give up," I tell him, then gulp. "We need you out here."

He shakes out his arm and nods. "Yeah. All right."

"Just do your best."

I jog back out to short. Jake takes a long time to start his next windup. When he finally does, he unfurls a great pitch, low fastball, tailing in. Parker swings hard at it, going down to one knee as he catches hold of another one.

There's nothing to do but watch. The ball arcs high, heading for the fence again. Craig backs up, his eyes on it the entire time, one hand reaching out behind him to make sure he doesn't run out of room. It's gone, I know it. We all do.

Except for Craig.

I remember when he first moved to Mira, just last year. He joined the Giants, and I saw right away how good his glove was. So did Coach. He was going to try him at short. My position.

"If it's okay with you, Coach, I play left," Craig said. "I always have."

Sometimes I wonder why. Craig had a chance at the infield, but he passed it up. I mean, I'm glad he did—I love shortstop—but I kind of don't get it.

Now, his eyes are fixed on Parker's smash. His fingers find the fence, close on top of it. Craig's as far back as he can go, and the ball's still coming down. At the last second, he leaps up, mitt up high. There's so much force, it looks like our left fielder's glove will tear right off his hand, but he holds on, turning Tim Parker's sure home run into an out. We all cheer.

I wait for him on the infield. "You play left," I say as we trot toward the dugout together.

"I always have," he says. Smiling, he flips the game-winning ball out to me, and I snag it with my bare hand.

- 23 -

After ringing the bell, I wait a long time on Courtney's porch. Maybe no one's home, which would be kind of weird on a Monday. We've met around this time almost every Monday for weeks now. I take a few steps back, check the garage, the upstairs windows. No movement. I count to ten before allowing myself to hop back up on the porch and try again.

This time I hear footsteps. They reach the other side of the door, and I swallow hard as the knob turns. When the door opens, Courtney's standing there. She tilts her head and frowns. "Oh, look, it's Captain Hurry Up. Here to save the day?"

I thought I'd planned out something to say, but it floats

right out of my head. Courtney just keeps looking at me.

I stare back. I don't know. I guess I kind of hoped she would've forgotten about the other day, that we could just go back to the way things were. We really need to get back to work, but I'm pretty sure I should keep that opinion to myself after her Captain Hurry Up dig.

"I, um . . . I'm really sorry," I tell her.

She starts to say something, then stops. After a brief glance at her feet, she looks up again. "It's okay. It's a lot of pressure. Probably we're all feeling it."

"Can I come in?"

She steps back and opens the door wider. "So what are you doing?" I ask as I step through.

"Just watching TV."

I start heading down the hallway toward the office before I realize she isn't following me. I find her in the front room. She sinks onto the couch and picks up the remote control. She's all slouchy. I've never seen Courtney like this.

"Don't you want to talk in the office?"

"What's the point?"

I chew my lip until it hurts. I ruined it. Our project. My only chance of waking Nate.

"Oh, hey," she says, sitting up a little. "I know you're probably going to freak, but my mom brought back some of the stuff I left at my dad's." She points to a bench in the foyer. There's a backpack, a plastic grocery bag, a three-ring binder, and a pair of ripped sneakers piled on top of each other. "Your comic's somewhere in there."

The backpack is crushing the white plastic bag. I try not to run to it. Pushing aside the shoes and the binder, I pull the bag from under the pack and open it. Inside there's more of the lined pages Courtney writes her scripts on, and three comics. A *Green Lantern*, the cover folded almost in half, a *Mockingbird* with curled corners, and, under them both, my *Alpha Flight*.

It's wrinkled. *Wrinkled*, like someone let it get all bent, then tried to set something heavy on it to straighten it out again. But it was way too late.

I'm gazing down at it so hard I don't even realize Courtney's behind me until I feel her breath on my shoulder. "I'm really sorry. I tried to take care of it." She tilts her head. "I don't think I'm so good at that."

A month ago I would've given her a huge lecture. You can't treat a comic this way. Where are the board and bag? But I guess things are different now. Seems like no matter how many bags you hide them in, how many boards you protect them with, comics are always going to end up looking like somebody read them.

"It's okay," I tell Courtney slowly.

She backs up a step. "Really? Ollie thought you'd lose it."

I shrug.

"Come and watch TV." She heads back into the living

room and snatches up the remote.

"Isn't your mom home?"

"She's up in her bedroom. She takes all her lawyer calls up there lately, so she can whisper like she's in the CIA or something."

"Oh." I'm still in the foyer, my comic in my hands. I jump when, two feet away, the doorbell rings. Which is awesome, because I wasn't sure what else I should say to her.

"Probably Ollie." I hope my voice sounds as cheery as I'm trying to make it. "I'll get it."

"Ollie isn't supposed to be coming over," she calls out as I turn the knob.

I open the Hoffmans' front door expecting Nate's little brother but find an old man waiting on the porch instead. He's my grandfather's age—sixty, maybe seventy—and he's wearing a basic blue button-down shirt and plain khaki pants. My gaze goes straight to a webbed scar on one side of his neck. It winds up from under his collar, covering his neck and cheek all the way back to his ear. Under one arm he has a black leather portfolio brimming with paper. With his other hand he leans on an ancient, carved wooden cane. The head looks like one of those gargoyles on the old building Dad's been restoring.

The old man's expression breaks into a lopsided grin as he extends his hand. "Ollie Templeton. Son, I can't tell you how honored I am to meet you."

"I—"

I've left him hanging, but he doesn't miss a beat. He lurches past me, his cane clonking on the foyer's hardwood as he takes the time to tousle my hair with the hand I guess I should've shook. "Where are your parents? I have to meet them, too."

I catch Courtney's eyes in the other room. Stunned, she watches the old man pace into her house for probably a second before she launches off the couch, slinging the remote behind her. "Excuse me, you can't just come in here like that. . . ."

He freezes, puts a hand up to the side of his mouth, and whispers to me. "Your sister?"

"No!" I shout it for some reason. Courtney stops, tucking her fists onto her hips. "I mean, we're friends."

"You should be very proud of your talented friend, young lady," he says in a tone that's almost scolding. "He's going to be in the *Tall Ship Annual*."

The old man slides a single page out of the jumble of them leaking out the top of his portfolio. "Ollie here does some incredible work," he continues, jutting his chin at me. "His submissions were by far the best ones I judged." The shiny certificate has curling script and a golden emblem.

Tall Ship Comics
Captain Nexus Fan Art Contest
Grand Prize Winner
Ollie Templeton

He offers it to me. "Go ahead, take it. You earned it."

"No, I didn't. I'm not Ollie," I say.

"You're not?" The old man frowns. He pulls the certificate back, then licks one finger to make it easier to fumble through the other pages in his portfolio. "Did I get the wrong . . . ?"

"No. No, this is the right address," Courtney rushes to say. "We submitted for him. He lives a few streets over."

He gives up on his searching. "Well, then, I should get over to his house."

"No, he can be here quick," she says. She lifts the pile of junk and sneakers with a single scoop of her arms, grabbing her phone off the bench underneath. She manages to twist it from the charger using three wriggling fingers. "I'll text him," she says as she dumps the pile down again.

Her fingers fly across the screen. "Oh my gosh, what do I even tell him?"

The old man smiles. "Tell him he won a *Captain Nexus* award. Tell him George Sanderson is here to give it to him."

- 24 -

For a long time I can't move. I gaze up into the old man's face—his webbed scar, his white hair with the matching bushy white eyebrows, his sideways grin. I guess I always assumed George Sanderson would look like a movie star or something, not somebody's grandpa.

"Excuse me. Can I help you?" It's Courtney's mom. She's at the top of the stairs, and she's holding her cell to her chest so that the person on the other end can't hear us talking. The expression on her face is halfway between annoyed and perplexed as she stares at the old man in her foyer, leaning on his cane.

All three of us start to explain at once.

"Mom, we entered Ollie in this contest—" Courtney.

"Hello, ma'am, my name is—" Sanderson.

"Ollie actually won!" Me, shouting at the top of my lungs, as if sheer volume has the power to clear everything up.

Instead Mrs. Hoffman raises the phone to her ear. "Isaac, let me call you back." She ends the call, then starts down the stairs toward us.

"He's George Sanderson," Courtney tells her mom when she joins us in the foyer. "He *created* Captain Nexus!"

"Congratulations," Mrs. Hoffman says. "I'm Lily Hoffman. What can I do for you?"

"If I may," Sanderson offers, "perhaps I can show you." He struggles with his cane and papers, juggling both, then casts a longing eye toward the kitchen. "Would you mind? It's this leg, you see."

Mrs. Hoffman's expression loses some of its tension for the first time. "Of course. Please come in."

Sanderson stumps on his cane deeper into the house. We follow him like lost puppies. When he reaches the kitchen, he dumps his messy portfolio onto the table.

"Let's see here." He bends over the haphazard pages, shuffling through them. "How about I use some quick sketches from yesterday as my ID?" He slides out a rumpled page and shows it to us. "Look familiar?"

It's the Hollow. His menacing figure—jagged, evil grin, slumped posture—faces us in the largest image. Two smaller drawings show him from the side and behind in equally disturbing poses. The creature looks ready to strike.

They're George Sandersons, for sure. No one draws the Hollow like that. "But," I start, still searching for words, "how are you here?"

"My publisher had me judge the annual contest blind. I'm understanding now these kids entered their friend in our competition," he says in Mrs. Hoffman's direction, and she finally shows a glimmer of understanding. "Maybe you knew already."

Courtney's mom glowers at us both. "No," she says, her voice icy. "Nobody tells me much of anything around here."

"I didn't know a thing about the submissions—names, ages, addresses, nothing," Sanderson continues. "I could've picked a grand prize winner from Australia for all I knew." He twists to put his drawings back in the portfolio. His next words come between grunts. "Once I chose the winners, though, I was allowed to see their names. The rest of their info, too. Your friend really stood out. Eleven and already that gifted? And so close, too, only an hour away. I couldn't wait to meet him. So I decided I would come to him first. I could visit his studio, and maybe later he could visit mine."

My heart skips. Visit George Sanderson's studio? "Hold on. An hour?"

"That's right. I live in Brooksburgh. It's about an hour

north, if you don't—"

"Brooksburgh?!?" Courtney shouts. "You've been in Brooksburgh this entire time?"

"It's where I came up with *Captain Nexus*, yes. Originally I'm from Nebraska."

"But—how—" I've never seen Courtney at a loss for words before.

"I keep sort of a low profile up there." Sanderson straightens and raises his voice. "Now, I think you know who I am, but I'm afraid you still have me at a bit of a disadvantage." He turns over one hand in my direction. "You are?"

"Oh, sorry. I'm Dan," I say. "And this is Courtney. We're Ollie's best friends."

Courtney cuts her eyes at me. One corner of her mouth turns up. "Yeah. That's right." She introduces her mom, too.

"It's nice to meet you all," Sanderson says. "So, you were going to text that best friend of yours?" he reminds Courtney. Then, turning to her mom, he adds, "If it's okay with you, of course."

Courtney looks at her phone like she forgot she was holding it. "Oh, yeah. Right." She waits for her mother to nod permission, then finishes tapping out a quick message.

After a minute, her phone buzzes back Ollie's reply.

"He's at the hospital. There's a complication with Nate." Courtney's voice cracks a little, and Mrs. Hoffman reaches out and wraps her arm around her daughter's shoulders.

I don't think my heart can beat any faster, but it does. "What kind of complication?"

Courtney's eyes scan the screen again. "He had some trouble breathing. They . . . they had to do a procedure."

"What do you mean, procedure?" I come around to her other side, trying to read her phone, unwilling to wait for her answer.

"I'm . . . I don't know." She taps a response and waits before dropping her hands to her sides in dismay. "He's stopped answering."

Mrs. Hoffman raises her phone again. "Let me see if I can find out." She sends a couple texts of her own, and her phone rings almost immediately. She wanders into the next room as she takes the call. "Hey, Jen. Have you heard anything from Pam?"

Both Courtney and I stare after her. Behind us Sanderson clunks his cane down, reminding us he's in the room. If someone had told me I'd meet George Sanderson, then forget he was even there not a minute later, I'd have definitely said they were describing another dimension, some alternate Dan Summers. A dumb clone, maybe. *Really* dumb.

"Sounds like I might've come at a bad time," he says.

"It's Ollie's brother," I say. "He's in a coma. We had . . . it happened at baseball practice. I was . . . it was my . . ." *Fault*. I still can't say it.

Sanderson seems to detect my hesitation and staggers back a step or two, like someone just stabbed him in the chest. "I'm . . . that's terrible. I'm so sorry." He heaves a breath and starts to pull out one of the chairs. "Do you mind if I sit?"

"No," Courtney says. "Go ahead." She watches the old man slowly lower himself into the seat. "It's why we're doing our comic. And the reason we entered him into the contest. We were trying to help him feel better. You know, because of his brother."

Sanderson narrows his eyes at her. "Your comic?"

I try to help explain. "We wanted to draw Nate—"

"That's Ollie's brother," Courtney adds.

"My other best friend." I nod. "We wanted to draw him into a *Captain Nexus* adventure."

"Fan fiction only," Courtney says quickly. Then she lowers her voice. Her mother is still on the phone in the next room. "We're having a little bit of trouble with the story."

"That's not surprising. Getting stories right isn't easy." Sanderson's gaze lingers on Courtney. "You're the writer, aren't you?"

She crinkles her nose. "How did you—?"

"We writers recognize each other." He turns to me. "And you?"

I suddenly feel about two inches tall. Courtney's the writer, Ollie's the artist, I'm just . . . the backup.

"He was . . . he is going to do the lettering," Courtney says. "He has a perfect comic style."

Sanderson regards me a moment, then nods appreciatively. "I see," he says. "Good letterers are hard to find." He scratches at his scar. "And you're hoping this project will help your friend how?"

"We're not sure," Courtney answers. "It just seemed like the right thing to do. Like, maybe . . . we could change things. Like, somehow, if we wrote a story, the real world would . . . follow, I guess. I don't know." Courtney's tone grows frustrated. Her voice fades. "Maybe it's dumb."

Sanderson rests both hands atop his cane. "No, that makes perfect sense. Stories give us ways to figure things out."

Courtney and I exchange hopeful glances. Maybe it didn't always feel like it, but we were doing the right thing after all. The only problem is that we didn't finish.

"I like to stay busy with my stories. Sure, they stretch my creative muscles, but that's not all. My stories, they keep my mind off . . . other things." Sanderson sighs. "Art, stories, they have power. Lots of it. They give us strength when we need it most." He stares hard at Courtney. "Keep writing. And your friend Ollie needs to keep drawing, too. It'll help all of you in ways you won't see right away. The line between your work and real life can be thin—very thin."

"I am. I mean, we are, definitely," Courtney assures him. "We'll keep it going." She trades a smile with me.

"I'd love to have a look at your project someday. Maybe your friend Ollie could bring it to my studio."

"In Brooksburgh?" Courtney hops up on her toes.

"In Brooksburgh," he confirms with a little chuckle. "You're all welcome there, but I do need you to get your parents' permission first, okay?"

We nod together.

Sanderson digs through his portfolio for a business card. He hands it to me, then winks. "Guard that with your life, now. It's your ticket to a whole other world."

- 25 -

"Thanks, Pam," Mom says into her cell that night. She ends the call with Mrs. Templeton, then sets her phone down on the kitchen island. "Nate's stable."

I let go of the top of the kitchen chair. I hadn't realized I'd been gripping it so hard. "What does that mean?"

"It means he's okay. They just had a little scare."

"Can we go see him?"

She shakes her head. "No visitors for now. I'm sure we'll be able to go when he's doing better."

"But it's . . . he's stable. That's good, right?"

It sounds like a strong word, so I want to keep saying it. *Stable.*

Mom nods and glances at the still-lit screen of her phone. It winks black. "Listen, Dan, Pam told me she's willing to let Ollie go to that art studio as long as you and Courtney go with him. And Courtney's mom seems to believe this man was who he said he was. You're sure as well?"

The Hollow crouching down in that sketch, ready to spring into an attack. "He was definitely George Sanderson."

"And he gave you his address and phone number?"

"Yeah. I have it all upstairs. We should go soon."

I try not to smile, but man, it's all happening just like I planned it. Ollie winning the contest, meeting Sanderson. Now the old man just has to tell us how to break out of the Nexus Zone, how to save Nate, and we'll be able to finish our project. I can't believe I forgot to ask him about #16 at Courtney's, but everything happened so fast.

"Hold those horses," Mom says, and the balloon pops, sending me crashing down to my feet. "I'll need to call him and have a chat first. Assuming that goes okay . . ." Mom takes a step toward me. "Well, Mrs. Templeton told me Ollie was really bummed about missing this Mr. Sanderson. Guess it's pretty important to you guys?"

"The most important," I agree.

Mom bites her bottom lip. "Okay, here's the thing, though. The Templetons are kind of busy with Nate. I'm happy to take you kids, especially if it'll help Ollie, but I can't drive an hour away like that until the weekend, okay? I have appointments all week. That Greek restaurant tomorrow. Gyros are always questionable. Then Un Poco Loco on Wednesday . . ."

"Mom." She stops and looks at me. I hold up both my index fingers and make a swapping motion. "You have your appointments flipped again. Freaky Greeky is Wednesday. Un Poco Loco is tomorrow. And I know all about the rest of the week, too." I'm more up to date on Mom's schedule than she is.

"I'll take them." I turn around to see Dad leaning against the kitchen doorframe. His shirt is rumpled, his tie loose. His end-of-another-long-day look, same one he wears every night around this time, before he heads into his office off the foyer for round two.

"You will?" Mom and I say at the same time.

Dad smiles. "This is that art studio I heard about, right? Your comic guy?"

"He's not just a comic guy, Dad. He's George Sanderson. He *created* Captain Nexus."

Dad waves a hand in the air, like he knows all about my favorite comic book, even though he's never asked me a single question about it. "Yes, yes. *Captain Nexus.* The Nexus Zone. Lake Carol. He does some wonderful work."

Lake Carol? Wonderful work? How does he . . . ? I rack my brain for some moment we might've discussed the landscape of the Zone in that much detail, but I can't find anything in my memory.

It doesn't matter anyway. Like he's really going to taxi us all the way to Brooksburgh. I wait for the inevitable, for him to change his mind, for reality to dawn on him, but Dad just stands there, smiling. "You'll really drive us?"

"How are you going to do that, Mike?" Mom asks.

"Maybe I'll take some time off. Think your friends can do it tomorrow?"

Did he just say time off? Tomorrow? "Definitely."

Mom taps one finger on her lip, assessing us both. "I'm calling this studio place first. I need to make sure this guy actually works there."

"Mom, he's George Sanderson. It's *Captain Nexus*."

"Then I'm sure he won't mind a few questions. Assuming he's legit, then . . . okay."

"Okay?" I have to try really hard not to leap out of my shoes.

"Yes, okay, but it's in Brooksburgh. So if he suggests getting lunch—"

"I know, I know. No Meatball Emporium."

As I race upstairs for Sanderson's number, I hear Dad asking, "Is that Luigi's Meatball Emporium? On Post Road, right? The guys took me there last week. Those meatballs are delicious."

"Mike!" Mom screams.

- 26 -

I'm beaming at Dad for a full ten minutes of the ride—as we pick up first Ollie, then Courtney, while we swing through Mira onto the ramp for the highway. We're on our way to save Nate, and Dad's actually driving us. It's a miracle.

As soon as we reach top speed, though, his cell rings. Dad spends the entire hour-long trip on a Bluetooth call with his office. He keeps mouthing "Sorry" and "Just a few minutes more" to me and my friends while words like "balcony" and "baluster" and "buttress" stream out of the car speakers.

Dad's still on the phone when we exit the highway in Brooksburgh and wind through town to the Brooksburgh

Art Coop. I'd seen the name of the place Sanderson worked on the card he gave us, but I didn't understand what it meant.

Now, though, as Dad slows down to navigate around groups of chickens pecking the ground lazily, I understand it. Art *Coop*, as in . . . chicken coop? This entire place is covered in chickens. On the sides of the roads, in the doorways, along the sidewalks. Some of them are even hanging out in the trees.

Dad keeps checking a sheet of paper in his lap, but the chickens are making him roll through the complex so slowly, it's not even dangerous. "Barry, I have to go," he tells his balcony-obsessed work colleague, then hangs up his Bluetooth.

"B," Dad says, mumbling a little. "Building B, where are you?"

He steers his way through the haphazard collection of ramshackle structures, some with broken-out windows, most built of faded brick. Dad slows down even more when a new pack of chickens decide to park themselves in the middle of the road, just as we pass a big dedication sign. We're almost at a complete stop, so I'm able to read the first few lines.

THE BROOKSBURGH ART COOP
DONATED BY DR. LAURA ANN ACREE FOR THE SOLE PURPOSE

OF HOUSING SHARED ARTIST STUDIOS, THIS FORMER CHICKEN FARM HAS OTHERWISE BEEN PRESERVED . . .

"Apparently the only rule they *do* have is that the chickens can do whatever they want," Dad grumbles as he comes to another stop in front of one more collection of the clucking birds. "That's it there. Building B." He points to a particularly run-down-looking building to our right. It's the largest in the complex, lone and rectangular, with a flat tin roof.

I'm not sure what I expected to see—the Batcave, Avengers Mansion, Dr. Doom's Latverian castle—maybe at least the science building the Nexus Five operate out of, or the Captain's remote New Mexico lab.

But the decaying building that apparently houses George Sanderson's studio isn't any of these. It seems like a strong wind could blow the whole place over. There's a wide wooden porch that looks like it's been rebuilt and added to more than a few times by people who just might've been using the wrong end of the hammer. A group of very tattooed and pierced twentysomethings sit or stand on one end of the scary porch, collected around what look like a couple of pizzas and a rolled-out sheet of paper.

Dad stretches forward to get a better look at what they're up to, then reaches up and loosens his tie. "Well, okay. It says Building B. I hope this is the right place."

As we mount the steps up to the porch, one of the artists, a tall, skinny white dude with a neck tattoo and dreadlocks, passes us going down, ignoring our group as he shouts to his friends. "I'm thinking we throw up some walls right about here." He stops a few feet from the porch and spreads his arms wide. "We can fit at least one new studio." He shrugs. "It's a start."

Dad stops at the top of the stairs. He turns and gazes at the young man, shifting his laptop bag so that it's hidden behind his back. I glance at the rest of their group, noticing that the paper they're hovering over looks like an amateur version of one of Dad's blueprints. Great, just what I need. More architects. Are they building another one of these crazy, twisted, ready-to-fall-down-as-soon-as-it's-up buildings?

"Can I help you, man?" the guy with his arms spread asks when he notices Dad staring at him.

Dad blinks and glances back at the paper in his hand. "George Sanderson's studio?"

"George who?" a woman with pink hair sitting on the porch says. She looks Dad up and down, like he's a rare bird she only gets to see once in a great while. Dad loosens his tie some more.

"Oh, never mind," he shouts back. "We're good." Then he whispers to us, "I hope this is it," while he punches a code from the paper into a keypad. The big metal door in front of us buzzes and unlocks. Dad swings it the rest of the way open, but we can't go in yet because two chickens strut out, stopping long enough to look at us with annoyed expressions until we shuffle out of their way.

All four of us step inside. There's an immediate set of rickety wooden stairs to the right with a bike locked to the railing. Straight ahead is a hallway that continues for about ten feet before bending off to the left. I grab for my nose at the same time as Courtney. I'm not sure what chicken feet smell like, but the odor in this hallway has to be pretty darn close.

The door slams shut behind us and I jump at the loud clang, turning around to make sure that's all it was. That's when I notice the sign taped to the door's back.

> ***REMINDER TO ARTISTS: DO NOT FEED ANY CHICKENS INSIDE THE BUILDINGS***
> *(It only leads to trouble. They are not able to control themselves.)*

"Dan." Courtney's calling and gesturing from the end of the hall. Dad and Ollie have already disappeared around the bend. I chase after them.

When I catch up, they're waiting near the second closed door on the left. The door to the studio straight across the hall is wide open. A woman inside is humming along to some old rock music, the Rolling Stones, I think, and painting away on a canvas attached to her easel. On the wall outside her studio is a brightly colored sign filled with hand-painted flowers that reads, *Joys by Joyce, Custom Oil Paintings.*

Outside the door Dad's knocking on, there's no sign at all. In fact, there's a big white space and holes where it looks like a sign used to be, but someone ripped it off the wall.

I watch Joyce the painter work and dance at the same time. She's the opposite of the artists outside. Older, maybe Sanderson's age, and her piercings are limited to her ears. Her hair is gray. She must hear us knocking because she looks up, sets her brush down, and leans out of her doorway.

"Oh, he won't answer, dears. A real recluse, that one. None of us even knows what kind of work he does in there."

"We've been invited," Ollie assures her.

"You don't say," she replies, genuinely curious now. "Wonders never cease."

Just then, the door in front of us pops open, revealing George Sanderson. He's wearing the same clothing he was when we met him at Courtney's: a blue button-down and khaki pants. He notices Joyce craning to get a peek behind him and hustles us inside.

"Quickly, quickly," he says, waving his hand and keeping

one eye fixed on his art neighbor. Once we're all inside the small front room leading into what's clearly a much larger studio, he slams his door shut and regards us. He strains to smile, his scar fighting him the whole way by forcing one side of his mouth down.

"Dan, Courtney, it's good to see you again so soon." Sanderson shifts his gaze to Ollie. "And this must be our talented young artist."

Ollie reaches out and shakes George Sanderson's hand. "It's an honor to meet you, finally," Sanderson says.

"No, I'm . . . the honor," Ollie stammers. "For me." His cheeks flush.

Dad's phone buzzes and his eyes jump to it, but he resists its call long enough for introductions. "Mike Summers." He and Sanderson shake hands. Sanderson inclines his head and leans on his cane, his fingers closing over that gargoyle face. The rest of us are straining to get a look into the next room.

This is it. George Sanderson's studio.

What I wouldn't give for Nate to see what I'm seeing. *Captain Nexus* is everywhere. There are pages on easels, scattered across desks, in piles on chairs and shelves and every available surface. It's like we're about to step into a living, breathing comic book, to walk through the gutters separating one panel from the next.

Except Dad's still talking. He's wandered toward the only

visible window, a narrow sliver of glass covered by a dark sheet. Dad pulls it to one side and I catch a glimpse of the porch again, from behind this time. "Those young people out there. Any idea what they're thinking of building?"

"None at all," Sanderson grunts back. He steps over to the window, but instead of joining Dad in inspecting their progress, he yanks the sheet out of my father's hand, blacking the window out with it again.

Dad's phone buzzes, somehow louder and more insistent, like it knows he ignored it the first time. He reads the text, then looks up with a frazzled expression. "I need to send some plans off, if that's okay." He pulls out his laptop and nods at a small desk. "You don't mind if I hang out and work here a few minutes, do you, George?"

"Fine with me," Sanderson says.

Dad meets my eyes. "You kids go on ahead. I'll be right here. Take me two minutes." His eyes get that unfocused look they always do when work passes across his vision and becomes the only thing he sees. I can't believe he isn't even going to compliment Sanderson on his art space.

"Two minutes, buddy," Dad says again without even looking at me this time. Instead he clears some space off the tiny desk and starts to set up his laptop.

Two minutes. Sure.

- 27 -

"Shall we?" Sanderson asks as soon as it's clear Dad isn't joining us. We're about to explore the studio of the world's greatest living comic artist and he'd rather send emails.

None of us are going to make the same mistake, that's for sure. As soon as the old man gives us permission with a gesture of his hand, Courtney, Ollie, and I crash into his studio and separate.

The surfaces aren't just covered with Sanderson's work. His tools are everywhere, too. Most are the same ones Ollie uses—T squares and French curves, triangles and pencils—but there's also a laptop with some kind of tablet connected to it. A tall mirror stands right next to an easel. There are inks and brushes and pens on one table, and another computer, a big desktop with a scanner, on the next.

Ollie skips toward the laptop. "This is a Wacom," he cries, running his hand over the tablet.

Sanderson follows him. "Yep, that's where I do my Photoshop coloring after scanning—" He reaches out to turn on the power, but Ollie's already scampering to the inking table.

"And you have a complete Winsor and Newton Series Seven set." He reaches up to feel the end of one of the brushes. "Sable?" he asks, eyes still wide.

The old man struggles to keep up, following Ollie to the brushes, picking one out and laying it flat in his hand. "I use them for inking my rough layouts. Also these Rapidographs, for the finer work." He points to a row of pens clamped to the back of his desk.

"You do all that right here?" Ollie asks, touching the tilted table with a fingertip like it's a hot stove. There's a page on its glass surface, divided into panels, each containing penciled layouts. The image of Captain Nexus leaps off it. A bloodied, bruised Captain. He seems to be hiding in a cave. Something's wrong with his hand. It's from issue #16, has to be. I lean in, trying to identify the rest of the story, but the pencils are too light and unfinished. There are no speech bubbles, no words. It's not alive yet.

"That's right." Sanderson reaches down and flips a switch, and a bright light beneath the glass flares on.

Ollie's whisper is full of awe. "A light table. I always wanted one like this."

Sanderson sits on a stool in front of the table. He leans his cane against an easel. "How'd you learn so much about comic art?"

"Geeker.com."

"Ah, Geeker." Sanderson sounds impatient. "One of the many reasons I'm not big on the internet."

"It's great for fans," Courtney says. She starts explaining the best features of the site.

"You know, some people on that site would probably pay a lot of money to find out where I work," Sanderson says when she finishes.

"We would never," I say.

"No," Courtney and Ollie add, shaking their heads.

"I know." He smiles. "Just to be sure."

Ollie reaches toward the page on the light table. "Can I ask . . ."

"You can ask me anything," Sanderson reassures him. "That's why you're here."

Ollie hops once. "So why do you keep your layouts so rough? Is it because you ink them yourself?"

"That's right. They'd be more precise if I were sending them off for someone else to ink. I'd probably use a harder lead, too."

Ollie nods. "And why don't you work with a team, like the way a normal comic is created? Separate inker, writer, letterer?"

Sanderson straightens. He turns a pencil over in his hand for a moment before answering. "I'm just . . . better off alone right now."

It's a strange reply, and I don't think I agree with him.

"How did you get your own comic, anyway?" I ask.

Sanderson shifts, then settles. "I spent years doing other things. All kinds of odd jobs. Whenever I had the spare time, though, I drew. I practiced and practiced. It kept my mind quiet. One day I decided to bring my work to a convention, and it caught the right eye. Good things that happen aren't just luck, and they aren't just hard work. They're both."

"Were you drawing regular heroes first?" Courtney asks. She's flipping through a stack of printed pages she lifted off a nearby desk. "Like Spider-Man or the X-Men or Batman?"

He shakes his head. "No, it was always this. Always Captain Nexus."

"How did you come up with the idea?"

Sanderson snatches the papers from her hands. "I'm afraid my origin story is private," he says. "As are all my new scripts." He inspects the pages as if he's concerned one might be missing, then flaps them on top of Courtney's head playfully. "No spoilers. They actually tried to buy me a safe to hide these in." He falls quiet, eyes on the script in his hand, then sighs deeply. "All I can tell you is Captain Nexus helped me get through something important, something that happened a long time ago. He's still helping me."

Ollie reaches out and rotates the page toward him. "I'm surprised you're working on the current issue still. I've read that most creators run a few issues ahead. Your publisher doesn't mind you cutting it so close?"

"They don't bother me, I don't bother them. If they want Captain Nexus at all, then they'll get him when I decide he's ready."

"Does that mean number sixteen will be late?" I ask, alarmed.

Sanderson sounds insulted. "I'm never late."

"But you're still working on the story," I say. "So they haven't seen it?"

He shakes his head.

"But they showed the cover in the last issue, like they knew what was going to happen. How is that possible if you're still writing it?"

"I'm not writing," Sanderson says. "Not exactly. I'm just transferring it from my mind to the page." His eyes lose some focus. "The truth is, this story's been written for years."

- 28 -

"Stories," Sanderson says. "No matter how much you think you know, they're never quite what they seem. They change and shift all the time, like they're alive."

After a short pause, he reaches down to a table-side magazine rack, his hand coming back with a newspaper. The *Brooksburgh Gazette*. "But enough of all that. Tell me about your baseball tournament. Says here Brooksburgh has a pretty good team. They're in some kind of tournament this summer, too. Same one?"

"Yeah," I say slowly. "Brooksburgh. They're supposed to be really good."

Brooksburgh isn't just good. Their team's been steam-rolling every opponent, with final scores like 16–2, 9–1, even 22–3. The tournament's meant to get tougher as time goes on, but each win seems to only come easier for the Tigers. Their pitcher, a big kid named Ray Yumido, is like Bizzaro-Nate. Tall but maybe not quite as tall. Same great fastball, but sports a curve in place of Nate's change. Rumor is Yumido has an uncle who played professionally in Japan.

Like all good catchers, Kurt studies breaking balls as much as a pitcher would. I think maybe he's been trying to teach Jake a curveball, but Coach isn't too keen on the idea, so if they've been working on it at all, they've been keeping it quiet.

Sanderson slaps his table, suddenly filled with energy. "Let's do some work. How about I draw and ink a panel, and you can all watch?"

"Seriously?" Ollie says.

The three of us press together as we peer over Sanderson's shoulder. He sketches for a while, effortless strokes that quickly develop into a faint image of the Captain's head. He stops and describes some technical choice he's made to Ollie. They're like two people from another country speaking a language only they understand.

Still Courtney and I follow along. I'm watching Sanderson scratch lines into the page, and it's amazing, but I keep thinking how much I wish Nate were here with us.

Ollie's been asking art questions nonstop, but now I add one of my own, the question I've been waiting to ask since we walked in the door. "Mr. Sanderson, can you tell us . . . ," I start out all eager, but trail off into a pause.

"Ask me anything," he reminds me without stopping his pencil or looking up.

"How does Captain Nexus escape the Nexus Zone?"

Sanderson's hand freezes. He turns. "Well, anything but that. I told you, no spoilers. Don't worry, number sixteen will be out in a few weeks."

"We can't wait that long. We have to know now."

Sanderson's eyes narrow and his gaze intensifies.

"We're trying to save Nate. Our story's stuck. You have to tell us . . . you have to give us . . ." I need to catch my breath, so I stop.

"I'm sorry, Dan, but it doesn't work that way. No one can give you your story. You have to find it yourself."

"But—" What am I even doing here then? We're wasting time on this guy. "I really need to know how he escapes, though."

"You and half the internet, kid," Sanderson says. I stare at him and he spreads his hands helplessly. "Really. I can't tell you what happens. The publisher would kill me."

I have to ask him again, to keep asking until he gives me something we can use in our comic. I have to *make* him tell me, but my throat constricts. I can't talk. And I know: I'm letting go of my only chance to save Nate.

Ollie points out something about the thickness of Sanderson's lines, and they both hunch over the drawing again. I back away, shocked at how Ollie can care so much about art when his brother's still trapped.

Courtney's the only one who notices me wandering off. She glances at me as I step back; then Ollie yells out "Awesome!" and she turns her attention back to Sanderson and his drawing. I drift around the studio aimlessly.

My angry, disappointed eyes scan the paper-covered desks and chairs until they fall on a bookshelf lined with art manuals and novels. The top shelf features action figures—mini sculptures, more like—of Captain Nexus and the rest of the team. I've seen them in the back ads of the comics, even asked for some for Christmas, but they were too expensive. There's a framed photograph there too, but it's too small for me to see clearly.

Sanderson's voice floats toward me as he teaches Ollie when to ink with a brush and when to use the fancy pens instead. Ollie peppers him with more questions. I reach the bookshelf and stand up on my toes to get a closer look at the incredible sculptures on that top shelf.

It's as if the figures have been pulled straight out of the comic—Sanderson's drawings made real. I inspect each one until my eyes are carried all the way across the shelf, to the photograph.

"Tell me about your brother," Sanderson says to Ollie. "This comic you're doing for him, the story you're trying to find."

Ollie tries to tell him about our idea, how we thought we could show Nate how to escape the Nexus Zone using our comic. Part of me wants to turn and help him explain, but I'm too mesmerized by what I'm looking at.

The black-and-white photo isn't large. I have to squint to take it in. It's old, one of those family poses the photographer has obviously choreographed, almost a glamour shot. There's a clear husband and wife, and the husband is a younger version of Sanderson. They have their hands on the shoulders of a boy, obviously their son. Two more figures fill the frame—a man and a woman about the same age as the two parents.

It's an ordinary scene. Only this photo isn't ordinary at all. Because the wife looks exactly like the Blue Witch, and the son is the spitting image of Nexus Boy. The man standing beside them could be the Red Flame's twin; the other woman is unmistakably Spark.

And the younger version of George Sanderson, pictured here without his facial scars, is . . . well, he's Captain Nexus.

The Nexus Five . . . it's as if I'm looking at an old picture of the team, from years ago. Which isn't possible, because they're not supposed to be real. I grip the shelf with both hands and pull up, standing higher on my toes. Sanderson's art is always so vivid, I've sometimes wondered if he worked from a photograph. I never imagined this, though.

"It's probably stupid," Ollie says. His voice sounds louder, like he's purposely calling his words out. "We're not even sure what we're doing. I mean, we get that it's just a comic book."

"I understand completely," Sanderson replies, and all of a sudden he's right behind my ear. I jerk around in surprise.

His pencil still in his hand, he reaches above me, turning the frame facedown. The image of the family—his family—disappears from view.

"Trust me." He's talking to Ollie, but his eyes bore a warning into mine. "No one knows better than I do. There's no such thing as 'just a comic book.'"

- 29 -

Time freezes. It's so quiet I hear the clack of Dad's fingers on his laptop keys. The noise suddenly stops, though, and he appears in the doorway between the two rooms of Sanderson's studio.

"Told you," he says to me with a grin. "Two minutes." He checks his watch. "Okay, maybe that was more like ten."

Sanderson finally takes his eyes off me and looks toward Dad. "So you're ready to head out, then?"

"Oh, no," Dad says quickly. "Don't let me interrupt."

"Yeah," Ollie protests, his voice shrill. "We just got here."

Sanderson limps away from me, back toward Ollie and the light-box table. For the first time I notice his wounded leg is on the same side as the scar on his face.

"Actually, I think you kids better get on home now," the old man tells Ollie.

Ollie gestures at the page next to him with a wild hand. "But you haven't finished."

"Need to get back to work," Sanderson mumbles. "Number sixteen can't be late. You said so yourself."

Ollie's face drops. Sanderson struggles toward him, reaching for his cane with his other hand. "You really are the most talented little artist I've ever met." He squeezes Ollie's shoulder. "And I can't wait to see your submissions printed in the annual."

Ollie looks up into his hero's eyes and nods. He might be about to cry. I think if Sanderson suggested he move into this falling-down building and do nothing but watch him draw all day, Ollie would tell him he just needed to check with his parents first, then start packing his toothbrush. Or maybe he'd just start with the toothbrush and worry about the permission later.

"Well," Dad says. Even he sounds disappointed. "Seems as though Mr. Sanderson would prefer to be left alone after all."

A few minutes later, as Dad attempts to steer around a chicken who seems to feel he owns the gravel road between us and the Art Coop's exit, I spy Sanderson peeking out of the slender, curtained window of his studio at us.

All I can do is shake my head at him. I don't even care if he sees it. This trip was for nothing. The guy didn't help us at all. We're completely on our own.

"They were like this," Ollie's shouting when I walk into the Hoffmans' office the next day. He's penciling Captain Nexus so frantically he doesn't seem to notice me come in at all. "It's this type of stroke here," he says, sweeping his arm in a broad arc. "So much freedom on the page."

Courtney smiles at me from the window. "Hey," she says. "Some day yesterday, huh?"

"Yeah." I nod toward Ollie. "Who's he talking to?"

She rolls her eyes. "I'm not really sure."

I step toward the whiteboard. There are real ideas there, not just scribbles and cross-outs. I skim them. Some aren't bad, not bad at all.

Courtney picks up the eraser and eliminates a stray line, tidying up her list. "I worked a little last night. Hope that's okay."

"It's awesome," I say.

Ollie's in his own world. He casts the page he's been working on to one side and starts in on a new one. He's still narrating what he's doing. "He was using a .4 millimeter. Is that possible? I think I heard Jim Lee uses a .4, too. Man, I need to get one."

"A .4 millimeter what?" I say. "Brain?"

Courtney snorts but Ollie ignores me, more insulted by his pencil than my try at a burn. He turns it over in his hand like something's wrong with it, then chucks it across the room, immediately picking up a different one.

"So what'd you find on that bookshelf yesterday?" Courtney whispers. "When Sanderson noticed you over there, he jumped up like someone shot him out of a cannon."

"It was a photo."

"Of what?"

How can I explain this? "His family, I think. From a long time ago."

"Why would that be a big deal?"

"Because his family—" I exhale. "They're the Nexus Five."

She squints at me. Across the room, Ollie says, "He pulled out the lead, then held the pencil sideways." He tries it, quick flashes of his hand across the page. "This is unbelievable."

"I don't get what you're trying to say," Courtney whispers to me.

I describe the photo in detail, making sure she understands how closely each person resembled a character from *Captain Nexus*. "I don't mean kind of," I tell her. "I mean *exactly*."

She bites her lip, thinking. "Okay. Could it be from an ad, maybe, like something Tall Ship did as a promotion?"

"I've never seen any kind of promotion like that. Have you?" She shakes her head. "And if it was just some gimmick, why did Sanderson get so worked up about it?"

Courtney trades chewing on her lip for gnawing on her thumbnail. She thinks some more.

"The brow sets the stage for the eyes!" Ollie shouts, sounding a little like Dr. Frankenstein bringing his creature to life. "The brow sets the stage for the eyes!"

"Dan." Courtney's eyes darken. "Have you ever googled George Sanderson?"

"Only, like, a thousand times."

"And what did you notice?"

I scratch my temple. "I mean, once you get past the random stuff, there wasn't much about him except *Captain Nexus* news. Definitely no mention of a family."

"No, there was *nothing* before *Captain Nexus*," she says. "That's what always jumped out at me. It was like George Sanderson didn't exist until the day he created the Nexus Five."

"So?"

"So maybe he didn't."

"Didn't what?"

"Didn't exist."

"The man's seventy. *Captain Nexus* came out last year. Of course he existed."

"You're not getting it. What I mean is . . . maybe it's

not his real name. Maybe he was someone else before, and something happened. Maybe he changed his name to George Sanderson. Maybe the person he originally was had a family. The people in your picture."

She's nodding to herself, like she already knows she's right. I try to keep up. "So what happened to his family, then?"

Courtney stops chewing on her nail and stares me straight in the eyes. "That's a good question, isn't it?"

A question we aren't able to come up with an answer to over the next hour. When Ollie finally settles down, we go back to the idea board.

So far we've agreed on one aspect of our plot. We know that the Hollow develops a new power, and we know that he uses it to knock an innocent bystander into the Nexus Zone. We're sure that Captain Nexus feels responsible for the accident and wants to help return the kid to Earth.

But what we still don't know is how he does it. We'd brainstormed seven ideas, then spent the last hour deciding between them, crossing each one off as soon as we realize its problems. Only three are left.

#2—Nate finds a new team of heroes living in the Nexus Zone, and they help him escape.

#5—Captain Nexus goes in after Nate while the team keeps a portal open long enough for their leader to bring Nate back through.

#6—Captain Nexus goes into the Zone alone, afraid to tell his team because he thinks it will put them in danger.

"It can't be number two," Ollie says after several minutes of staring.

"Why not?" I ask.

"Because," he sighs, "who's this other team? I don't think they exist. Besides, you can't always wait for somebody else to fix your problems, you know?"

"He's right," Courtney says. She steps forward and runs a dark line through number two. "So I guess it's ether five or six."

We stare some more at the two remaining options. Finally Courtney and I speak at the same time.

"He can't do it by himself," she says.

"They're a team," I say.

We smile at each other. "So it's number five," we say in chorus.

"Has to be," Ollie agrees behind us.

"I think they'd all want to help the Captain," Courtney says, "if he gave them a choice."

"Definitely," I agree.

The story locks into place, and suddenly all we want to do is get started.

- 30 -

That afternoon we work feverishly on the comic. I'm pretty sure we all realize the same thing: no choice left, it's all up to us. No one's going to fly off some rooftop or swing down from a skyscraper to save us.

The story pours out of us. Before it felt like our project might take forever, but now it comes together all at once, like magic.

We move around the office and each other, jotting notes on the board, encouraging Ollie, shouting out new ideas.

Ollie draws faster. His pencils become looser, more abstract. Sometimes there's no talking, the only sound the scritching of his pencil across the page. We hold our breath as each wild image escapes his fingers. He's self-conscious about it at first. "I should do this page over," he says after a particularly savage depiction of the Hollow leaps off his pencil.

"Don't," I say. "It's really cool, like a new style. Unique but all you at the same time."

Courtney agrees. "Yeah, it's super creative. Let's keep going. Rough it in. It doesn't have to be perfect."

Nodding, Ollie hunkers down and works on another panel, using the same quick strokes of his pencil, mimicking Sanderson's techniques, narrating what he's doing the entire time. "Nice and light, don't let the pencil dig into the page . . ."

Courtney talks over his ramblings, making sure he understands her script. "No, his hand comes right out of the panel, like he's breaking through it, almost 3D. . . ."

We keep bumping into each other. Papers flutter into the air. Uncapped whiteboard markers are scattered about the room. Half-empty bags of chips and half-drunk sodas line the windowsill.

None of us wants the session to end, but as the afternoon wears on into evening, Mrs. Hoffman stalks in to break it up. "Okay," she says, "both your parents have called now. It's dinnertime, and they want you guys home."

Courtney moans. A red dry-erase streak divides the bridge of her nose neatly in half, while a blue slash runs down her cheek. "Mom, we can't stop now."

After some negotiation, Ollie agrees to let me bring a stack of his completed pages home, along with Courtney's in-progress script, scribbled into a lined notebook in a mad rush. I'd managed to letter a few panels during our session, thrilled to bring the characters to life as I gave them Courtney's words, but I couldn't keep up. I offered to put a few hours in on my own.

The garage door's open when I get back to my house—both cars home for a change. I park my bike too fast between them; it topples over with a loud clatter and almost clangs into the Volvo. I consider picking it up (I can already hear Mom yelling, "Daniel Lee Summers, why is this bike on the ground?"), but Ollie's pages under my arm are too precious. I can't risk setting them down out here. They might get dirty.

I race up the stairs for my room, drawings of Captain Nexus and the rest of the team flapping under my arm. Halfway there, Dad calls out to me. "Hey, Dan?" I halt in my tracks and turn. Dad reaches the base of the steps and looks up at me. "Mr. DeLeon stopped by to borrow a shovel." His eyes narrow. "Weird, but . . . couldn't find mine. Know anything about that?"

"I . . . yeah, I know where it is. I can get it after dinner."

"Dan, you can't just—" Dad stops and points. "Hey. What's all that?"

I inhale. I'm not sure how he'll react, but I can't hide

our project now that he's glimpsed it. I pace back down the stairs and turn over Ollie's work so Dad can see it. "This is the comic we're working on." I watch his eyes scan the pages, searching for some sign of what he thinks. The last page is half-lettered. "Here's where I come in," I tell him, pointing at Captain Nexus shouting at the Hollow.

YOUR REIGN OF TORTURE IS NEARLY OVER, CREATURE!!

"This . . ." Dad looks at me and a smile creeps across his face. "This is great work, Dan."

My heart leaps. "I have to finish tonight. I don't want to be the one delaying the project."

"No, you shouldn't. It's important to hold up your end of the bargain." Dad hands the pages back to me. "Listen, the shovel can wait. Richie has his own, he just likes to have an excuse to stop by and chat." He grins and rolls his eyes.

"Thanks, Dad." I take the stairs up two at a time.

He calls after me. "But from now on, if you need to borrow something, ask me first!"

After dinner, I get to work on the lettering. It's an hour before my hand starts to hurt. I'm almost done with my pages, but I feel like I can't draw another letter without some kind of break. I keep thinking about Dad calling my work great, and the shovel I took without asking his permission. It's a quick walk down the narrow path at the back of our yard to the pond and the trail. Just long enough to stretch out my aching fingers.

I find Dad's shovel leaning against the base of a tall pine. In my rush to fetch it, I trip over a heap of dirt, landing in a pile of leaves with an "Oof!" I roll and make sure everything's still attached and nothing's broken. From the ground, I get a new view of my progress.

I've been trying to re-create the Nexus mountain range that looms over Lake Carol. The launching hill gave me a great start, and it's easy to see how closely it matches the largest mountain. But to really make the entire range, I need to finish the three or four new hills I started way back when Dad was first helping me. The ones Nate and I never bothered with.

It took a lot of hot, sweaty work to bring enough dirt over for them. I tore down the old jumps, but I still didn't have as much as I needed. Luckily, I also had to create the valley at the base of the mountains, otherwise known as a "big, giant hole." After that, I had all the dirt I could ever want.

There's still a ton more to do. I get to my feet and head for the main hill, the highest vantage point. On top, I sit and wonder what Nate would think of me replacing our jumps with this weird imitation of the Nexus Zone. Man, he should be here to tell me himself. I squeeze my eyes shut and wish it for about the thousandth time.

There's a rustling in the trees behind me. Something's lumbering through the woods. Blinking, I wait, hold my breath. The noise gets louder. Closer.

Nate?

No sound of a turning chain or switching gears reaches my ears, but something, someone, is definitely on the way. Not as fast as Nate's bike—more like a slow, plodding movement. Step by step for the clearing, clumping over brush, snapping branches in half, trampling saplings.

A dark, hunched shadow. Like the Hollow.

It's just beyond the final line of trees now. Closer. Closer.

I can't breathe.

The creatures—I see there are two shadows now, in single file—break through the last line of saplings, the first one leading the way with his arms out like some stumbling monster, the second right behind. They're in the clearing with me now. Not Nate, but not monsters, either. The one in front leans on his cane and breathes in deeply, clearly exhausted. He reaches into his back pocket for an old, yellowing handkerchief and uses it to wipe the brow above those bushy white eyebrows, then to clean the sweat off the rest of his face, leaving his bumpy scar for last. Finally, George Sanderson straightens and collects himself.

"You've got a visitor," Dad says. Having made his delivery successfully, he lingers at the edge of the trees. He looks around, and for a second I think he's going to notice my work, say something about the project that started out as ours.

I guess he really has forgotten all about it, though, because he only sends me a quick salute. As soon as his hand drops off his forehead, he turns and leaves, fading into the trees toward the lights of our house. I watch him go as long as I can, all the way until he disappears completely.

"Well," Sanderson pants once we're alone. "Found you."

- 31 -

Sanderson heaves breaths so deep it kind of scares me. "Feels like I just ran a marathon. Most days, I'm lucky if I make it from my car to the door of my studio."

"I'm . . . you all right?"

"Just need . . . a second." Sanderson limps forward a few steps, then cranes his neck so he can see me clearly at the top of the hill. He glances back, only noticing now that Dad is already gone. "Nice of your father to give us this moment."

I shrug. It would've also been nice if he'd wanted to be a part of whatever conversation was about to happen, if he'd stopped long enough to notice my improvements to the project he'd once been so excited about. It would be nice if I was surprised.

"He doesn't mind us talking for a minute, right?" Sanderson asks, his head still turned slightly.

"I guess not."

The old man faces me completely again. "I'm sorry to burst in on you like this. Your dad said you'd been spending a bit of time back here lately. I couldn't quite tell how far into the woods you were."

I'm still too confused to reply. What's he doing here? What does he want?

Sanderson points over his shoulder. "I was really hoping you'd be home tonight." He pauses, rubbing his hand over the grooves in the wood of his cane, massaging the gargoyle's forehead. "I drove all the way down here to . . . Dan, it's about that photograph. I wanted to apologize in person."

He comes forward and puts a tentative black shoe up on the base of the hill, testing his footing. Before I can say something that might stop him, he starts to climb, using his cane to lever himself up one struggling step at a time.

"I'm really . . . sorry I reacted the way I did." He grunts before taking another step up. Higher. Closer. "It's just that I don't . . . get many visitors. I shouldn't have left it out like that, and it isn't your fault you saw it."

"I wasn't supposed to be there to snoop around your studio. I'm sorry." I leave out how angry I was that he wouldn't tell me how to escape the Zone, because it doesn't matter anymore. We're figuring it out for ourselves now. We don't need him.

"No," he says, digging the end of his cane in deeper. "I invited you." He stops, checking how far he has to go to reach the top, and for a second I think he might topple backward. I scramble to the edge and offer him my hand. He reaches out to grasp it.

Sanderson is heavy, and I have to use my other hand and lean back with all my weight to help him through the final, steepest step up. His struggle reminds me of all the times Nate and I played King of the Hill in this very spot. He'd always let me get only so far, and when I went for the final push, he'd send me skidding back down.

No mercy, he'd announce, and I wouldn't say anything back, because he was right. If I ever got to the top, I wanted to do it on my own, not because he let me. So I would clench my fists, back up for another running start, and try again.

At the top now, Sanderson leans on his cane and looks out over the pond. Suddenly he checks behind him, then, still breathing heavily, spins around once completely. "Amazing," he mutters. "You did all this?"

"Sort of. It used to be a bike trail. My friend Nate and I built it. But lately I've been changing it, kind of on my own, into—"

"The Nexus Zone," he finishes, his eyes wide with wonder.

"You can tell?"

"Of course." He spins around again. "I created this place. I've seen it in my head a thousand times, drawn it on paper a hundred more, but I never imagined . . ." His hands are shaking. "Dan, you made my dreams real." I look into his face, shocked at the way his voice is trembling. "Thank you."

"I wanted . . . I thought . . . maybe Nate needed a place he could come back to." I gaze down at the pond, feeling my throat tightening. If I don't keep talking, I'm going to end up crying again, like that first day with Nate in the hospital. So all of a sudden I say what I haven't been able to say for weeks now. "It's my fault he's in the coma."

And with that, the floodgates open. I tell him everything, what I haven't been able to tell anyone else. Not Mom. Not Ollie or Courtney. No one. My hand grabbing Nate, turning him, how that memory has haunted me for weeks. George Sanderson doesn't interrupt, doesn't claim what I'm saying can't be true, doesn't try to tell me the guilt I'm feeling isn't real. He just listens.

"I can't stop thinking about it," I say. I kick at a stone. It tumbles down the side of the hill, smacks into a bigger rock, and takes a giant hop into the pond.

"So that's why you made this place?" he asks.

I nod.

"And your comic book, the project with your friends?"

I nod again.

"Do they know?"

I shake my head. "Not exactly, anyway."

"Does anyone?"

"Not . . . no." My heart skips. Did I make a mistake? Is he going to tell everyone else?

Another long pause before Sanderson seems to come to a decision. "That's okay. You can only share something like that when you're ready. It might take a long time, longer than you realize." He scratches at his scar. "It's a good thing, what you're doing. This place, the comic book, all of it."

"But I don't think it's helping Nate any. Not the way I wanted it to."

"No, it's not." Surprised, I jerk my head up at him, but Sanderson pokes my foot with his cane playfully. "It's not helping him. It's helping you." He pauses. "I think it's my turn for a confession. Mind if I tell you a story?"

I shake my head.

Sanderson smiles softly, then looks out over the pond, Lake Carol. "Imagine a scientist building a machine, one that he believes could create a new kind of clean energy. He's so optimistic, this scientist."

"Captain Nexus," I say. "Bruce Peters."

He tilts his head, then shakes it, like I'm right and wrong at the same time. "Imagine he's so excited he doesn't test his machine properly. He wants to show it to his family and friends right away. So one night, after a dinner party that went very late, he invites them out to his garage, where he's been tinkering." Sanderson's gaze shifts to his feet. "Something goes wrong."

I don't get it. He already knows what a huge fan of the Nexus Five I am. I've read this story. Not just once, but over and over again. It's how the team got their powers. Bruce Peters's machine, the Nexus Turbine. He was trying to discover a new energy source, but instead got pulled into the Nexus Zone in #1. When he came back in #3, everyone got powers—and the Hollow returned with him.

"You remember what I told you about stories? Sometimes they make real life easier. Sometimes that's exactly what they're for." Over Sanderson's shoulder the sky is gray, but there are no stars yet.

"I don't remember much about that night." He runs a hand over his scar. "These burns . . . I lost consciousness pretty quickly. My son woke me up—I thank God to this day he was thrown clear—but my wife"—his voice breaks—"my sister, and my best friend . . . they were gone."

A rattling breath escapes him, and Sanderson looks down and away, hiding his face. "The doctors weren't sure if I'd ever walk again. The nerves on this side of my body"—he gestures at his cane-leg—"are pretty much shot. There was a trial. I should've gone to prison for what I did, but they said it wasn't my fault. They said it was an accident." He spits out the last word like it disgusts him. "My son, though . . ." He looks down at me. "He was about your age then." Sanderson shakes his head slowly. "He didn't want to live with me anymore. My wife's sister and her husband sued for custody and won. I had visitation rights, but Jason refused to talk to me. Not that I had any explanation for him.

"I couldn't accept that, so I made up a story. Told myself that story so many times, I started telling other people, too. So many people, it became real even to me."

Sanderson sighs. "So maybe you'll believe me when I say I do understand what you're going through. I know how critical it can be to create stories and worlds—on paper, on land, in your head, anywhere, really—that help you feel like you're bringing the people you love back to life again.

"That's why I told you it's important that you and your friends keep working on your book, Dan. It'll keep Nate alive."

Keep him alive.

"Really?" I ask, my heart beating like a jackhammer inside my chest.

"All I can say is it's worked for me." He straightens, pushing against his cane. "And I wish I could tell you how it ends, Dan. How to escape. The truth is, I don't know."

I don't think I've ever breathed out so long and hard. It's a good thing we don't need him. It wasn't that he held back the answer. He never had it to begin with.

Sanderson looks at me sternly. "Now, I would say we're officially secret sharers. But we keep each other's secrets, right?"

I nod so hard my neck starts to hurt.

- 32 -

LET US HELP YOU, the Blue Witch says. *WE'RE A TEAM.*

I'M RESPONSIBLE FOR THE HOLLOW, CAROL, Captain Nexus tells his wife. *ME. HE BANISHED THAT POOR BOY INTO THE NEXUS ZONE. I HAVE TO TRY TO FIND HIM.*

YES, she agrees. *BUT THAT DOESN'T MEAN YOU HAVE TO DO IT ALONE.*

I tilt the bright desk lamp toward me and slide Courtney's script closer. I can't make any mistakes. This job is too important.

It'll keep Nate alive.

It's only been a couple of hours since Sanderson left, and I keep hearing those words again and again. I couldn't possibly sleep now.

I'm trying this first pass in pencil, but the eraser marks are really obvious, and I don't want even one to be showing. These pages have to be perfect.

Ollie gave me one of his tools, something called an Ames Guide, sort of a stencil-ruler thing made of clear plastic. It's supposed to help me keep the letters the same size, but I can't make heads or tails of it. I decided to trust my hands more.

Leaning back, I double-check the completed panel—making sure nothing's misspelled, that I've given the right lines to the right characters, that I've emphasized particular words with bolder lines—before moving on to the next one. Ollie's pencils are awesome, but Captain Nexus wasn't alive until I added these letters, Courtney's dialogue. I can almost hear his deep, hero-like voice.

LET'S BRING THE BOY BACK, THEN. TOGETHER.

So far our story's been focused on the Nexus Five. There's been only one distant image of Nate, the innocent bystander in the crowd watching the team's epic battle against the Hollow. The Five's archenemy had unleashed his new power, a beam capable of opening a portal straight into the Nexus Zone. He'd demonstrated his strength and covered his escape by propelling one of the onlookers, a young boy, into the very same place Captain Nexus had once been trapped. With a maniacal laugh, he closed the open portal, trapping the surprised kid.

Trapping Nate.

I don't know how Courtney's able to write this. If it were me, I'd feel like I was sending Nate to the Zone all over again. And actually, I was: in a weird way, I had to agree to send him back so that I could show him the way out.

My best friend hadn't had any dialogue yet, but once the Captain found him in the Zone, they'd both get lines. The words I gave Ollie's drawings of Nate would spark life into his eyes.

I start in on a new page. I can't visit Nate, but I can do this. One word in, I hear Mom start up the steps. Three, two, one . . . I count off in my mind until she reaches the top and trips with a loud *ba-dump*. Every night, like clockwork, Mom stumbles over that top stair.

"Hey," she says outside my closed door. "You're supposed to remind me of the time." I'd watched bedtime come and go but kept quiet because I was busy. Sometimes it's good to have a mother with clock issues. "Lights out in there, kiddo."

"One second," I call back.

"How about no seconds?" she counters.

This is working, I know it is. I don't want to stop. Still, I snap the bright lamp off. My room descends into darkness.

"Good night," Mom says, satisfied.

"Night."

I sit at my desk watching the winking, glowing stars and listening for the sounds of Mom and Dad closing their bedroom door, their TV coming on. They'll both fall asleep watching the news, same as always.

I flick the desk light on and get back to work.

The next morning, it's Thursday. The day the doctors plan to wake Nate is less than a week away now. I'm not surprised they picked a Wednesday. It'll be a better Wednesday than even a *Captain Nexus* Wednesday. As long as we're done by then. As long as we show Nate the way home by then.

I expect to find Ollie's bike parked in the Hoffmans' driveway, but it isn't. "His parents had an appointment with Nate's doctor at the hospital," Courtney says as we head toward her dad's office. "He wanted to be there."

"Are they letting him see Nate?"

"He wasn't sure. He wanted to."

"I hope Ollie tells Nate how much progress we're making." I spread the completed pages across the desk. She leans over to take them in.

Courtney straightens, then punches me in the shoulder. "I knew you were right for this job!"

I'm still not completely satisfied. I see an *N* that tilts too far to the right. But maybe it's good enough. "Wish I could show Nate. Or that my dad didn't always have to leave so early."

Courtney peeks out the office door, eyeing her mother, who's sitting at the kitchen table, concentrating on her checkbook. Quietly, she clicks the door shut. Which is weird, because normally we work with it open.

"I did some research," she whispers.

"On what?"

"The French Revolution. What do you mean, 'On what?' What else? Sanderson."

The image of Sanderson standing beside me on the hill flashes into my head. *But we keep each other's secrets, right?* I gulp. "What could you research? We don't even know his real name."

"No, but he said he was from Nebraska, remember?"

"Did he?"

"Sure." She points. "Right there in the kitchen. First time we met him."

"Oh, yeah."

Courtney removes some printed pages from the lowest desk drawer. She glances at the door again, as if her mom will burst in any second. "I found a few Nebraska stories that would fit the timeline. A man who lost his family in a car crash." Shaking her head, she tosses that page to the side. "A political scandal that led to a divorce. Guy's whole family left him." That sheet is quickly discarded, too. "And this one." She taps a finger on the final page.

Cautiously, I peer at the article she's printed. It's been scanned in from an old newspaper, then archived onto whatever site she pulled it off. The headline reads, *Local Inventor Franklin Loses Family in Freak Accident.* It's dated September 1, 1984.

"Check it out," she says with an awestruck whisper. She tries to wait for my eyes to scan the page before breaking in and telling me anyway. "There was a gas . . . his wife, she couldn't breathe . . . did you know your skin turns . . . ?"

Blue, I think. The Blue Witch.

Courtney inhales before continuing. "There was a fire, too. Sanderson got . . . he . . ." She shakes her head, and when she speaks again, her whisper is even lower. "And his best friend, too. Sanderson—I—I mean, Franklin—he crawled out, but the friend . . ." Courtney bites her lip.

The Red Flame.

"The inventor's sister was on the other side of the room. She tried to unplug the machine, hoping to save the rest of them, but they think she might've grabbed the wrong cable. She—" A slow, desperate shake of Courtney's head.

Spark.

I'm holding my breath as I read the reporter's account of the horrific accident. It's worse than what my mind had imagined when Sanderson confessed at the bike trail.

"Sanderson and his son were the only ones who made it out," she says.

I make one last attempt to protect the secret. "But that was some guy named Franklin," I say. "Not Sanderson."

Courtney hops up and down once. "Are you kidding? Read it again. Tell me that doesn't sound exactly like the machine Bruce Peters tried to build in number one. It's the same accident, except in the comic, no one dies. In the comic, they get powers that would've helped them survive. He must've . . . it's like . . . wishful thinking or something."

"Sure," I say, every word still coming slow. "Maybe . . ."

"And look at the inventor's first name!" She nearly shouts it. She reaches up to cover her mouth. I think for a second she's going to tap her nose, and my heart skips a beat.

Courtney narrows her eyes. "Seriously, *Carl*? You know every *Captain Nexus* issue cold. Don't try to tell me you don't remember number four, when the team was still trying to figure out their powers and the Blue Witch's parents stopped in for a surprise visit?"

"Sure, the Franklins," I say, and my voice chokes a little on the last name. The last remnants of Sanderson's secret float away like smoke. I feel a little relieved to have someone in on it with me now. A friend.

"Which means her real name, her maiden name, is Franklin. Carol Franklin? That's only one letter off from Carl. You're telling me you can't see how this Franklin guy and George Sanderson might be the same person? He's hiding little details based on true stuff in his story. What did he say? About the line between your work and real life?"

I bite my lip. "Thin," I whisper. "That it's very thin."

"Exactly!"

I exhale and meet her eyes. "Okay, I have something to tell you, but you can't tell anyone else." This time it's me who glances at the door. "Not even Ollie."

- 33 -

"I knew it!" Courtney hisses when I finish telling her Sanderson's story. She stands straight and triumphant, fists on her hips. "At least now we know why he acted so weird when you found that photo." Her eyes grow distant. "Must've been awful. That scar . . ."

"Yeah."

Courtney pulls one of the pages I lettered closer, a full-pager showing the entire team fending off the Hollow's attack. "I can't believe we're the first ones to find this. If the people on Geeker knew—"

"You can't!"

"I won't! I'm just saying. Imagine the hits *that* thread would get." She spreads her hands apart in the air above her head, like the headline she's imagining is floating there. "'Captain Nexus: More Real Than Ya Think.'"

Courtney drops her arms to her sides. "It even seems kinda obvious now, doesn't it? I mean, he didn't change much."

"Let's focus on our own project," I say. "What happens to Nate and the Captain next?"

"We should wait for Ollie. He'll be here in a half hour."

"If you want." I really don't want to wait, but what can I say? I turn to the whiteboard, pick up a blue marker, and start to doodle, trying to act as if allowing more precious time to tick away isn't bothering me.

"So what's this bike trail thing? Where you said Sanderson found you."

So we can't work, but she wants to pry her way into our space? No way. "It's just a place. Somewhere Nate and I used to go."

"But where—"

"It's private, okay?" What is this, twenty questions?

"Fine, yeesh," she says.

"How early does your dad leave?" She starts to reorganize the pages I brought.

"I don't even know. Way before I get up. He's, uh . . . he's pretty busy."

"That's what time my dad used to leave, too. I-don't-even-know-o'clock. When he lived here, anyway." Courtney bites her lip, like she wants to say something but is having trouble getting the words out. "One more question?"

"I really don't want to talk—"

"It's not about your stupid bike trail, okay?"

I stare at her, waiting.

"Just . . . okay." Courtney inhales. "What in the world is a squeeze play?"

I laugh, surprised.

She frowns at me. "It's not funny."

"You really want to know?"

Courtney throws her hands out to her sides. "I asked, didn't I?"

What could it hurt? I love talking baseball, and at least it's not a bike trail question. So I explain the strategy of bunting with less than two outs and a runner on third, how the idea is to sacrifice yourself but give your teammate a chance to score. "In the suicide version, the runner leaves third with the pitch," I finish. "So it's really important the bunter makes contact or he'll be dead meat at home."

Courtney seems to replay my description in her head, her mouth moving silently, like she's memorizing the capitals of every state for a test. I turn back to the whiteboard again.

"And," she says, "what's the difference between a curveball and a slider?"

"A curve drops. Mostly. A yakker breaks away."

"What's a yakker?"

"Just another name for a slider."

Courtney flexes her hands open and stamps one foot. "*God.* Can there *please* be one name for these things?"

"There's never one name. Why are you asking all this, anyway?"

She doesn't answer but continues peppering me with questions. We go over pitchouts and hit-and-runs, balks and catcher interference. I explain how the infield rotates so that every bag is covered, where the cutoff men stand in certain situations. Occasionally Courtney calls a time-out, like Kurt taking a trip out to the mound, so she can memorize some new detail. She never writes anything down, though.

I tell her how a hitter recognizes a curveball's coming. "The seams spin a certain way, too fast to see, but it makes a red dot. . . ." I go on to detail the little signs to watch for when stealing a base off a righty. "The pitcher's back heel, gotta keep your eye on the back heel . . ."

I start to get impatient waiting for her next question. It's so weird to see know-it-all Courtney this way, off-balance by a subject she doesn't already know everything about. And watching her learn, absorbing everything I say so quickly . . . it's sort of amazing.

And it makes me want to tell her everything.

I open my mouth to explain more, but Ollie bursts through the office door. Two steps in and he freezes.

"What are you guys doing?"

Courtney pops up off the floor and sends me a look of warning. "Waiting for you, Dr. Latehead." She grabs his pages from under his arm and spreads them out beside mine.

"How's Nate? Any change?" I ask as we gather around the desk.

Ollie adjusts his glasses. "Not really. He's breathing a little better, at least, so I guess that's good."

"Are they still waking him up Wednesday?"

"I think so. They always quiet down about the plans when I'm around." Ollie sighs as he sits. He takes a quick look at my pages, nodding approval. "These are great. Where'd we leave off?"

He's right, no time for chitchat. We need to finish.

It takes only a few minutes for the room to explode with activity again. We get to the pages featuring Nate. Ollie uses a bunch of old photos he brought to draw his brother from all sorts of angles. The speech bubbles he adds call out to me. *Bring me to life*, Nate's black-and-white eyes beg.

Soon.

Courtney's pacing back and forth, shouting out dialogue and concepts and ideas, when she suddenly stops, her wide eyes fixed on the doorway. I turn to look at what's caught her attention.

A man's standing there. I'm not sure how long he's been

there or how much he overheard, but he's smiling as he watches us work.

"Dad!" Courtney shouts. She surges forward to hug her father. Mr. Hoffman rubs her back as he returns the embrace. They separate. "We're working on the comic I told you about."

"I see that," Mr. Hoffman says. "Glad to know this old office is being put to some good use. How's it going?"

"Really great." She takes a few steps back from him, as if she's realized she allowed herself to get too close. "What are you doing here?"

Mr. Hoffman's expression grows serious. "Your mom and I are going to have a little talk out on the deck, all right? You guys just keep working."

Courtney's reply is soft, containing none of her usual confidence. "Okay."

After he leaves, I want to ask Courtney if this "talk" means her parents are getting back together, but I don't. Our work slows way down, because she keeps stopping to gaze out the window. Her parents are only twenty feet away, but we can't hear them through the thick glass. They might as well be on a different planet, or in another dimension altogether.

"Maybe we better stop," she says a half hour later. A moment ago, her parents' voices rose, drifting in toward us.

I want to keep going, for Nate. Of course I do. But

Courtney's slouching again, the same way she was the day she told me her mom was talking with her lawyer. And it's weird, but I'm starting to get just as worried about her as I am about Nate.

"Yeah, probably," I agree. I point at some of the pages in front of Ollie. Nate and the Captain in the Nexus Zone together, tons of speech bubbles just waiting for my letters. "How about I take them home again, do some more lettering?"

After all, I think, Wednesday isn't that far away. Less than a week now.

Courtney returns to the window. Her hand, a green marker wedged between the fingers, grips the sill hard, like she's hanging off the edge of a tall building. She doesn't answer.

Ollie and I exchange glances. I try again. "Courtney?"

She turns. "Hmm?" She sees me pointing at Ollie's pages and the little bit of script she was able to complete. "Oh . . . yeah, sure. Do what you want."

I try to use my telepathy to help her. *It'll be okay.*

Nate would've turned around and tapped his nose, made sure I knew he heard me, but Courtney doesn't move. She's still at the window when Ollie and I leave. We say goodbye, out loud this time, but she doesn't respond to that either.

- 34 -

That night I spread Ollie's pages out on my desk and stare for a long time at the panel-by-panel images of Nate, side by side with Captain Nexus, searching for an escape from the Zone. The Giants have another game tomorrow, so we aren't meeting back up at Courtney's until the weekend. I don't have to letter them tonight, but they're calling to me. I click on the desk light, tilt it so that it shines on the first page, and sit down to work.

Pencil in hand, I take a deep breath. In the first panel, Captain Nexus has just found Nate stranded in one of the Zone's lonely deserts. *DON'T BE AFRAID, YOUNG MAN*, the Captain says to Ollie's drawing of my best friend.

I'M NOT SCARED, Nate answers. I letter the dialogue

into the bubble above his head, my fingers tingling with excitement. They're the first words I've given to our version of my friend. I'm keeping him alive with them.

When I lift my hand up to double-check my work, though, I look closer into the face of the lost kid trapped in the Nexus Zone. His eyes aren't alive at all. They're still distant, unfocused. Afraid.

My hand's trembling. I stare at my fingers, trying to make the shaking stop, to keep them working, but I can't. Nate is lost. Nate is trapped.

My best friend is alone in a strange place, and he's terrified.

I burst up out of my chair and snap the light off, then cross the room to fall into bed, pulling the covers over my head. Tomorrow, after the game. I'll letter the pages tomorrow. We're so close to finishing; we still have plenty of time before Wednesday.

Sally slings the first warm-up grounder out to me. I bend and field it, then hop once to make my throw. My elbow spasms and I double-clutch, trying to get it across the diamond with all arm, a pitiful heave. My ankle turns in the dirt. The awkward throw skips off the ground, kicking up dust and chalk. It scoots under Sally's glove, skidding along the grass and clanging into the fence behind him.

Sally sidesteps the skinny Garvey first base coach to

chase the ball. He gives the grinning, glasses-wearing kid a dirty look, making less of an effort to avoid bumping into him on his way back to the bag. As he steps onto the dirt, Sally pumps the ball in my direction. "Come on, Summers. I've seen better arms on a beanbag chair."

Mark fields Sally's next practice grounder and straightens. I can see the white cowhide and red stitches in his webbing. He looks first at me, then Sally, clearly confused. "But beanbag chairs don't have arms."

Sally rolls his eyes. He taps one finger against his temple. "You got a steel trap up there, Lefferts." He nods at the ball in Mark's glove. "Get that in."

Mark tosses it back across the diamond. "Still doesn't make sense," he mutters.

I sigh, testing my ankle by flexing my toes and rotating my foot in place. I feel a little twinge, but it doesn't seem too bad.

Mom's wearing a worried expression in the front row of the stands. I know it's because she noticed my bad throw. Mom notices everything. She's constantly inspecting me like a suspicious restaurant. I almost think she's going to stand up and come out to the field to check on me, but then Jake's dad squeezes in front of her to sit farther down the row. He's carrying a Burger Bonanza take-out bag, and Mom's eyes dart to it like a dog who's spotted a squirrel.

She gave Burger Bonanza about the lowest score you

could give a restaurant last year. Something about roaches and rat poop. She tries to get Mr. McReynolds's attention.

Which gives me a chance to scan the rest of the crowd. Dad's about the only family member missing today. More than parents are here; a lot of grandparents made it, too. Even a few of my teammates' aunts and uncles are eagerly craning their necks to find their nephews on the field. Ollie's here, too, parked on the bleachers between his parents. I can't imagine how hard this is for the Templetons, to attend a Giants game without Nate out here pitching.

Lately Ollie usually watches from his bike, in foul ground next to Courtney, but today Courtney's nowhere in sight. At first I assume she's not here at all, but then I find her in the top row of the stands, sitting with her father. She points at the field, talking a mile a minute.

She's describing everything that's happening. She's talking baseball. All her questions for me yesterday suddenly make sense. All those times she hung out with Ollie at our games and practices, when I thought she had no reason to care about baseball.

I grin then, wider than I have in weeks. I can't help it. As sad as she was when I left her yesterday, I never expected to see her here today, talking to her dad so fast and with so much excitement. But then I should know better; Courtney always has a plan.

When Sally's next warm-up grounder skitters toward

me, I snag it cleanly and, tuning out the lingering pain in my twisted ankle, blast a strike right back at him.

By the fourth inning, it's a lot harder to ignore the way my ankle is starting to ache. Maybe I turned it worse than I thought. I smack a leadoff single and jog out to first, not even considering a wide turn. After Kurt flies out to short right and Jake sacrifices me over to second, Mark laces another single into left. I do my best imitation of a sprint toward third, but it seems like it takes months to get there.

Coach Wiggins, though, doesn't know anything about my injury. He waves me home. I lower my head and will my legs to churn, rounding the bag hard, my helmet peeling off. I'm only halfway when I catch sight of the ball bouncing in to the catcher. The Garvey backstop fields it on two hops and sets up in front of the plate, waiting for me.

I'm dead.

I think about sliding feetfirst like I normally would, but then I picture my ankle crumpling as it slams hard into his shin guards. At the last moment I decide to try headfirst.

I don't even reach the plate. I tumble to an abrupt stop two feet short, and the Garvey catcher simply taps me on the shoulder with the glove and ball. The ump shouts "Out!" at the top of his lungs, and the game remains scoreless.

• • •

At the bench I gather up my glove and hat to take the field for the top of the fifth. Coach pulls me aside. I follow his gaze down to my foot. "You hurt?"

After what happened to Nate, he'll pull me in half a second if he thinks I'm injured. So I stand firm on both feet. "I'm fine, Coach."

Sally gets up off the bench and grabs the front of my shirt as he heads out to the field, pulling me with him. "Rub some dirt on it, Summers," he tells me. Then, "All that's injured is his pride, Coach."

We leave Coach Wiggins scratching his head. "We're not forfeiting," Sally whispers when we're almost at the pitching mound.

"No kidding," I reply in a low voice. I split off for short, trying to convince myself with each step that my ankle isn't lighting up the rest of my leg like the freakin' Fourth of July.

- 35 -

As he waits for Kurt to return his latest pitch—another ball four, second walk in a row—I see Jake jerking his shoulder in a strange way. He keeps rolling it over. Bending, then straightening his elbow.

We're in the last inning. It's still 0–0. There's one out, but those two walks mean Garvey has runners on first and second now. I jog in to the mound. "You okay?"

"Arm's dead." Jake isn't joking. His eyes are wide.

"What do you mean, dead?"

He shakes his arm out from shoulder to wrist. "I mean dead. I can hardly feel it."

"You should've been icing it down."

He frowns. "Super helpful, Summers."

I kick at the back of the mound. "Sorry. We just gotta get these last two outs, okay?"

Jake rubs his elbow with the back of his glove. "It can't go into extras. I won't make it."

"Hey," I say harshly. He stops fiddling with his arm and looks at me. "Just toss it in there, like batting practice. You got a whole team out here backing you up."

Jake surveys the field. The rest of the Giants are in position, rocking back and forth on their heels. "Yeah," he sighs. "I'll try."

The next pitch smacks the new Garvey hitter square in the center of his back. He trots to first, and the other two Garvey runners advance to second and third. Bases loaded. Jake breathes deeply, in and out, on the mound as he waits for the ball back from Kurt. I close my eyes and pray he doesn't hyperventilate or something.

Jake soft-tosses the first pitch to Garvey's lanky pitcher, grooved down the middle. I wince. The Garvey kid swings way too hard, though. He rolls his bat over on it, sending a high-hopping grounder toward the hole between me and Mark at third.

Mark will never get there. Still, he starts toward it, his reflexes kicking in. Just as I think, *No. Cover the bag,* he reverses field and races back to his base.

Mark stretches his glove toward me. Did he hear me? I almost think he'll tap his nose. He doesn't.

The grounder takes a sweet, magical hop into the pocket of my glove. I don't even bother to transfer it to my throwing hand. Instead I just swing my glove hand toward third, and the ball streams out. I lose my balance, head up as I fall face-first into the dirt.

The runner who was on third is fast, almost on top of home plate already. The lanky pitcher who hit the ball, though, isn't quite so quick, even with his long strides. He's only halfway up the line.

"First base," I yell from the ground.

The ball lands in Mark's glove, his foot on the base. He trusts me. Without even looking at second or home, he turns and wings the ball toward Sally, already stretching for it at first. It arrives a split second before the runner, completing the double play and ending the Garvey half of the inning with the game still tied.

I let my head fall to the ground and stay there for a few seconds. The infield dirt is warm and safe, and I sort of don't want to move, but I have to. We still have a game to win.

In the bottom half, I draw a walk with one out. Kurt sends a hot shot over the first-base bag. The ball streaks into the corner, which I know is tricky to field sometimes. But it's behind me. I can't know if the right fielder is having trouble. I have to rely on Coach.

As I near second, I look up and see him, in foul territory

at third, waving me on again. It's a huge risk. I'm not sure I can make it. My ankle feels stiff and swollen. My foot flops on the ground like a wet pancake.

Still, I run.

Three-quarters of the way to third, I want to quit. Coach is almost home himself now, hollering and waving. "All the way!" he shouts. "All the way!"

The crowd is yelling. Cheering. Screaming.

I close my eyes and I'm not on the base paths anymore. I'm at the bike trail, with Nate.

"When Coach came to the mound, I was so pissed I almost told him to take me out," he said last summer. "Put Jake in."

"Why didn't you?"

"I knew you guys needed me."

I open my eyes again. Almost to third. Behind Coach my team isn't sitting, not a single one of them. Their fingers are wound into the fence, rally caps are on their heads. Jake's on his toes, his pitching arm dangling uselessly at his side. *It can't go into extras. I won't make it.*

I round third. I keep running.

Sally's screaming at me. "You better score, you freakin' sloth. Score!"

Now that I'm sprinting down the line, I can see the throw coming in from right field. The cutoff man snags it and spins. I'm almost home. Push, I think. *Push.*

Nate looking at me like it was so strange that I didn't get why he wouldn't quit.

I knew you guys needed me.

My friends, the wire fence digging into their fingers. All those rally caps. The slowest kid on the team calling *me* a sloth.

Push!

The ball is in the air. The catcher steps forward. I slide, feetfirst. My bad foot runs into his cleat. Pain flashes through my entire leg. I hear the pop of the ball in his glove, see him swiping his tag down for me. A cloud of dust rises up.

And then there's only silence and that fog of dirt. I can't see the umpire, but I hear him.

"Safe!" and the crowd noise surrounds us again as the smoky dust clears.

If I were forced to, I'm not sure I could stand on my ankle. Fortunately, though, I don't have to, because my team rushes around the fence and carries me off the field.

- 36 -

DiNunzio's is super crowded, but Coach knows the owner, so he finds us some tables in the back we can push together. Mom didn't want me to come; she'd seen me limping around the bench after the game, but I told her I was fine. She rolled her eyes a bunch but it didn't matter. I was sticking with the Giants tonight.

"Dude, one more win until the finals," Jake says. He grabs my shoulders and shakes them.

I look past him to Sally. "Hey. You call me a sloth?"

He answers through a mouth full of garlic knot. "Scored, didn't ya?"

A waitress starts dropping off pizzas wherever she can fit them. Pepperoni and cheese at the first table, sausage and mushroom at the second, and Coach's infamous anchovy and pineapple right in front of me and Jake.

"Aw, man," Jake groans. "Gross."

I'm in such a good mood I reach out and tear the biggest slice off Coach's pie. I plop the pineapple-and anchovy-covered wedge on my plate.

"You wouldn't," Jake whispers.

The whole team is watching me now. Pizza slices freeze halfway to open mouths. I stand, lifting the plate with me. Throw back my shoulders. My ankle throbs when I put weight on it again, but not too bad. I raise the slice up over my head and the Giants start chanting my name. "Dan! Dan! Dan!"

The scent of pineapple dunked in a fishy swamp wafts toward my nostrils. The room goes quiet. I chomp down on the end, the sweet fruit mixing with the salty fish and cheese and sauce. My eyes widen. My toes curl. I'm trying to chew normally, but I feel like a dog lapping away at peanut butter.

"That sloth has lost his mind!" Sally yells. All I can do is chew and chew, until I can't stand it anymore. I swallow the disgusting bite, mumbling through my horror, "Coach, how could you . . ." I pick a piece of dead fish off my tongue. Gross.

The Giants roar, and I laugh with them. We're one game closer to the championship, one game closer to another great story for Nate. We can't win the whole thing by Wednesday, but still. The more stories, the better.

I should really go home, work on my pages, but there's still plenty of time. I have the whole weekend, plus a couple of days after that. So when Sally invites us over to watch the latest Marvel movie for about the fiftieth time after DiNunzio's, I say yes. It's after ten by the time Mom picks me up. I have to really concentrate to hide my limp as I make my way down the driveway for the minivan.

"How's that ankle?" Mom asks, one eyebrow arched.

"It's fine," I say.

"You sure about that?"

"Mom."

"You should've been home icing it."

She frowns and tries to peer at it, like she can determine how badly I'm hurt with some sort of mom-vision that sees through my sock and shoe. "When we get to the house, I'll give you an ice pack and I want you straight into bed, elevating it. Promise?"

"Mom, okay!"

When I wake up Saturday morning, I roll toward my window. The sun streams in through the blinds, casting slanted beams of light onto the pages I left on my desk. Suddenly today the Wednesday deadline feels like it's coming fast.

I still have some time, but I better hurry. Ollie's working on getting his parents to let us visit Tuesday, right before the doctors bring Nate back. Excited, I jump out of bed without thinking and my ankle falters as soon as my foot hits the floor.

"Agh," I cry, catching myself with one hand on the bedpost. I test my leg some more. The ankle's definitely stiff and a little painful, but now that I'm up, I think I can at least limp around on it. I start to worry, though. The next game's only two days away, and we still have just nine players. If I can't play, the Giants might have to forfeit.

Mom'll know what to do. Maybe I just need more ice. When I open my door and step out into the hallway, though, I hear hushed voices downstairs. Did Dad stay home this weekend? It would be the first Saturday in a while. Maybe it's someone else. But who?

Using the railing for support, I hop down the stairs, occasionally testing my ankle with a little weight. I limp into the kitchen.

Mom's at the table and Dad's on the other side of the counter. He was drinking a cup of coffee, but as soon as I enter the room, he sets it down.

I look at Mom. She sniffs. Her eyes are red. Has she been crying?

I hop forward a step and put my hand on the wall to help me balance. "What's wrong?"

Mom shakes her head.

"Sit down, Dan," Dad says. He swipes at an eye with his finger, and I realize he's been crying, too. Dad never cries. Well, almost never. Last time was when Aunt Megan passed away around Christmas three years ago.

My heart starts to beat really fast. "Why are you home?" I ask him. My voice is too high. It breaks when I say "home."

"Son, it would be better if you sit—"

"Tell me!" I shout. "Why are you—what's wrong?"

Dad starts to come around the counter toward me. "Dan, Mrs. Templeton called this morning."

I take a step back from him.

"Nate . . . son, he had some more trouble breathing last night. And the doctors, well, they had to try to help him." He crouches down, so we're eye level. "They were going to bring him out of the coma later this week anyway—"

"Yeah, I know. Wednesday."

"Well, they had to change their plans. They tried last night instead. And . . . well, it didn't work."

"It didn't work because we weren't ready!"

Mom sits up. "Dan, honey, this is something the doctors do. It has nothing to do with you."

"N-no, we had to show him . . ." Ollie said if it didn't work when they tried to wake him up, Nate might not come back at all.

Dad reaches out for me, but I use both hands to push him away so hard that he rocks back on his heels. "They were supposed to wait!"

"Hold on, Dan," Dad starts.

"No," I say, backing away some more. "No, I was supposed to help him. I was . . . he wouldn't—" Those pages on my desk, the ones I was supposed to be working on. The ones I was too scared, too busy celebrating, to finish.

They're still there.

I race back down the hall, half limping, half hopping for the stairs. I clutch the railing as I climb. When I reach the landing, I forget and step up with the wrong foot. The pain in my ankle sends me crumpling to the ground.

There's no time. I crawl into my room, past my bed, to my desk. I use my chair to pull myself up onto my knees. Reach for my pencil. Slide the top page over. Find Nate in the panels.

I dig words into the bubble over his head. I'm not even looking at Courtney's script. I just want to reach my friend. He's still out there. It's not too late.

Right?

NATE! I scratch. More words come in spurts, whatever pops into my head. *CAN YOU HEAR ME?*

CAPTAIN, DAN. Each word another stretch of my searching fingers. *HELP.*

DON'T.

I'm pressing down so hard on it, the pencil snaps in half. I pick up the pieces, try to keep going, but it twists and I slash a dark line straight down the page, right across Nate's face. I throw the useless pencil against the window and scream.

It didn't work. Nate's still trapped. And now his chances of making it back might be gone forever. I slide down, the weight of my realization melting me into the floor. Mom rushes in. She kneels, wraps her arms around me, lifts me into a hug. She starts crying.

"I could've saved him," I say, pressing my face into her shirt.

"No, honey," she says, stroking my hair. "The doctors'll find . . . you can't blame yourself. None of this is your fault. None of it."

She squeezes me tighter and tighter. I nod against her warmth as we sob together, and she murmurs the same things again and again.

"Nate's not gone," Mom says.

"The doctors will try again," she says.

"It wasn't your fault."

I keep nodding and nodding, like I believe all those words must be true, that she has to be right.

Even though I know she's wrong.

- 37 -

Monday evening, we're playing Lollar. Brooksburgh had crushed them, dropping them into the losers bracket with us. I almost didn't bother showing up for the game. I really couldn't believe there'd been no meeting about whether we should play, no talk about that being a decision at all. It was as if I was the only one on the Giants who knew the real truth.

The doctors had tried to bring Nate back without waiting for our story. And, of course, it didn't work. So now it doesn't matter if the machines in his room keep blinking and beeping, it doesn't matter that Mom believes he might still have a chance to come back, it doesn't matter how many times his chest rises and falls with breaths or how many thumps of his heart the doctors hear when they listen to it.

Nate's stuck.

Nothing matters anymore—not our stupid comic, not my weird bike-trail-slash-Nexus-Zone project, especially not this dumb baseball tournament. But here I am, playing in this meaningless game anyway.

First inning. The Lollar leadoff batter lines a hot shot right at me. I hop up on my still-sore ankle and stick my glove out, but the familiar sound of an out slapping into the pocket never comes. I jerk my head around, watching the ball touch down in shallow left and bound toward Craig. I search the inside of my glove for a hole that isn't there.

The other Giants are studying their own mitts, their cleats, kicking at dirt and grass. Anything but making eye contact with me. Jake gets the relay back from Greg, bites his lip, then sets up to take on the next hitter.

The leadoff kid steals second on Jake's first pitch to Lollar's lefty third baseman. I'm supposed to cover the bag but I forget, freezing in place. Kurt has no one to throw to.

Mark hisses at me from third. "You all right?"

"Yeah," I say, waving him off. "Fine."

After a couple of lazy fly outs, the Lollar cleanup hitter smacks a double to the right-center gap and the leadoff kid scores easily. Jake strikes the next hitter out, but the damage is done. We're down one before we even get a chance to hit.

At the bench I pull on my batting gloves. Coach stares me down. I hold his gaze. He opens his mouth to say something, but after a second closes it and weaves through the Giants to the other end of the dugout, like he needs to get as far away from me as possible.

The rest of the Giants are avoiding me, too, like I have a no-hitter going and they don't want to jinx it. Or maybe more like I just made two mental errors in one inning.

So what? Seriously, what's the point anymore?

Sally grounds out, and I'm up. I dig into the dirt and wait for the first pitch. It comes in blurry, already past me before I can even think about swinging. I try to close my eyes and clear my head, to visualize like Coach always says, but all I see are Nate's eyes in Ollie's drawing, deep with fear. I swing right through the second pitch. My bat never leaves my shoulder as I take the third strike.

In the second inning, the first grounder eats me up. I try to stay in front of it, but it hops up into my chest and skitters away from me. By the time I pick it up, it's too late to throw to first. Another Lollar hitter on base.

Sally snags a soft liner for the first out of the inning. The next hitter pops a fly into shallow left. I'm backing up, keeping my eye on it.

Behind me, I hear Craig calling for it. What's he doing? I have this one. Craig calls out again. I feel him charging in. I call back, louder, then settle my feet, waiting for the ball.

Right before it drops into my glove, I'm struck hard from behind. Craig and I tangle together as we both go down. The ball lands on the grass a few feet away, then rolls away from both of us. While I reel in pain, Craig scrambles on his hands and knees for several feet until he can finally stand. He jogs toward the ball and tosses it in. Too late. The runner from first has already scored, but the hitter, thinking he was out for sure, didn't run hard. He's still at first. The Giants are down two now.

"What do you think you're doing?" Craig yells. "I called it."

It takes another second to get up. Everything hurts. "I had it."

"You're supposed to peel off when an outfielder calls for it."

All I can do is say "I had it" again.

He frowns at me, snatches his hat off the ground and turns back for his position. "Okay, Summers. You had it. Meanwhile, they're scoring. Or haven't you noticed?"

- 38 -

As I trot back to the infield, I notice Ollie stand up in the bleachers. I didn't see it before, but he has his sketchbook with him, the same one he used to keep pressed tight to his chest when he teleported into our dugout after all our other games. He slips past his mom and streams down the metal steps. Mr. Templeton reaches out to stop him, but he isn't fast enough.

Ollie rounds the chain-link fence and rushes onto the grass, the heavy sketchbook under his arm causing him to cant to one side. Where's he going? He reaches the third base line and trips over the chalk, as if some invisible hand thrust out and grabbed his shoelace. The sketchbook flies out of Ollie's hands and lands a few feet away. There's a long "oooooh" from the crowd. In the bleachers, Mr. Templeton stands. His wife puts a hand on his arm and eases him back down.

Ollie lies face-first on the grass for what seems like a long time before pushing himself up to his knees. His glasses are off-kilter on his face. His hands wander out for his book. He slides it along the grass until it's close enough for him to dig his fingers underneath and lift it back up again.

I haven't moved since he left the bleachers, still frozen on the line dividing the infield dirt from the outfield grass. I step forward, both cleats on the dirt now. The field is so quiet, I almost think I've lost my hearing, like Nexus Boy back in #3. But when Ollie rises to his feet again, one of the Lollar parents hoots out a cheer. He claps once, twice. When he sees he's the only one applauding, though, he stops.

The home-plate ump steps out from behind Kurt and rips his mask off. Coach appears in an instant, pushing the ump back with both his hands on the ump's chest protector, whispering in his ear. The anger in the ump's face fades. He twists his black, backward cap around so that it faces forward. He glances into the bleachers at Mr. and Mrs. Templeton, both of them leaning with their hands on their knees. They seem about to leap down and save their son at any moment, but for now they don't move.

Ollie starts to jog again, and this time it's clear that he's heading in my direction. When he reaches me, he stops and seems aware for the first time that everyone is staring at him. All the parents in the bleachers, the other Giants around the diamond. The umps. Our opponents, the Lollar Mets. His eyes widen.

"Hey," he says through a deep inhale. "Never realized how big it was out here."

"What are you doing?" I ask.

"Did I ever show you my sketchbook?" Ollie boosts it up on his hip, same way he used to do after games when he and Nate would head for their car. He flips through the pages.

"You can't be out here, Ollie."

"Just look." He finds his page, and holds the book up toward me. It's Nate. Not the Nate in our comic, trapped in the Zone, afraid. This is an older drawing of Ollie's big brother, as a pitcher. Confident, in mid-windup. My best friend, about to strike someone out, probably.

I look away from the image. "Ollie . . . I'm sorry, I can't look at Nate right now."

He twists the book toward himself, then back to face me. "The other page, dummy."

The opposite page has a kid leaping in the air over an oncoming runner. In the first drawing, at the top, he's throwing toward first to complete a double play. Then in the middle and bottom, two more drawings show him somersaulting when he hits the ground.

They show *me* somersaulting.

Because the drawing is me, I see it now, the one Courtney told me about. My play last year, against Shale. I guess it's me, anyway. You never really think about someone drawing you like that, what you'll end up looking like. It's like when you hear a recording of your own voice. Not quite what you expected at first, but the more you listen to it—yeah, that's you, all right.

"What is this?" I ask.

Ollie squints at me. "You were always best at the superhero-guessing game."

I stare at the drawings again. They're definitely me. And you know what? I look good. I look like I know what I'm doing. I look like a star.

I look, maybe just a little bit, like a hero.

And now I see something else. Right in front of me, like his drawing. Nate's always been my hero, but he was Ollie's too. But Nate isn't here now. And it's my job to take his place for my new friend.

I breathe in deep, then reach out and straighten Ollie's glasses for him. We stare at each other for a few seconds. I still can't tell him the accident was my fault. I can't tell him I had two whole nights to keep Nate alive but I didn't because I was afraid to letter those pages.

I can do one thing, though.

I can play ball.

• • •

The next hitter scoots a ground ball straight up the middle. I'll never get there, but I scramble toward the back of second base anyway. I lower my glove, almost stumbling to the ground as I bend. Somehow the ball, skirting close to the infield dirt, finds its way into the leather. But I'm racing toward right field so fast, my feet slipping under me, there's no way to twist and make a good throw back to Greg at second.

We need this double play.

I do the only thing I can think of, nothing more than a reflex, really. I swing my glove arm around my back and make a total guess at the right time to open my hand to let the ball fly. As soon as it's gone, my footing gives out and I slide headfirst onto the outfield grass. When I twist to look back over my shoulder, Greg is barehanding my glove toss, turning on the bag, and sending a great throw toward first.

Sally squeezes it at the same time the runner gets there, and I hold my breath waiting for the ump's call. He raises his fist. We're out of the inning.

The Giants start clicking at the plate and in the field. We're unstoppable. In the fifth we hit four consecutive doubles, and I make another diving stop at shortstop. It's not quite a somersault, but I do roll to my feet and gun down the runner sprinting for first.

As I'm jogging back to the dugout after the final out, an

11–2 score up on the board, I can't help but glance up at Ollie, nestled safely between his parents once more. Both their arms are around him, like they'll never let go of him again, not even for a second. He smiles at me, and then, struggling to free a hand from his mother's vice grip, he does something else.

Ollie taps his nose.

He taps his nose, and I tap mine back.

- 39 -

The morning after our big Lollar win, sweat streams down my face as I sidearm another flat rock across the pond, clear to the opposite shore. I'm finally doing it, every time now, but I can't even smile, because there's no one here to celebrate with me.

Sure, we made it to the finals against Brooksburgh. But because we got there from the losers bracket, we'll have to beat them twice to win the championship. The first game's in Mira. A win there would mean we'd still have to beat the Tigers a second time, on their field, way up in Brooksburgh. What an incredible story that'd be. Too bad I don't need one of those anymore.

At breakfast, Dad suggested maybe we could take a ride

to the comic store today, but there's nothing I need there. I came out to the bike trail instead.

I've been back here a couple hours probably, just slinging stones, using a branch to scratch patterns into the dirt, lying on my back, watching the clouds drift slowly overhead. I fire one last rock across the pond, then race up the hill again.

I get to the top and plant my feet, but I still hear movement. At the edge of the woods, creeping toward me. My heart doesn't skip, my breath stays even. It's not Nate, I already know, even before I catch sight of Ollie and Courtney pushing their way through the brush into the clearing.

For a second I think my friends might laugh at the idea of me spending so much time out here alone, turning this place into the Nexus Zone. Like it ever mattered. But then Courtney races forward and looks up at my partial mountain range, her gaze following the trail turned river flowing toward the pond.

She grins up at me. "The Zone?"

I nod.

"It's perfect."

"How'd you find me?"

She glances back at Ollie. "Followed you and Nate here last year," he admits.

My surprise must show on my face, because he adds, shrugging, "I could tell you guys wanted to be alone."

We stare at each other, me up on the hill, him at its base. All this time I thought I was winning a competition with Ollie for Nate, but I wasn't winning anything, because Ollie wasn't even trying. Not to win, anyway. To prove something? Sure . . . just that he belonged. He waited a long time for us—no, me—to figure it out, but I never did.

He knew about the bike trail. He knew about our nose tapping. He left us alone on purpose, allowed us to have our little secrets-that-weren't-really-secrets. And then this week, after what he did for me in the Lollar game, getting me back on track like that . . .

Nate has always been a hero to both of us. I wanted to spend all the time I could with my best friend. I'd already lost Dad to his work—I didn't want to lose Nate to his brother. But unlike Dad's job, which is just . . . just a thing, Ollie is a person, who tried his best to be fair. He gave up one thing after another to allow Nate to hang with me more. And I was too stupid to notice any of it.

A bunch of loose stones I piled into a pyramid tumble into the pond. Courtney saves one from the water and tries skipping it, but angles her throw wrong. It spikes up once before rudely plopping down in the center of the pond.

I'm about to scramble down the hill and show her how to sidearm it when someone else approaches through the brush. There's so much noise Mom must step on every possible branch as she picks her way into the clearing. She has her cell in her hand, holding it above the prickling vines and sharp branch saplings protectively. When she sees me, she points the phone at me.

"Dan? It's Mr. Sanderson. He has something to ask you. I think you should listen."

I stare at her, at the phone in her hand, like from way up here I can see the old man's expression on the screen. But Sanderson's face isn't there. It's just a black screen with a red button that part of me wishes Mom's thumb would run over accidentally.

I had it so wrong. I tried to use the *Captain Nexus* contest to call for help, like Jimmy Olsen's signal watch, or Commissioner Gordon's Bat-Signal. I thought that somehow Sanderson would drop out of the sky knowing how to save Nate, but Sanderson didn't have the powers I needed. Because he's not a superhero—he just draws them. This is real life, superheroes don't exist, and Nate is slipping away from us all, trapped deeper and deeper with every passing minute.

Mom reaches the hill. Ollie steps to one side so she can raise her phone in my direction again. What does she expect me to do? I don't get what Sanderson could possibly say that could matter right now.

The clearing is quiet. A crow flies overhead, squawking while Mom and I fall into a staring contest that feels like it lasts a long time. She blinks first, but then immediately puts one foot up on the base of the hill, stretching the phone closer to me. "Please, Dan."

I'm not going to escape this. Sighing, I slide sideways down the steepest part of the hill toward her, dirt avalanching down with me.

"Hello?" I say into the phone after I accept it from Mom's fingers.

Sanderson's voice is scratchy, like he's just recovering from a coughing fit. "Hi, Dan. I . . . thank you for talking to me. I was very sorry to hear about Nate's setback. How are you doing?"

"I'm okay."

"And Nate?"

"I don't know."

"I understand." He exhales into the phone, and it's loud enough that I pull Mom's cell away from my ear. "Listen, Dan. I think I need your help."

"How?"

"Come back to my studio," he says. "Help me finish number sixteen."

"Your studio?"

Ollie steps forward when he hears me mention his mecca, his eyes wide with naked eagerness.

"But you work alone," I say.

"Yes, I do. I have before, anyway," Sanderson says.

Another sigh. "The Captain's in real trouble. I've been trying to finish number sixteen on my own, but . . ." A long silence. "The issue . . . it's taking a lot out of me. Too much, maybe. I think I know what I need to do. I'm just not sure I can do it by myself anymore."

That day in the gym, the day of the accident, my best friend and I were the last ones to leave the locker room before practice. We sat side by side on a bench, tying our sneakers.

"You know, it actually would be kind of funny," I said. "Jake's idea."

"What was that?" Nate asked.

"If we sent you out there to the mound all by yourself some game. You know, just like a joke or something. To see how shocked the other team would be."

"That wouldn't be cool, man."

Nate was so serious about it. "It's just a joke," I muttered.

He finished with one sneaker, then paused before starting on the other. "Why would I ever want to play alone? How much fun would that be, with no team?"

"Dude, sorry," I said, tossing a towel in his direction to hide my reddening face.

Nate ducked and half caught the towel between two fingers. It slipped away from him, but he grabbed it with his other hand. "Being on a team with you guys is the best part of playing."

I wish I'd known. I wish I'd understood it was the last time he and I would talk. I think I would've said something more if I'd known. At least told him I felt the exact same way about being on his team as he did about being on mine.

All we did was finish tying our sneakers and race each other into the gym for practice. I thought we'd have a thousand more practices together.

A breeze blows through the clearing. Dust flies up from one of the fresh mounds of dirt. I check on my friends. Ollie's eyes couldn't get any bigger. He so wants another chance to work with Sanderson.

I know I can't let him down. I owe him too much. But it's not just for Ollie and Courtney, it's for Nate, too. He wouldn't want me to pass up a chance to save the last issue of *Captain Nexus* because I was too busy being sad about him.

"You really need our help?" I ask Sanderson.

There's a click on the phone line, and for a second I think I've lost him. My heart sinks, and I realize how badly I want to go back to the studio, too.

Then Sanderson answers, and I breathe out relief at the sound of his voice. "Yes, I really do. I think . . . it might be what I need more than anything right now."

For the first time, I'm not scared to try to be Nate. To do what I know he would do. To say what I know he would say.

I don't even let a second pass before I give Sanderson my answer, because Nate wouldn't have hesitated either. "What time should we be there?"

- 40 -

I can't believe it, but Mom is super late again. Dad had some important meeting this afternoon, of course, so I had to turn to my mother for a ride to Brooksburgh this time. I even set the alarm on her phone. She should be home by now. The drive is at least an hour; we were supposed to leave over twenty minutes ago.

I call her again. All I've been getting is voice mail, and she doesn't answer texts, either. Sure enough, her recorded message clicks on. "You've reached the office of Claire Summers. I'm not available to take your call now, but if—"

Argh! I should've known. Friday inspections always get kind of crazy. But Sanderson had wanted us to come for a little while today so he could show us how we'd be helping him next week.

I'm going to have to text Courtney and Ollie soon. They're probably waiting in Courtney's foyer already, staring at the driveway through the narrow side window, wondering where the heck I am.

My mother's supposed to be coming back from inspecting that beef and custard place on Route 20, but I can't remember the name. Something starting with *L*, I think. Lisa's? Laura's? Lulu's? Maybe she has something in her office with the phone number. I head down to the basement, tapping Mom's name one more time as I turn the corner at the bottom of the stairs.

Mom's desk is a mess. Something's buzzing underneath a stack of papers, half of them photos of rotting food: moldy bread, flies all over grayish meat, something else white and bumpy and disturbingly close up. Sliding the scary pictures over, I uncover Mom's phone, vibrating away, the screen lit with *DAN*. She forgot it again. And knowing her, she's so wrapped up in her inspection she doesn't even realize it's missing.

"Dan?" Dad's voice, calling down from the kitchen.

"Down here," I shout back.

"I heard from your mother. She forgot—"

"Her phone," I finish as I reach the bottom of the steps

and show him the trail of alerts—all my voice mails and texts, plus the never-heard alarm that went off an hour ago—running down its screen. "No kidding. We're supposed to be on our way to Brooksburgh by now."

"Well, she's stuck at a diner inspection in Tonawanda. Something about French onion soup and dishwater." He shakes his head. "I'm the cavalry."

"Really? You're taking us again?"

"So surprised," he scolds. "Yeah, I'm taking you, as soon as you're ready."

"I was ready an hour ago," I say as I race up the stairs.

"Are you coming in?" I ask Dad as his Volvo idles in front of Building B of the Brooksburgh Art Coop. A lone chicken struts and clucks across the porch, stopping in front of the door. One of the tattooed girls, this one with a blond buzz cut, taps in the code and lets the chicken in, then shuts the door before rejoining her friends at the far end of the porch.

I can't stop picturing Mom wandering around this place, imagining what she must've been thinking as she stepped over and around stubborn chickens. She hadn't been completely comfortable allowing us to work with Sanderson all week, but she'd had to go back to Brooksburgh to reinspect the Meatball Emporium on Wednesday. While she was out this way, she decided to add a side trip to the Art Coop. I guess she met Joyce and some of those goth artists while she was here. After that, she seemed okay with Sanderson's proposal. I wanted to sprint across the porch and thank them for whatever they'd said to her.

Only thing is, I really hope those dudes weren't eating pizza at the time. Mom probably would've issued a citation because of the chicken feet odor alone, never mind the poop covering every available surface.

Dad had talked with us the entire drive up—about comics and baseball, movies, the Sabres—he'd even asked Ollie so many questions about art I started to feel a little jealous. There'd been no business calls, not a single one. I couldn't figure him out lately.

Dad shakes his head, answering my question. "I'll stay out here. I think George is only interested in working with you three."

"You're sure he didn't say anything else?" I ask for about the fifth time.

Dad repeats his answer, which is getting kind of old for both of us now. "All I know is Mr. Sanderson asked for you kids," he says. "Just you guys. Besides, I have a project to work on out here."

I glance at his shoulder for his laptop, but Dad hops up the steps without it. No phone in his hand, either. Before my shock can sink in, Mr. Neck Tattoo separates from his friends and skips toward my father. They do a sort of a secret handshake. I watch with my mouth wide open.

"Mr. S!" Neck Tattoo shouts.

Mr. S? I want to—need to—stick around and figure out what's up, but Courtney's already punching in the door code. All I can do is call back to Dad before following her inside, "Hey, Dad? Thanks for bringing us. I know you're busy."

Dad grimaces out a smile. "Anytime. You know that, right?"

Do I?

"We won't keep him long," the girl who had pink hair last time, now green, assures me.

"It's just that the dude is a structural genius," Neck Tattoo adds. "And there's a lot of work to do around here. We really appreciate him donating his time like this."

"Awesome," I say slowly. I look toward Dad for answers, but he's already bent over some blueprints.

"This door is *heavy*," Ollie complains, and I can't stay out here focused on what Dad's up to, because he's not the reason I'm here. I follow my friends into Building B.

We don't have to knock, because Sanderson's door is already open. He's standing outside it, in the hallway, having a friendly chat with Joyce. She sees us coming and, smiling, says, "Well, here are all your adorable little helpers now. Have fun, kids." She crosses the hall back to her studio, winking at us.

Sanderson looks relieved, as if he wondered whether we'd really come. He leads us through the first room of his studio space and into the inner room, all tidied up now. Papers are neatly stacked, brushes and pens in their proper places, the chairs and stools pushed up under their desks and tables. A stack of paneled pages waits in the middle of his light box.

Sanderson reaches down and flips on the light. "First things first. You need to see what I have so far." He pulls the first page closer, revealing the cover to *Captain Nexus and the Nexus Five* #16.

It's amazing, more detailed than anything he's ever drawn. The image is similar to the final page of #15, with the Captain and the Hollow locked in combat. The Captain still grips the Hollow's wrists; the same energy floats off the creature's upturned hands. But where the drawing in #15 had been against a stark white background, this one is in the foreground of a Nexus Zone bursting with color. Every tree, bush, rock, distant mountain, shimmering lake—all of it—is rendered in mind-numbing detail.

Ollie's hand shakes as he reaches toward the drawing. Sanderson blocks him.

"Art later, story first." Sanderson taps the cover page. "I'm more than halfway done." We lean in. We must be the very first people to be reading the final issue of the greatest comic book ever.

"It's amazing," Courtney says.

"Yeah," Ollie agrees. "Awesome."

"I'm sort of stuck," Sanderson admits.

George Sanderson, stuck? It doesn't seem possible.

He flips more pages, and we watch the epic fight between light and dark—the Captain and the Hollow—unfold before us. It's the best comic I've ever seen. But when the stack ends, nothing is resolved. Captain Nexus and the Hollow are still locked in struggle. It's not nearly enough pages to make a full issue.

I'm confused. The issue must be due soon. The next Captain Nexus Wednesday is only twelve days away. How can he have so much work left?

We're all quiet for a minute. The old man is still staring at his table, thinking. Or . . . I don't know. Remembering, maybe.

"Mr. Sanderson?" I manage.

Sanderson takes a moment before responding. "Hmm?"

"I'm sorry, but . . . why are we here?"

He inhales and looks up at the ceiling. Slowly, his gaze drops back down to the pages.

"Because I don't think I can tell the world this particular truth all by myself. Because I'm finally ready to admit who the Hollow really is, and you guys are going to have to help me be brave enough to do it."

- 41 -

We'd heard rumors about how big and strong the Brooksburgh Tigers are, but you can't really appreciate it until you shake their hands before the game, until you're dwarfed by one of them trotting past you after his homer almost reaches the parking lot. I half expect, when they're done trouncing us, that some of them will hop in cars and drive themselves home. They don't even bother to pitch their star, Ray Yumido, in this first game. He's out in left field, looking bored.

The Tigers smack two home runs off Jake in the first, both solo shots, and another here in the second, with one man on. It's four to nothing already.

It's hot today. The fiery Saturday afternoon sun beats

down on us as we stand in the field watching balls sail over the fences. Two in a row? There's no way we're beating these guys even once.

After the third bomb, Coach takes a trip out to the mound. The entire infield joins him. "Hey," he says to Jake. "Settle down, all right? Trust your fielders."

It's clear Jake's lost all his confidence. "That's not gonna work, Coach. I can't just let these guys hit it. They keep knocking them over the fence."

Most of us look down at our feet. Jake's right. These guys are too good. Maybe if Nate . . . I sigh. Sally kicks at the dirt. Kurt plays with the curved bars of his mask, as if he's strong enough to straighten out the steel.

Coach presses his lips together. He rips his cap off. "So that's it, then?" He points his hat at the Brooksburgh dugout. "I should let their coach know we're done? We don't want to play? Yeah, how about that? Let's forfeit." He stabs a single step in the direction of the Tigers' bench.

"No!" Kurt slams his mask against his chest protector. "Come on, you guys."

"We can do this," I agree. Because maybe I'm not playing for Nate anymore, but that doesn't mean the rest of my teammates and their parents couldn't use a good win right about now, too.

Coach scratches at his hairline. "Dan, what would Colonel Neutron say to get us going?"

It starts with Jake. He raises his glove to his mouth. Sally catches the laughter bug next. Then Mark. Kurt. I'm squeezing my mouth closed, trying not to erupt, but soon I'm practically doubling over, the entire Mira Giants infield with me.

In the distance, the Brooksburgh players stand off their bench. They gaze at us in confusion. This is the championship game, a serious thing. And somehow their opponents, losing bad already, are downright yukking it up in the middle of the field. Most of them seem bewildered, a few angry. They murmur and point.

"What's all this, then?" Coach asks. He pulls his Giants hat back on with force, like he's as annoyed as the Tigers are.

"His name is Captain Nexus, Coach," I say. "No idea who Colonel Neutron is."

"Isn't Colonel Neutron on Nickelodeon?" Kurt asks.

"That's the other dude," Sally says. "The one with the ginormous head."

We burst into more laughter. Coach squints at us for a second before an embarrassed smile spreads across his face. "Come on. What do I know about comic books?"

The ump appears. He glances around our huddle curiously, then rests a hand on Coach's back. "Time to break this one up, men."

Our laughter dies down. The Giants' expressions harden.

I can't be the only one thinking about Nate. When we used to laugh together, he was always loudest.

"Hey, team?" Coach Wiggins raises his voice. "Don't think so much, all right? Just play."

My teammates start heading back to their positions. "Dan," Kurt calls out to me. He's still on the mound in front of Jake. I stop and wait. "Seriously. What do you think Captain Nexus would do?"

Over Kurt's shoulder, I catch a glimpse of George Sanderson limping up into the stands. He's late, but he made it. "Remember when the Captain beat the Hollow by tricking him into that containment unit?"

Kurt nods. "Sure. Issue nine."

"I think the Captain would say, 'Do something they'll never expect you to do.' I think he would say, 'Trick 'em if you have to.'" Our pitcher and catcher look at each other with questions in their eyes.

"How's that curve been coming?" I ask.

Their confused looks fade away. They start to grin.

"Worth a shot, isn't it?"

Jake ends the inning by striking out the next two Tigers. His curveball is amazing, a big looping pitch that half the Brooksburgh hitters think is going to hit them. They keep bailing out of the batter's box just before the ball dives down through the strike zone.

Kurt does a sort of disco dance at the bench as he stores his gear between innings. "Told you," he says to a smiling Jake, jabbing his fist into the center of our pitcher's chest. "That thing's unhittable."

"Where'd that come from?" Coach, stalking toward them, asks.

"Something we've been working on," Kurt says proudly.

Coach shakes his head. "No way. Don't do it again."

Jake's smile fades. "Why not?"

"You're too young. Curveballs will damage your arm."

"Coach . . ."

"I'm serious. Throw another curveball and . . . and I'll put Sally in to pitch."

Sally stops Velcro-ing his batting glove and looks at Coach with super-wide eyes.

"Locate your fastball," Coach orders Jake. "Move it around the zone. Keep them off-balance. No curves."

Kurt and Jake drop onto the bench, dejected. The entire team is quiet. That inning, Brooksburgh's pitcher holds us scoreless again. We're still down four as we retake the field.

Jake follows Coach's instructions. He keeps getting into trouble, then out again—one huge guy sends a deep fly to left that Craig narrowly tracks down, and the bases end up loaded with two outs—but when the Brooksburgh shortstop screams a line drive over my head that I somehow snow-cone with my glove, we escape still down only four.

"Dude, you skied for that ball," Sally says as he picks out the right bat. "Never seen anything like that."

I shrug. "Just got lucky, I guess."

"No, you got air is what you got," Mark agrees.

"Big ups, man," Kurt adds. "Like you were levitating."

I'm on deck, so I concentrate on finding my bat and they leave me alone. When they're gone, though, I allow myself to remember how that jump really felt. Must've been the highest I've ever risen. Almost like I got as high as I could on my own, and then someone invisible boosted me up the rest of the way.

I glance into the stands. Ollie's got his sketchbook open on his lap. He's drawing like mad, his tongue clenched between his teeth. Courtney's next to him, watching him work. She looks up and smiles at me. Weird, because she doesn't move her lips, but somehow I hear her voice anyway.

"It's you," she says without talking. "He's drawing *you*."

- 42 -

Jake settles in, moving his pitches around the zone, keeping Brooksburgh off-balance. A couple innings later, we finally break through against the Tigers' pitcher. Greg walks and Sally reaches on an error. I bunt, sacrificing myself for the team and advancing each runner one base. Kurt laces a single to center and we cut the deficit in half when Greg and Sally both score.

In the next-to-last inning, the Brooksburgh pitcher appears to tire, issuing two walks with two outs. Their coach calls for a pitching change by tapping his right arm as he paces toward the mound.

Ray Yumido trots in from left. He's huge—*their* team should be called the Giants, since they seem to have an endless parade of them. He swaps places with their starting pitcher. Their coach sends the dejected kid off the mound with a pat.

I watch Yumido warm up from the on-deck circle. This is their star, the kid who pitched a shutout in their last game against Lollar. The one they were saving for their home game if by some miracle we actually won this one. Guess their coach decided it would be easier to finish us off today.

Yumido fires blazing fastball after fastball into the Brooksburgh catcher's mitt. I try to time the speed, getting into my stance and swinging as each pitch screams through the zone, but it seems impossible. I've only seen one person throw with this much heat before. And he's . . . well, he isn't here right now.

My stomach turns over.

Yumido signals he's warm and the ump calls for me to step up to the plate. I take a deep breath and try to tune everything else out. The first pitch is a ball, way outside, but it doesn't matter because I swing wildly at it. Sally's on first, shouting for me to settle down. I take another deep breath. My bat doesn't leave my shoulder as I let the second pitch groove past me. I'm hoping for another ball, but it's straight down the middle.

Strike two.

I step out of the box.

The voices of the crowd and the bench and my

teammates on the bases seem on top of me, right behind me, and, at the same time, far away. In #15, when the Blue Witch finally figured out how to beat the Hollow, she said, *We'll use his own power against him.* I see Sanderson's panel in my mind now, her determined never-give-up expression.

I climb into the box again, holding my hand up to request time. Deep breaths. The Blue Witch is right. Yumido's throwing so hard, all I have to do is make contact. He's generating all the power. I just need to turn it around on him.

I wish Nate were here, but he's not. The Mira Giants are losing 4–2, and this might be our last good chance to push some runs across. No one's coming to save me. I'm on my own.

Maybe. Or maybe my friends are right behind me on the bench, in the stands sketching heroic versions of me. Maybe all I have to do is be who they already believe I am.

Yumido gets into the stretch. I crouch. He checks the runners. I adjust my grip on the bat. He starts his windup. I screw my back foot into the dirt.

He rears back and pitches. A fastball, tailing outside. I step toward it and swing.

Contact.

I can't see the ball at first. I know I popped it up somewhere. My eyes search the sky until they find it. It's high in the air, deep to the opposite field.

Really deep.

The Brooksburgh right fielder is retreating, his throwing hand extended back, searching for the fence. He raises his glove to his head, shielding the sun. At the last moment, he leaps, reaching out. I'm halfway to first. I should be running harder, but I can only hold my breath and wait.

I expect to see him come away from the fence with his victorious glove in the air, but he doesn't. Instead he leans over the top of it, staring at the ball rolling through the open grass beyond it, toward the parking lot. He turns and smacks his frustrated mitt against his thigh.

A home run. I just hit a home run.

And now we're winning—actually winning—5–4.

Sally leaps up and down as he rounds the bases in front of me. I start to run, hitting first base, pumping my fist, hopping up and down. And I don't stop running as fast as I can, either, not until I cross home plate.

We still have to hold Brooksburgh scoreless for one more inning. The first two outs come quick, but the third Tiger hitter sends Jake's first two offerings deep into the stands. Either could've been a homer.

Clearly rattled, Jake takes a moment to compose himself on the grass. He returns to the rubber, staring in at Kurt's signs. He starts his windup and takes a long stride forward, looking for all the world like he's trying to give this next fastball everything he's got. But instead one of those forbidden, looping curveballs leaves his fingers. It's headed straight for the hitter's head. He locks up, like a statue. Then Jake's pitch drops straight down into the bucket of the strike zone.

Kurt doesn't move his glove. Someone's pressed stop on the world. Only the ump can hit play again. He does, yelling, "Strike three!" and we all race in to smother Jake in a huge pileup on the pitching mound.

- 43 -

On Friday, when he showed us #16, Sanderson had seemed so lost, scared even. He's completely different Monday. He even starts to joke around a little. When Courtney, Ollie, and I take a break to eat some sandwiches in the front room, we come back to discover he's sketched out a quick page with the three of us in it. We all have baseball gloves on, and so do the Hollow and the Captain. The five of us are playing catch, and the Hollow in particular looks completely ridiculous wearing a Mira Giants cap twisted off to one side.

"You're wasting time!" Courtney scolds him, but she's laughing while she does it.

"What? You don't think this fits the story?" Sanderson asks.

"Only because the Hollow's so *not* a baseball player," I say, chuckling. "Hockey, maybe. Football, definitely."

"Okay, okay," Sanderson says, pushing the page away and bringing back a piece of blank paper.

"Focus!" Ollie orders. For a second his voice is deeper. For a second he sounds like Nate.

"Yes, sir," Sanderson says, saluting him as if he heard the change, too.

Maybe we're helping Sanderson. Maybe he's helping us. Maybe they're the same exact thing.

Tuesday, Dad picks us up at the end of another long day. I catch him chatting again with the Art Coop crowd. Even oil painter and Rolling Stones fan Joyce has joined in this time. He hands over some plans to the group. The girl with the once-pink-then-green-now-blue hair jumps up and down with excitement. We feel the questionable porch shake all the way on the other side. When Dad turns to face us, he notices us waiting near the steps and separates from the crowd.

"All set?" Dad asks us in a nothing-to-see-here tone.

I just nod, and we climb into the car. Everyone's as tired as I am. There's hardly a word exchanged all the way back to Mira, but I'm thinking about the amount of time Dad must be spending working for the Art Coop crew. After dropping off Courtney, then Ollie, we turn into our driveway, and I'm about to finally work up the courage to ask him what's going on. But then I notice Kurt and Jake sitting on their bikes across the street.

I twist in my seat as Dad pulls into the garage. My friends don't take their eyes off the Volvo. Something's up.

Dad checks his side mirror. Kurt and Jake have straddle-walked their bikes to the end of our driveway. "I think your friends were waiting for you," he says.

I open the door and hurry toward them. I see different emotions in their expressions: worried annoyance in Kurt's, pained dejection in Jake's. Our pitcher's arm looks weird, like it's barely attached to his shoulder.

"Where do you go during the day?" Kurt asks when I get there. He's rubbing his hands together, no doubt after another plop of sanitizer. But they're moving extra fast, like he's nervous.

We're supposed to keep our project with Sanderson quiet. "Nowhere. What's going on with you guys?"

Kurt rolls his eyes but seems to have bigger concerns than my secrets. He gestures in Jake's direction. "We got a huge problem."

I study our pitcher. "What's wrong?"

Jake tries to bend his elbow and winces. "I think it was that last curveball. Something popped."

"Did you tell your parents?"

Jake shakes his head.

"Who'd you tell?"

Jake glances at Kurt.

"I think it's his UCL," Kurt offers.

"The only person you told was Kurt," I say, and Jake shifts uncomfortably. I look toward Kurt. "I don't know what UCL means, man."

"Your ulnar collateral ligament," Kurt says. He runs a finger along the outside of his elbow. "It's right here. I googled it. It's one of the most common pitching injuries."

"So you're a doctor now?"

Kurt shrugs.

"Jake, you need to go to a doctor."

"But if I can't play, we'll have to forfeit. We don't have enough players." Jake glances at the darkening sky. "Man, I should've listened to Coach."

"You gotta find out what's wrong," I say. "Tell your parents. Go to the doctor. Once we know for sure, we'll figure something out."

Jake nods. "Yeah, okay." He jabs Kurt's shoulder with his good hand. "Told you Dan would say that."

I watch them pedal away, Jake unable to bring his right arm up to help him steer. I'm thinking that before, they would've gone to Nate—same thing I would've done. I'm thinking about something else, too—I actually have no idea what we're going to do. Except maybe forfeit.

• • •

The next day, the smooth, effortless strokes of Sanderson's pencil bring Captain Nexus to life once again. Sanderson lifts his hand up so we can see his latest drawing clearly. "How's that one?" he asks.

"It's great," I say.

"Yeah," Ollie agrees, pointing to a spot on the page. "Especially in through here."

But Courtney frowns. "I don't know. Don't you think . . ." She sighs.

"What do you see?" Sanderson asks her. "Tell me."

"I'm just not sure that's what the Captain would do, now that it's on the page."

"Well, he can't do it over," Ollie protests.

"Yeah," I agree. "That's a whole page. We gotta get this done by the end of the week, for the fans."

"No," Sanderson says, tapping his pencil on his chin as he thinks. "Maybe Courtney here is right. If something in your story's wrong, you have to fix it. We owe it to ourselves and our readers to get everything right."

Ollie shifts, still full of doubt. Sanderson spins his stool toward him. "Listen, you can't be afraid of new things. If you live right, you'll be doing new things your entire life. And you remember what we said about starting over, don't you?"

"Sometimes you have to," Ollie, Courtney, and I say

together in a chorus. It's not the first time Sanderson's thrown away some work he wasn't happy with. We've been hearing his mantra about starting over all week.

But this time I really listen to him. Suddenly I know what to do about Jake. Suddenly I know how the Giants can survive the last game of our season without having to forfeit.

- 44 -

There's traffic coming back from Brooksburgh that evening. By the time I get to practice, the rest of the Giants are shuffling out to the parking lot, heads down, texting their parents. Coach is alone at the bench, packing up equipment.

"What's the deal?" I ask Kurt.

"It's a strained UCL," he says, pointing at Jake's arm, in a sling now. "At least it's not torn. But he can't throw. We have to forfeit. No sense practicing."

I step in front of him and he's forced to stop walking. "We're not forfeiting."

Kurt makes a face like he's just swallowed a bit of anchovy and pineapple. "How do you figure?"

I call out to the rest of the team. "Hey!" One by one, the Giants stop their slow progress away from the field and turn. I shake my head. "We're not forfeiting."

"You can't bend reality, Summers," Sally shouts back, followed by a mutter under his breath. "Too many comics . . ."

I turn to our pitcher. "Jake! You want to play, don't you?"

He sends me a *duh* look of exasperation. "Of course I do. But the doctor says no throwing. I can't pitch."

"You won't have to." I turn and start marching toward Coach at the bench. Halfway through the outfield, I check to make sure my team is following me. Most of them, still staring at me with slack-jawed expressions, haven't moved. "Guys, I can't do this by myself."

For a second my voice is deeper. For a second I sound like Nate.

They glance at each other, shrugging, then start to follow. We reach Coach Wiggins together. "Coach, we can't forfeit."

"I won't send an injured player out to the field, Dan. We're out of bodies."

I turn to Jake. "You can still catch, can't you?"

"Sure, but—"

"Nothing wrong with his left hand, Coach. He can play first."

"Dan," Coach says, his voice stern. "You know first base still has to throw some. And he'll need to hit."

"So we help him. He can glove-toss the ball to someone else. They can make the throw for him." I look Jake up and down. "And he can bunt. Or pretend like he might swing, even if he won't. Maybe he'll work a walk or two."

"But I play first," Sally says. "It's the only position I know."

"You move to third."

Mark, who's been playing third since Jake became pitcher, backs up a step. His mouth drops open. "I'm at third."

"You move to short."

"That's your spot."

"Not anymore." I look up at Coach. "I'm pitching."

His eyes widen but he doesn't say anything.

"You?" Sally cries. "I've seen better arms on a . . . on a . . ."

"I can't believe it. You actually stumped him." Jake lifts his slinged arm to mock Sally but stops, grimacing.

"For good, I hope," Kurt adds.

"Shut up, both of ya," Sally says. He turns to Coach. "I've never played third."

"And I can't play short," Mark agrees. "I'm barely getting used to third."

"That's four players out of position," Kurt warns. "In a championship game."

"Guys," I say, spreading my hands out like my next words are the most obvious in the universe. "If you live right, you'll be trying new things your entire life."

The bench is quiet, cars racing past the park the only sounds in the early evening air. I wait, gritting my teeth and tapping a foot. Somehow I know that for this to work, someone else has to say it. Come on, come on . . .

It's Jake. He turns his face up suddenly, like he's just gotten a great idea. "Dan's right. It might actually work." He sinks his head down and slips out of his sling. "It'll be a secret, but the good kind. Brooksburgh will never know. I can fake a lot. Mom thinks I'm singing in church, but I really just move my lips."

Coach Wiggins frowns. "I've asked you boys not to tell me things like that." He sighs. His gaze passes over the team.

"We have nothing to lose, Coach," Craig says.

Coach glances back at Jake. "I can only let you do this if I hear from your parents that it's okay."

Jake nods. "They'll say yes. This is for Nate. They've known him since he was a shrimp."

Coach starts to smile. "Well then, I guess we better use the practice time after all. Jake, you watch for now."

The Giants hoot. We high-five. My teammates race out

to their new spots. I turn to join them but Coach stops me. "Hey, Dan. Hold up a second."

He opens his mouth to say something, but nothing comes out. He twists his head from one side to the other, like he's surprised and happy and maybe a little bit impressed all at the same time. He reaches out and tugs the brim of my cap down, pulling it so low it covers my eyes.

"Nate would be proud, kiddo," Coach tells me.

I run out to the pitching mound, climb onto it. I thought I'd feel small up here, but actually, it seems like I'm bigger than I've ever been.

- 45 -

At the practice field Jake said, *It'll be a secret, but the good kind.*

I keep thinking about that. It's the reason I end up in Dad's office the next morning. It's on our first floor, near the front of the house, right off the foyer. He used to use it a lot, but lately he's always downtown, so it's mostly just a dumping ground for papers. I'm supposed to stay out, and I usually do, but I have questions I haven't been able to ask. I still can't understand what's made Dad so suddenly available.

It feels like a big secret. I need to know if it's the good kind or not.

Sure enough, a copy of the plans he drew up for the Art

Coop project are right on top of the loose stack on his desk. I sift through them, not really understanding what I'm looking at. Seems to be mostly guidelines for new buildings, but also some suggestions for shoring up the existing ones before they fall apart completely.

There's a plain file folder at the bottom of the pile. I slide it out and open it.

The first page is a printout of an email Dad wrote to his boss. He's begging for time to conduct some pro bono—pretty sure that means free—work for the Brooksburgh Art Coop. He explains he never expected that accepting the downtown restoration would steal so much of his family time away, that the company owes him a little of it back. He mentions me, how much I love comics and *Captain Nexus*, that I recently found a way to meet the creator of my favorite comic, how Sanderson's studio is housed in the Art Coop.

I know it would mean so much to Dan if we were able to add studio space to the Art Coop so that other young artists with potential, maybe even his good friend Ollie one day, when he's older, could work in the same vicinity as the great George Sanderson.

My heart skips. We were supposed to be keeping that part quiet. But then Dad goes on to tell his boss how

Sanderson knows all about what he's working on, his proposed improvements to the Art Coop studios, that the old man has even agreed to mentor a few young artists once the new space is ready. Dad's company will help select the participants and get some free publicity for donating time and energy to the shared studios.

Dad closes his argument by describing, of all things, my bike trail, telling his boss that he'd started working with me on it last year but had to stop.

> **If you take a look at the attached plans, I think you'll understand why the opportunity to help Mr. Sanderson teach the next generation of art students is so important to me. And to my son.**

I flip the page. I have to turn it sideways to recognize Dad's original design for the bike trail. There's another sheet paper-clipped to it, a photocopy of Sanderson's earliest drawing of the Nexus Zone, from issue two, with red circles over the awesome comic-book images of Lake Carol, the Nexus Mountains, and the rest of the key landmarks.

I go between the first page, his bike trail design, and the comic image again and again. There are new marks on Dad's design. They weren't there before, but I can't miss them now.

Underneath *Pond* there's smaller writing, surrounded by

parentheses: *(Lake Carol).*

Where the hills are, including the biggest one, our starting ramp, there's another handwritten comment, again in parentheses: *(Nexus Mountains).*

The series of smaller hills I had to finish on my own: *(Nexus Range).*

The river, winding from mountains to pond: *(Scott River).*

All this time I'd thought it'd been coincidence that our trail looked just like the Nexus Zone. Noticing it had kept me going these past few weeks, thinking that Nate might come back there, filling my time working on ways to turn it even more into a place he'd recognize.

But it wasn't lucky chance. It wasn't coincidence at all.

The unseen force guiding Nate and me to make the trail look like the Nexus Zone wasn't really unseen at all. It was Dad.

He'd *planned* the trail out based on the Zone from the very beginning. He must've pored over every little detail in Sanderson's work. How long had it taken him? No wonder he remembered Lake Carol.

For a second the image of Dad photocopying one of my issues of *Captain Nexus* distracts me, but maybe it's okay to flatten out a comic and press a heavy lid down on it, if it's for the good kind of secret.

I thought he didn't care anymore. Sometimes I wondered

if he ever cared. But he definitely had, enough to line up all those little details, to learn about the thing I loved. And now he's trying to show, by helping the Art Coop, by helping my hero, that he still cares, that he never stopped. Why didn't he just tell me?

My hands are shaking as I reassemble the folder and the pile, trying to put them back in the exact spots they'd been in. When I finish, I drop back into Dad's office chair and stare at his desk, all those pages of hard work. I've sat here before, but the leather seat never felt so big. My feet dangle off the end. I'm super tiny, like Ant-Man.

Or maybe I'm the same size, and Dad's the one who's gotten bigger.

Way bigger. Hulk-sized.

A lot of baseball fields in small towns only have porta-potties, but Brooksburgh Park has bathrooms that actually look pretty clean—a brand-new cinder-block building right behind the concession stand. I hustle there, nearly slipping when my cleats leave the grass for the pavement.

I've been nervous tons of times before games, but tonight is the worst yet. Maybe because it's the championship. Maybe because I'm just now realizing what I agreed to—standing on the mound and trying to pitch, something I've never done in a real game before. Maybe because after volunteering to pitch in practice Wednesday I could hardly throw a strike, and when I finally did, I had to slow my pitches way down to control them enough. They were coming in so fat it would be like batting practice for Brooksburgh. And now it's Friday, the big game is here, and there is no magic learn-to-pitch-in-two-days pill. At least Google knew nothing about it.

Whatever the reason, I sort of feel like I have to puke. I rush to the bathroom, hoping I make it in time.

A big line of people waits at the concession stand, buying popcorn and peanuts and Popsicles, but when I round the far end of it, I sigh with relief because the bathrooms seem empty. I make horrible noises when I puke—Mom, who grew up on a farm, says it sounds like a cow giving birth.

I don't puke, though, I just spend some time alone in front of the mirror, taking deep breaths and inspecting my face, gray with worry. Wondering what the heck I was thinking volunteering to pitch in the biggest game the Giants have ever played.

Eventually I hear cleats clacking onto the pavement and rounding the concession stand. They echo into the entrance of the bathroom. I know it must be one of the Giants trying to find me, so I scramble into one of the stalls and lock myself in.

"Dan, I can see your feet." It's Craig's voice.

I unlatch the lock and let the door swing open. Craig's out of breath; he must've ran all the way here from the field. His glove dangles from his hand. "What are you doing?" he asks me.

I take in my silver-walled surroundings. "Stalling?"

"Very funny. Coach says you gotta get back. Now."

"Give me one second," I say.

"For what? The game's gonna start."

He's right, and so is Coach. I can't hide in here, hoping for escape. I have a responsibility to play, to be in my spot no matter what might happen. We take off together, heading for the field. Heading for the championship game.

Coach spreads his hands out but looks more relieved than angry when he catches sight of me jogging back to our dugout. He follows me along the bench, clapping several times right behind my ear. "Come on, come on, come on," he says. "What happened? You fall in?"

"Sorry."

"Championship game, Dan," Coach Wiggins reminds me. "Championship game." I guess it's a night for firsts, because I've never heard him sounding nervous like that before. It actually makes me feel a little better about trying to hide.

We're up first. As I get ready to hit, a shadow as giant as the Hollow's falls over me. I spin around and almost yell out, but it's only Sanderson.

"Where'd you come from?" I ask a little too loudly.

Some of the Giants look our way, but Coach is too busy at the far end of the bench giving Kurt tips on keeping his swing level to hear me.

"I may be an old man, but I still have some sneaky skills," he whispers. "How are you feeling?"

"Nervous," I admit.

"Listen, remember something for me?" I stare at him. "Something I'm remembering for myself, lately, too."

"Okay."

"Just this. The people closest to us never leave us. Not really, and not all the way. Got it?"

I nod. I remember what I found out about Dad. He came home from work so late and left so early I haven't even seen him since I snuck into his office. I kind of want to ask Sanderson what he knows about the construction going on at the Art Coop, but it isn't the right time. The most important game of my life is about to start; questions for Dad will have to wait until the next time I see him, whenever that might be.

"Close your eyes and listen," Sanderson adds. He reaches out and puts his whole palm on top of my hat, squeezing my head with surprisingly strong fingers. "You'll know when. Now go get 'em." He turns and limps toward the stands, climbing up into the front row. Courtney and her dad are here, too, at the top of the bleachers. And Ollie and both his parents. Everyone.

I check for Mom. I know she's here, she drove me, but I can't find her at first. Usually she sits alone in front, concentrating on the game. Finally I see her in the middle of the crowded stands. Her head was turned in an excited conversation with Jake's parents. She twists around now, facing forward, which is how I notice her. The guy next to her was wrapped up in the same discussion, and when he turns to look at the field at the same time as Mom, of course I recognize him, too.

Because it's Dad.

- 46 -

Brooksburgh's as backed into a corner as we are in this second game of the championship, so their coach wastes no time, sending Ray Yumido out to the mound from the start.

With Jake injured, Coach shuffles the lineup for the first time in weeks. In the first inning, I dribble a meek grounder toward third and sprint down the line with everything I have, expecting to see the Tigers' first baseman reach out for the ball before I even get close. Instead I hear a quick shout of "Safe!" as my foot thumps across the bag.

"Way to run it out," Jake, who's standing in the first-base coach's box, whispers. We fist-bump.

"What happened?" I glance at third.

"He flubbed it."

One out and Kurt steps up to the plate. I walk into a modest lead, check the stands. Dad's leaning forward with both hands on his knees, smiling. He can't wait to see what happens next.

As soon as Yumido moves toward home, I steal second. I don't even think about it. It's not like Coach gave me the sign, but man, I got such a great jump.

The next pitch gets away from their catcher. When he chases it to the backstop, I take third. That's two errors already. Almost seems like the Tigers are the nervous ones.

Kurt sends the next pitch deep to left. "Tag up," Coach says in my ear.

I retreat to third and get into position, one foot on the bag and the other forward, like I'm in the starting blocks on a track. I wait, watching over my shoulder as the ball spins toward their left fielder's glove.

It lands in the pocket with a loud smack.

"Go!"

I take off. Head down, I don't look back. In what seems like only a moment later, I'm sliding into the plate safely.

And the Giants are ahead 1–0.

I take the mound for the first time ever in a real game, stepping up on the hill I always thought of as Nate's place. My warm-up pitches are all over the place. The Brooksburgh leadoff batter grins hungrily as he watches me struggling to locate. He whispers something to the next two hitters. They all laugh together.

My infield's watching me closely, too. They're not warming up because Jake can't send grounders their way with his injured arm. I try not to meet their eyes. All these low pitches, bouncing before they even reach the plate, are bad enough without having to see how worried and nervous my teammates must be.

I uncork another worm burner toward Kurt, then signal I'm ready (I'm actually far from ready, but I might as well get this over with). I send him one more fastball. He has to reach across his body for it. He stands and fires a throw off to Mark at second. The infield goes around the horn with the ball, ending at first. Jake walks it to me. I take it out of his glove so he doesn't have to lift his useless arm.

"Nice and easy," he tells me. "Trust your fielders." Sometimes the advice you give comes right back to you, like Captain Boomerang's um . . . well, his boomerang. Duh.

Jake trots back to first. I inhale.

This is gonna be bad.

The first Brooksburgh hitter steps into the box. I continue throwing ball after ball, walking both him and the second batter, too. Kurt trots out to talk. "You need to find the strike zone."

"Helpful." I toe the rubber and tuck the ball behind my

back. Ray Yumido comes up next. He looks ten feet tall. I check the runners, let loose another fastball. He has to duck out of the way.

Kurt lobs the ball back. I pace away from the mound. Third hitter and I haven't thrown a strike yet. I need help, big-time. "Close your eyes and listen," Sanderson told me.

I'd try anything right about now. I squeeze my eyes shut and wait.

Nothing.

Sighing, I open them again. Another one of Sanderson's stories. He's full of them. I get back on the rubber and set up in the stretch again, thinking about what I'm doing wrong. Maybe if I come over the top more—

"No, not like that." Nate's voice speaks to me like he's right behind me. I close my eyes again, and I'm not on the mound anymore. I'm at the pond, the bike trail.

I listen.

"Sidearm," he says. "Like this." He sends a flat stone skipping fast, a half-dozen times along the surface of the water before it lands on the opposite shore.

Sidearm.

How many stones have I slung sidearm across the pond in the past few weeks? Dozens. A hundred, maybe.

Always thinking Nate wasn't there to see I'd finally learned to do it. Maybe I was wrong. Maybe he was watching me the whole time.

I breathe in. Open my eyes.

Standing straight, I start my motion. Arm dropping low, I sidearm a pitch toward home. It loops up, then falls off the table at just the right moment, almost like a curve, straight through the strike zone.

Yumido freezes, doesn't swing. The ball lands in Kurt's glove and he keeps it fixed in place. The ump shifts but doesn't say anything. The stands are silent.

It's like the whole field's in shock. The ump rises from his bent stance, peering over Kurt's shoulder. He rips his mask off. The words seem stuck in his throat, but finally he calls the pitch, softly. "Strike one."

The crowd cheers. Kurt stands up out of his crouch and steps to one side to fire the ball back to me. He points at me with his mitt. "That's the way, Dan! More like that one!"

I exhale. Okay. More like that one.

- 47 -

Sidearm slurve. Brooksburgh grounder. Slurve again, grounder again. I escape that first inning without allowing a run, then keep slinging pitches at the Tigers, each time imagining stones skipping clear across the pond.

Inning by inning the Giants cling to our one-run lead over the biggest, baddest team in all of Western New York—until it almost seems like we'll actually win.

Every once in a while I hear, "That's it, more like that one." The words come from different voices. Kurt, behind the plate. Coach, in the dugout. Mom, Dad, and Sanderson, all from the stands.

Nate, in my head.

Slurve after slurve. Out after out. I watch my team back

me up with everything they have. Jake, running around with that useless, flapping arm, tricking Brooksburgh into thinking he'll throw them out anyway. Diving stops from Sally, Mark, the whole infield. Incredible coverage of the outfield by Craig and the other outfielders, like there's ten of them back there instead of just three.

Even though I'm the one pitching, it's almost like I'm watching them all from somewhere else. The Nexus Zone, maybe, peering through an open portal at them like we're not in the same dimension, let alone the same field in the far corner of Brooksburgh Park. Watching my team fight for their tournament lives.

Maybe I am on the other side of the Zone. Maybe that's why I can hear Nate so clearly.

Maybe it's why time passes the way it does, too. Because before I know it, we're in the last inning. It's 1–0 still, and all we need is one more out.

"One more!" Shouts echo across the field, and I can't even tell who's yelling. Everyone, I guess.

Brooksburgh sends up a pinch hitter. The infield plays back. I wind up and sidearm another pitch toward home plate.

The ball loops up, then drops. The Brooksburgh kid stays back, waiting for it. He connects but gets under it, popping it straight up. I point for Kurt, showing him it's above and behind him.

He'll have to get it, because I can't move. I can only stare from my side of the portal.

Our catcher tears off his mask, casting it to one side. He finds the ball in the sky. It looks like it's going to stay in play. The ump shuffles out of the way.

The ball's super high. Kurt calls for it, then camps under it, taking a step forward, then back, as he tries to stay on it. I hop up once on the mound. This is it. It's really it.

From the corner of my eye, I catch movement down the third base line. It's Sally, lumbering toward home. Another figure flashes, this time to my left. Jake, racing in from first. I stare at them a moment before it clicks.

I'm the pitcher now. And that means I'm not supposed to be staring at this foul pop like an idiot, because they might need me. I'm the backup, and I should get to my spot before it's too late.

I start in toward the plate.

Jake gets there first, just as the ball descends toward Kurt's glove. The wind blows or the ball spins, something, because our catcher needs to take a surprised step back to reach it. It's too far, though. Stretching, he gets his mitt on the dropping foul but can't squeeze it. He stumbles as the ball pops back into the air. Jake dives headfirst for it, tipping it with the end of his glove. It pushes toward third, straight for Sally, arriving late, sliding in on his knees. The awkward ball hits him in the center of the chest, and he flips up his hands to try to grab it, but he was coming in too fast. It floats up and away from him, from all of us, toward the backstop.

My three friends roll on their backs and stomachs, helpless, watching the last out spin away and start to drop toward empty dirt again. None of them will be able to get up in time.

I rush past the plate, hop over Kurt's legs, and slide, turning my glove backhanded. My cleats run into the links of the backstop and get hung up, but I don't lose my concentration. I keep my eyes on the white cowhide, the red stitches, my glove turned over, until . . . *POP!* The foul that Kurt tipped to Jake, who saved it for Sally, who popped it up just enough for me, drops into the pocket of my glove for the last out of the game, the tournament, the season.

I don't move. Everything seems still and quiet. Frozen. There's only me and the ball I just caught, with my feet hooked into the fence. The ball I only reached because my team, my friends, kept it alive for me.

I breathe in. There's the smell of grass and leather and my own sweat.

There's the sun overhead, hanging on to the last few minutes of today's light.

There's shouting and screaming and cheering, but it seems a long way off.

One by one, a jumble of images flash into my head.

Nate. My teammates. Mom and Dad. Courtney, Ollie, George Sanderson, Dr. Tori.

Captain Nexus and the Blue Witch and the Red Flame. Spark. Nexus Boy.

The photograph on Sanderson's bookshelf. That first time in his studio, all those half-finished pages, like an incomplete life.

The bike trail, my makeshift Nexus Zone, Sanderson breaking through the brush into the clearing with his cane.

The tournament, how badly we—I—wanted to win it. For Nate. For us. Our comic, all those afternoons in Courtney's office, the last few days in Sanderson's studio.

All the stories we made. All the stories we saved.

Tying my shoes next to Nate in the locker room. His voice on the mound.

For a moment, I panic that the ball isn't really in my glove, that instead it rolled away, and I'll have to go through all that stuff all over again. I don't know if I can. But then I squeeze my hand, and I feel the ball there, right down to its frayed red stitches.

YES.

- 48 -

After the game we hit DiNunzio's, of course. By the time we get back to Mira, the restaurant's about to close, but Coach's buddy keeps it open just for the champs. He lets his staff go home but stays to takes our orders and make our pizzas himself. Our parents are starving, too, so most of them come along. Mom and Dad sit with the rest of the adults at tables on the other side of the restaurant, leaving the Giants alone to enjoy our win together.

The celebration is awesome, but I keep peeking over at Dad. I still really want to ask him about the Art Coop, talk to him about the bike trail. I don't understand why he kept all that work and planning to himself. He should've told me about his Nexus design so that I would've known what the trail was supposed to look like from the very beginning. He should've explained why he was working at the Art Coop, instead of leaving me to guess. Did he think I wouldn't realize what a cool idea that was?

"Hey, Dan, show me the ball again," Kurt says.

I've been carrying it with me since the end of the game, tucked into my glove. I pull it out and turn it over in my hand, rubbing my thumb over a rough spot on one side.

Kurt's eyes flicker as he stares at it, like it's some kind of jewel we discovered by random chance. "There's something about it, right?"

It's just a ball. Same weight as any other baseball. Same number of stitches. Scuff marks all over the cowhide. But I lift it to my nose and sniff deep and he's right. I can *smell* the difference. This little baseball is like victory itself. Not the sort of "Ha-ha, we beat you" type of winning. More like the kind of winning you worked really hard for, pushed through and climbed over tons of obstacles to reach. No, we didn't discover it by random chance at all.

This baseball smells a lot more like something we earned.

"Yeah," I agree out loud. "Definitely something."

When the last slice is eaten and the bill paid, we pile into the minivan and head home. Mom keeps eyeing me over her shoulder the entire drive, like she can see the questions

I'm holding in written across my face.

"You okay?" she asks me.

How does she do that? I avert my eyes from her gaze. "I'm good."

"I thought you'd still be on cloud nine."

"I am! I just . . ."

Dad yawns. "He's tired. We all are. I'm hitting the pillow the moment we get home."

That night, I gaze out toward the bike trail through my back window. I can't actually see it, there are too many trees between it and our yard, but I imagine it lit up like a pro baseball field, giant floodlights shining down on the mound and bases and infield dirt. I dream of ghost players moving around the base paths, Kurt's never-ending game. I stare in that direction for a long time, trying to catch a bat slicing through the air, a pitch diving out of the strike zone, but there's nothing but dark trees, leaves swaying in the wind. Exhausted, I finally give up, climbing into bed and falling asleep almost right away.

Early the next morning, I come downstairs to find only Dad at the kitchen table, his usual coffee and toast in front of him. He's leaned back in his chair, staring into his iPad.

Scratching my hair, I head straight for the fridge and my orange juice. I'm about to ask where Mom is, but before I can, Dad starts humming. It takes me a minute to recognize the tune, but when I do, I hear the words that go with it in my head:

We are the champions . . . we are the champions . . .

And, as if to make sure I definitely got it, he finishes by raising his coffee in a toast to me and singing, out loud this time but softly, "My friend!"

I snort. "Thanks, Dad."

He goes back to his reading—emails, probably—and I pour my orange juice into a tall glass. I take it to the table and sit across from him. He doesn't look up.

Dad sips his coffee. I gulp down juice. All this time I'd been waiting for him to notice what I'd been doing to the bike trail, not realizing that I'd actually been executing his original plan all along. I'd been waiting for him to show up at my games, too, and now that he finally had, he was humming victory tunes in our kitchen.

It's been kind of confusing, I guess, trying to figure out if he wanted to know about the things I've been doing or not. I keep waiting, as if time will miraculously give me the answer. Ollie waited all that time, too. But maybe that's not how you get people to see you the way you want them to. Maybe Dad has been waiting for me as much as I've been waiting for him. Or . . . maybe he likes coming to things at the end. Like, the last game of the season, for example. And if I was finished with the bike trail, maybe it's time I showed that to him, too.

"Dad?"

He still doesn't look up. Another sip, another drag of his finger across his screen. "Uh-huh?"

"Can I show you what I've been doing out back? You know, at the bike trail?"

Right away I wince. I shouldn't have asked it. He's going to say no. If he had wanted to see it, he would've said something a long time ago. The day he brought Sanderson out there to talk to me. A million other times.

"Would you?"

I meet Dad's eyes and he's wearing a huge grin. I feel my mouth drop open. "Well . . . yeah, I—"

Dad glances toward the stairs. "Awesome. Let's do it now, before your Mom wakes up and tells us to put on better shoes." He stands and shuffles to the sliding glass door in his slippers.

I bolt up out of my chair, pull on my sneakers without stopping to untie them, and race to his side.

"Hold on, though," Dad says, putting a finger in the air like he just got a new idea. "Gotta get something." He heads to the front of the house and disappears into his office, emerging a second later with a rolled-up set of plans.

My excitement deflates again. He's already thinking about what he's going to work on after we head out there. I thought I finally had his attention, but he's still focused on architecture. "Okay," he says, breathing a little deeper from his rush to the office. "Let's go."

"We really don't have to—"

Dad's smile fades slightly. "What? Come on! Are we doing this or not?"

"Sure." Apparently I have at least five minutes of his attention. Maybe no more than that, but okay, I might as well use the little bit I can get.

We stomp through the backyard, Dad shaking his feet out now and again as the dew wets his slippers. We slip down the trail and pace through the brush to the clearing. The pond shimmers in the early-morning sunlight. More dew glistens off the blades of grass and weeds sprouting up around my version of the Nexus mountain range. A few steps into the clearing, Dad stops and puts his hands on his hips, surveying my version of the Nexus Zone. "I've been meaning to tell you, Dan. This is really great work."

So he's been out here? He knows?

"But we're going to need to widen the river. It isn't quite right. And I was talking to your friend George, and there are some cliffs in those mountains we should imitate, and—"

My head spins. He's been talking to Sanderson about the bike trail? He knows about the cliffs in the mountains? But out of everything, my brain focuses on one simple word that he's said multiple times now. *We.* "You mean, you'll work on this with me again?"

"Are you kidding? I can't wait."

"So why did you forget about it up until now?"

"Forget?" He turns to me, and I stare at him. "I never forget about anything you're doing, Dan. I'm always thinking about you."

"But you haven't worked on this with me in like a year."

He pauses. "Okay, that's fair." He scratches the back of his head. "Listen, Dan, when we won the project downtown, I got super busy. You know that. I dropped the ball on a lot of things. By the time I had even a small opening of time, you were working out here with Nate instead. You guys made it into something different than I'd planned. It would've been awfully selfish of me to interrupt you and ask you to continue building what we started."

He looks at me sadly. "I was happy to see you guys having so much fun with it. I could tell you definitely didn't need me."

Dad turns and inspects the trail again. "Then you guys abandoned it, and I figured you were just on to the next thing. Your mom and I can hardly keep up with the sports and the comics and the video games . . ." He inhales. "Then Nate had his accident, and you started coming out here again, and . . . it just seemed like you needed time for yourself." He meets my eyes again. "But listen! I was so happy to see you pick up our plan again. After I brought Mr. Sanderson out here to talk to you, I started sneaking out with a flashlight to follow along. But, you know . . . I didn't want to insert myself into the work unless you asked me."

"Our plan?!?" I kind of yell it at him, I can't help it. "I had no idea this was supposed to be the Nexus Zone until I saw it on your—" I stop, realizing I'm incriminating myself by confessing my snooping from the other day.

Dad laughs. "Hold up. You didn't know?"

I can't help but laugh with him, shaking my head. "No."

"No idea? And you saw about . . . ?"

"The Art Coop. Yeah. Why didn't you tell me about all that?"

"We wanted to surprise you. George and I. And those other kids were in on it, too. They're really talented. Have you seen their work?"

I shake my head.

"Next time we go, we'll check them out together. It's been kind of neat to be around all that art and enthusiasm again. Makes me feel like a kid myself, if you can believe that."

We both turn away from each other to study our version of the Nexus Zone side by side. A huge blue heron swoops over the clearing, weaving along on the currents of the wind until it lands on the far side of the pond. I stare at it, and it stares back at me, like the stupid bird is daring me to say what's on my mind, the stuff I would usually keep to myself. "Dad?"

"Yeah?"

"You shouldn't have done that." I feel him turn toward me again, but I don't dare look at him. Not until I finish saying this first. "I don't care what happens at work or whatever. You shouldn't disappear, okay? Helping me is never selfish."

"I'm so sorry, Dan," Dad says softly. "You're right."

I don't know why I'm suddenly whispering, but I am. "And . . . and I always need you."

I finally risk turning my face toward him, and he's wearing the biggest smile I think I've ever seen on my dad's face. "That's the best news I've heard all week."

"Why's that?"

Dad lifts the rolled-up plans and unfurls them onto the ground with a flick of his wrist. "Phase two." He starts talking a mile a minute, pointing out the changes on his drawing as he describes them. "Like I said, the river is too narrow, we'll put the cliffs here, and then I think we need to lift the height of that whole range . . . there isn't much time."

My eyes scan the plans. There are so many changes. "There's not?"

He turns sheepish, shrugging. "I *might've* promised George

that he could bring some photographers out here for a news article in a couple weeks." He raises both eyebrows at me. "What do you think? Can we get it done by then?"

I wanted to finish this place for Nate so bad. Maybe he won't ever see it completely done, but George Sanderson will. And reporters? And photographers? My stomach does a little nervous roll.

"Dan?" Dad says. He's waiting for my answer, but I can't talk. Every time I try, I get this choking feeling in my throat. Besides I don't really want to answer with words. I take two giant steps toward him and wrap my arms around his waist in such a huge hug he's actually forced back a step.

- 49 -

C*aptain Nexus and the Nexus Five* #16 ends up being exactly one week late. Part of me thinks Tall Ship did it on purpose, to increase the hype, because by the time the issue actually appears on shelves, everybody in Mira knows about the secret project three local kids were working on with the most famous comics creator in the world. The Wednesday night group read in the Templetons' basement is so crowded there's barely enough room for all the people.

After he sent our completed pages to the publisher, Sanderson started granting interviews. First to the *Buffalo News*, then the *New York Times*, then a dozen other newspapers and websites. He even agreed to talk to Geeker again.

George Sanderson didn't want to hide anymore. He revealed his true name, Carl Franklin, and though he wouldn't answer questions about the accident, lots of reporters and bloggers had uncovered it. The head mod over on Geeker put together a superlong post comparing the themes in *Captain Nexus* with the events in Nebraska. It had so many comments on it I stopped trying to keep up.

It isn't just the Giants—the entire team this time—who are packed into the basement. For the first time ever, we let a few adults in, too.

I invited Dr. Tori. She arrives in full-out *Captain Nexus* gear—T-shirt, sweatshirt, cap. It's a little bit corny, but that's okay. She's still supercool. Besides, I'm wearing a *Captain Nexus* button on my shirt, too. The one she gave me.

I'd asked if we could read in Nate's hospital room, but Mrs. Templeton felt that might be too many visitors. She promised I could see him afterward, and then made her own request. Nate's mom wanted to listen in on the basement read. So did Mr. Hoffman. Courtney's parents still seem headed for divorce, but she's been spending a lot more time with her dad since she started bringing him to Giants games.

My dad's here, too. Lately, he's been a step behind me everywhere I go. Like earlier today. There never seemed to be any question in his mind that he would be the one to take me to Jackson Comics and Games to buy the very last issue of the best comic ever. With a heavy heart, I pulled together my loose change and brought one copy up to the counter.

"You can't buy just *one*," Dad complained. He turned to Reggie, opening his wallet. "I'll take as many as you'll part with."

Mr. Templeton stayed upstairs, waiting for our final arrival. The entire basement's buzzing with activity, but when the doorbell rings, we quiet down. When a cane taps across the floor overhead, we exchange eager glances. When the basement door opens, and George Sanderson carefully steps down the steep stairs, we all hold our breath.

Being in the same room with *the* George Sanderson isn't that big a deal for three of us anymore, but it is for the rest of the Giants. They're still reeling over the news that we'd *met* the creator of *Captain Nexus*, never mind that we'd been *helping* him with the last issue of the comic.

It's Dr. Tori, though, who zips up to Sanderson so fast she nearly runs him over. She's talking a mile a minute. "Comics-like-these-saved-my-life. I-can't-tell-you-how-much-your-work—"

"I think maybe we should let Mr. Sanderson sit," Mr. Hoffman interrupts.

Dr. Tori nods. She takes a step back. Before Sanderson can move too far, though, she leaps into him and envelops him in a big hug.

The old man lets out a surprised exclamation. "Oh!" He pats her on the back. "Thank you, dear. You're more than welcome."

He limps past her, his eyes falling on Nate's recliner. "This seat taken?" he asks. Somehow, despite the crowd, my friend's chair remained empty.

Mrs. Templeton, on the floor between Ollie and Courtney, sits up on her knees. "I . . ." She can't finish.

I jump in to help. "No, you could definitely sit there."

The thing is . . . it's Nate's chair and it always will be, but it can't stay empty forever. You can't keep things the same, no matter how perfect they started out. No matter how many bags and boards you try to protect them with, you still gotta read your comics.

Everyone turns their attention to the cover of #16. The Captain and the Hollow, squaring off. A bold red banner obscures the title, like a rubber stamp: *FINAL ISSUE.* Another splash of text angles underneath the combatants' feet. *WINNER TAKES ALL!!*

"Okay," I say with a sigh, opening to page one.

"Everyone ready?" The room's so quiet, I can hear Courtney working her gum like she's right next to me.

No one told me I was supposed to lead the final read. It just seems like the right thing to do, even though it's way harder than any of those pitches I threw in the championship. For a minute I almost think I won't be able to do it, that the words will remain stuck in my throat forever, that the whole room will just sit here staring at unopened comics, but then I remember I'm not really breaking *Rule One: No one reads before anyone else* at all. We're not about to read the last issue of *Captain Nexus* without Nate.

Because the people closest to us never really leave.

Not all the way.

- 50 -

The first full page shows a battle-ready Captain Nexus across from the menacing, hunched form of the Hollow. They're in a Nexus Zone clearing filled with purple and orange scrub brush and surrounded by lime-hued boulders. In one corner, the page features something else, too: a simple, single line of credits.

TEAM: George Sanderson, Courtney Hoffman, Daniel Summers, Oliver Templeton

There's movement and murmuring around the room. "Holy . . . ," Kurt mutters. He's so distracted and amazed that instead of rubbing his hands together, he smacks the

Purell in his palms onto his cheeks like aftershave.

Pages flipping. It's Dad, peeking ahead.

"Dad!" I point at our poster, still propped up in the corner.

Rule three: We flip the pages together.

"Okay, okay," he says, putting his hands up in surrender. He goes back to the first page.

Courtney and I glance at each other, exchanging grins. Maybe this thing, this talking without talking, maybe it's not telepathy at all. Maybe it's just friendship.

Captain Nexus's thoughts come in square gray captions, way classier than floating cloud bubbles. He considers reasoning with the Hollow. It's the first time, after all, they've faced each other like this, one on one. In all the other issues, the Nexus Five battled their enemy together.

The Captain wonders if he's strong enough to confront the creature alone. Perhaps, this one time, he can convince the villain to remain here in the Nexus Zone, where it belongs, so that our hero can find his way home in peace.

"Wait—" Captain Nexus starts, lifting one cautious hand, but the Hollow sends a thick black energy beam straight into the Captain's midsection. The impact cracks open the silence with a *Zap!* and the blast lifts our hero off his feet, slamming him into a boulder with so much force the yellowish-green rock splits.

Captain Nexus shrugs rocky debris away. He struggles to his feet. Another blast follows, and he ducks just in time. The violent energy flows over his head, taking out the stand of trees behind him with the force of a hurricane.

The Hollow's never been this powerful before. The creature shrieks with disappointment at its near miss, and the Captain seizes the opportunity to cast his own beam forward, sending the Hollow careening back into more rocks. The dark energy creature melts through the first boulder. Others crash and crumble, burying it under what must be a ton of rubble. Sanderson's art brings the battle to life, superimposing panels atop each other, with a single underlying image showing the culmination of the action.

The pile of rubble burying the Hollow stirs. The earth rumbles, trees shake, boulders that should be too heavy to move vibrate. A blast explodes upward and the Hollow emerges, levitating into the air, a twisted grin etched onto its face.

The creature raises both hands and beams more dark energy at Captain Nexus. This time our hero is hit with such force he's sent flying miles away, carving a deep trench into the Nexus Zone landscape where he meets the ground again. He skids through several panels to a dusty halt in the lower corner of the page.

• • •

In the basement, somebody gasps. I think it's actually one of the parents.

Captain Nexus crawls out of the trench. The Hollow flies toward him. The Captain closes his eyes, concentrates. He's only flown a few times before, whenever he's felt an odd surge of power rising in his very core, always in the middle of a battle with this nightmarish creature.

He feels that strength again now. He floats up, then aims another beam, forcing the Hollow to stop in midair and shield itself. The Captain's effort is deflected downward, incinerating dirt and rock and trees, creating a deep, quarry-like pit.

Large drawings of the characters float at the top of one page, their feet intruding on another panel at the bottom.

The Hollow streams forward again.

The Captain tries to create another blast, but he can't. He braces himself. The Hollow slams into him, driving him back and down to the ground. It begins to hammer away at our hero, pummeling him with energy-driven punch after punch.

Captain Nexus is momentarily defenseless. He can do nothing to resist the beating he's taking. His face bruises and swells. He tries to raise both hands up in front of him, but the Hollow is relentless. Dropping its knees onto the Captain's arms, it pins them straight out before continuing to batter him again and again, until our hero falters at the edge of consciousness.

The Hollow rears back for a final, fatal blow. Captain Nexus conjures just enough strength to free a hand. He expends his remaining power to deflect the attack. The Hollow's full strength shifts away, exploding into the Captain's other hand.

Jagged edges and a red background show us the Captain's searing pain. He rolls his head to one side. His eyes widen in shock.

Two of his fingers have been severed clean off his left hand. Red blood streams out onto the yellowing dirt, tinting it orange.

Captain Nexus screams.

- 51 -

The pain in the Captain's expression melts into rage. The Hollow attempts another killing blow, but Captain Nexus converts his fury and pain into raw power. He blasts the creature upward with a beam from his good hand and, cradling his injured limb against his body, pushes to his feet.

The Captain pursues his enemy into the atmosphere again, one-handed, in agony. Still, he doesn't let up on the Hollow, blasting the creature backward and upward with a continuous barrage. He flies high, outflanking the monstrous villain, aiming down now with every bit of power he can muster. The Nexus energy comes not just from his hand this time, but his whole body.

The Hollow can't withstand the sheer intensity of the attack. The creature is cast downward into the center of Lake Carol, which boils and bursts where it splashes in, launching a flood of cresting waves toward the shore. The water crashes out of the edges of the panels, spilling into the gutters of the page. That one was Ollie's idea.

Captain Nexus freezes in the sky, gasping for air, as if he's the one underwater, not his enemy. Exhausted by his injury, by this battle he's been waging for only minutes but feels as though it's gone on for weeks. He falters, spying a craggy range of mountains peaking in the distance. The Nexus Mountains. He falls more than lands, rolling to a stop on a short plateau high up on the tallest peak. He takes a moment to survey the Zone.

It's a two-page spread. The Captain's dismayed expression shows in the lower corner, while the rest is taken up by the most detailed drawing of the Nexus Zone Sanderson's ever attempted.

The land's been ripped apart. Great craters and fissures split the surface. Whole forests are hewn low, valleys flooded. Smoke even rises in the distance, and the Captain struggles to recall if they somehow ignited a fire.

This strange, wondrous Zone had been such a beautiful place, and together he and the Hollow have ruined it, turning it into nothing more than a desolate wasteland. The Captain's shoulders slump; he nearly falls to his knees. He catches himself with his good hand on a boulder.

Turning away from the destruction, he staggers up a short path and rounds a corner, finding a shallow cavern. He ventures inside, sits, and examines his injured left hand. Two fingers are missing—his pinkie and ring finger—and as soon as he's no longer applying pressure to the area, the bleeding resumes.

Using his teeth, the Captain manages to tear away much of his sleeve. He binds his wound with the strips of fabric. He leans his back against the cave wall, hoping to catch his breath and recover some of his strength. The Hollow's still out there, he's sure of it. In fact, he begins to doubt if the creature can be defeated at all.

Maybe Captain Nexus can escape, just go home.

He attempts to open a portal back to New Mexico again but conjures barely a spark. After it fizzles out, however, crackling sounds of Nexus energy still echo through the cave. Coming not from within, but from outside.

The creature. It's here.

The Captain crawls to the cave's opening and risks a glance out. The Hollow stands on the same plateau the Captain landed on, also staggering, clearly weakened. As Captain Nexus had, the creature glances at the terrorized landscape of the Nexus Zone.

The Hollow hesitates, gazing out across the flooding and fires, the craters and pits. And, just as Captain Nexus did, it nearly falls to its knees. It reaches out with one hand to steady itself on the very same boulder, moving so similarly to the Captain's memory of himself, it's almost disturbing.

One hand. The creature used one hand—its right hand—to support itself. Captain Nexus glances at the creature's other hand, at the end of an arm that seems to dangle limply at its side. Energy fizzles from it, as if his enemy has sprung a leak in the precise spot where its pinkie and ring fingers would be.

The Captain glances at his own hand. Somehow, they have the same injury.

His eyes widen.

The way the Hollow moves, just like Captain Nexus. Their matching injuries. The identical despair over what their battle was doing to this beautiful place. How he gasped for air when it was the creature underwater, not him. The way, sometimes when the Hollow attacked, Captain Nexus felt stronger rather than weaker, as if the energy his enemy battered him with belonged to the Captain somehow. As if it was merely coming home.

The Nexus Five had always assumed the Hollow was an inhabitant of the Nexus Zone, that it had managed to hitch a ride to Earth when the team saved Bruce. But if the creature came from here, where were the rest of its kind? Where were all the other Hollows?

What if this dark monster wasn't from the Nexus Zone

at all? What if it hadn't even existed before Bruce's family rescued him? That feeling that Bruce had when he was pulled back to Earth—like he was being ripped apart . . . could he literally have been torn in two that day?

Maybe the Hollow's path of destruction across Earth hadn't been fueled by rage and evil. Maybe it had merely been confused and desperate, searching for the part of itself it had lost, hoping to be made whole again. Maybe that's how it had always been able to hunt down Captain Nexus and the Nexus Five so easily. They had the same energy signature. They had the same . . . everything.

Clenching his teeth, the Captain pushes to his feet and stumbles out of the cave, still cradling his injured hand to his chest. He straightens and bravely positions himself across from the Hollow. The creature whirls around. Battle ready. Jagged sneer.

Captain Nexus inhales. He understands what he has to do now.

- 52 -

"Wait," Jake says, bolting up off the couch. With his good arm, he brings his issue an inch from his face, like he can't believe the words he just read. "So Captain Nexus was fighting *himself* this whole time?"

"Quiet, son!" It's Dad. I turn to him, and he's leaning into his issue, chin in his hands, both elbows on the pool table, staring at the pages like they're a set of brand-new building plans.

"Yeah, rule two, man," Sally agrees, pulling Jake back down onto the couch. "No talking. Shut up and read."

I glance at Courtney and Ollie, then Sanderson. Everyone else in the room is shocked, their faces buried in their comics, but the four of us?

We're smiling.

The day we reached this page in Sanderson's studio, I reacted the same way as Jake. "I don't get it," I said. "No way. The Hollow and Captain Nexus? The same person? They can't be. They're complete opposites. Enemies."

Sanderson had been in the middle of drawing the Hollow. He didn't look up, stayed focused on his work, but he did answer me. He spoke quietly, like his response was the most normal thing in the world, as if he was simply describing the curve of a line to Ollie, or some snappy dialogue to Courtney.

But he wasn't talking to them.

"It doesn't seem possible, I know," Sanderson said, touching up a line. "But the truth is, sometimes we can be our own worst enemies. Especially when we blame ourselves for far too long."

And I could be wrong, but when he finished that particular rendition of the Hollow, it seemed like he wasn't quite as menacing as he'd always been before.

The Hollow looked weak, unsure.

It was as if the creature already knew he'd been beaten.

When Captain Nexus summons his power again, it isn't to attack the Hollow. The beams he generates with both hands, even his injured one, don't strike the stunned creature. Instead they snake out toward it, more like . . . tendrils. They wrap first around its arms, then wind across the Hollow's waist, its torso, even its face and mouth, like gray bandages that cover and embrace the creature's black form.

The Hollow looks mummified.

The tendrils aren't just inside the panels, either. They surround them. Every gutter isn't simply a white space between two panels, it's a gray tendril, suffocating the page itself, squeezing the panels like belts pulled too tight.

At first the creature is only confused. But when the Captain begins to drag the Hollow toward him, it starts to struggle. Too late. Captain Nexus clenches his teeth, determined, and tugs. The Hollow's manic eyes widen; it tries to shriek a protest.

Step by step, the Captain pulls the twisting monster across the high plateau. When the Hollow is halfway to him, Captain Nexus begins to pace forward, closing the space between them even faster by wrestling with the rope like a cowboy who's lassoed a steer.

The two beings meet. The Captain isn't entirely sure what he should do next. He just continues pulling the creature, clutching at the Hollow now with both hands. Hugging his enemy close. Embracing it.

And that's where it starts. Captain Nexus's injured hand

makes contact with the Hollow's leaking appendage, and the Captain begins to absorb the escaping energy. Our hero feels immediately stronger, restored.

The Hollow's eyes widen. It twists and shakes, frantic, but it's too late. The absorption picks up speed. The Hollow fades, graying out, as more and more of its essence is returned to Captain Nexus.

Returned to where it belongs, returned to where it came from in the first place.

Soon the creature that has terrorized his family is gone, and Captain Nexus feels whole again. He staggers forward. His fingers are still missing, but the wound no longer bleeds. He's himself again. No, more than himself. After all he's been through, he's stronger than ever.

With his good hand, he draws a familiar circle in the air, and a new portal opens immediately. No shimmering. No flickering.

On the other side, the Captain's family is attempting to reassemble the Nexus Turbine. Captain Nexus doesn't hesitate. He steps through, landing in the New Mexico lab. His wife hears him and spins around.

"Bruce?" Carol drops some tools to the floor with a clatter. "Bruce!"

Nexus Boy charges forward. "Dad!"

Captain Nexus scoops up his son. The rest of the team follows. On the last page, the whole family embraces.

Hugh checks over the Captain's shoulder, peering into the still-open portal. "The Hollow?"

"It's over," Captain Nexus tells him. "That awful thing . . . it can't hurt us anymore."

- 53 -

"Just a few minutes, okay?" the nurse tells me. "I'll be right outside if you need me." She shuts the door, leaving me alone with Nate and the beeping, blinking machines surrounding him.

It's been over a month since I was last allowed to visit, for Nate's birthday party, but not all that much has changed. IVs still drip into his arm. His blankets are the same shades of blue and white. One of those meters that measure your pulse and temperature clings to his index finger. The nurse at my regular doctor's explained how it worked last winter, when I had the flu and missed almost a whole week of school. The only thing that's really different is all the chairs are gone, like everyone's already deserted him. Nate's more alone than ever.

Now that I'm here, I realize I don't have a firm plan. I mean, I asked to visit because #16 came out this week, and, sure, I brought it to show it to Nate, maybe read it to him, but right now I can't move. I think it's because, even though everyone keeps saying there's still a chance Nate might wake up, I know why I'm really here. It's to say goodbye to my best friend, and I don't want that to actually be happening. If I stay here, in the corner, like I'm trying to hide from being picked for the square dance, if I don't take another step forward, maybe I can keep it from being real.

I thought I could save Nate with a comic. First the one me and my friends were working on, and then, even better I assumed, *Captain Nexus and the Nexus Five* #16. Because in comics, the heroes don't die. Hardly ever. Or if they do, they always come back. Because their name's on the cover, because it's their story, because they're the ones with the power to save everyone else. But this isn't a comic book and there are no heroes in this story, just a bunch of ordinary people like me.

I don't know how long I stand there, wedging myself deeper into the corner, almost hyperventilating, before I realize I'm wasting the little bit of time I have left with Nate. I take one last deep breath. I'm ready. I have to be.

I start with one cautious step toward his bed, then another. Finally I will my legs to carry me all the way across the room, because I can't keep telling myself that things that are real aren't.

"We met George Sanderson," I tell Nate when I reach his bed. I hold up #16. "Did Ollie tell you we helped him finish the last issue?"

Nate's chest rises just a little, then falls again.

"Seriously, my dad drove us out to Brooksburgh every day for a week. I think maybe we saved *Captain Nexus*, if you can believe that. George Sanderson might not have finished the series without us."

A machine beeps. Above Nate's head, a glowing 74 flashes to 75, then drops to 74 again. I try not to stare at the numbers. They don't mean anything anyway.

"We won the championship, too. You should've seen the guys." I sigh and look down at my shoelaces. "I almost quit, you know. Mom wouldn't let me. I'm so glad, because it would've been really dumb. I kinda blamed myself for, you know . . ." I point at Nate's head, as if he can see me. "But Mr. Sanderson, he had an accident in his past, too, and he beat himself up for a long time about it. It's . . . I don't think that's such a good thing to do."

Nate doesn't want to hear your whining, I tell myself.

"Anyway, the Giants! Sally played third, and Jake was at first—you should've seen, he blew out his UCL"—I run my finger down my elbow like Kurt did—"but the Tigers had no idea. And, oh, man, did anybody tell you I pitched? Sidearm, baby, just like you taught me."

I make my pitching motion right there in his room. There's a double *beep-beep* from one of the machines. I freeze for a second, but nothing else changes. Nate doesn't move. The glowing numbers stay the same.

"Your brother sketched me in that stupid, awesome book of his. Did you know about that? It kind of saved me. Kept me from giving up, anyway. And man, I wish you could've hung out with Courtney like we've been doing. She's actually pretty cool. You know she messed up that Sasquatch *Alpha Flight* but I didn't even care?"

I lift #16 again. "I mean, I still think they're awesome, but also, they're just comics."

I should be reading it to him. Captain Nexus, the Blue Witch, they're the heroes, the ones with powers, the ones who Nate would want to hear about. What happened to them, how the series ended, that's the important stuff. Instead I'm blabbing on and on about our friends and parents.

The ordinary people. One of the machines starts beeping a little faster, and so does my heart. Ordinary. Maybe. I remember back to all those times Nate told me it wasn't powers that made someone a superhero. It was the things they did, every day.

I set the comic on the table next to him. He doesn't need me to read that story to him. I tell him about the tournament games instead, Jake's curveballs, Craig's incredible catch, my homer, Kurt diving for that last ball, how it bounced off my other friends and ended up in my glove for the final out. I tell Nate about all those days in the Hoffmans' office, the whiteboard, Ollie's art, Courtney's words. All her questions about baseball, Ollie winning the contest. George Sanderson's studio, the Art Coop.

"I have to say, it was really cool to pitch. I felt so tall out there. Did you always feel that tall?" I take a breath and keep going. "You know, I didn't pitch sidearm at first. But Mr. Sanderson . . . he told me the ones closest to us never really leave us. He told me to close my eyes, and I did, and it was you, Nate. I heard your voice telling me to pitch sidearm. It worked. Thanks."

I stop talking for a second and stare down into Nate's face. It would be so great to see him happy to hear that, a little smile maybe, anything, but he doesn't move an inch.

I close my eyes. I know it's the last time I'll use my telepathy with Nate, that I'll talk to him without talking, so I try to tell him everything I should've said a long time ago.

I tell Nate how much I liked knowing him. I thank him for being my friend for so long, for picking me out that first baseball practice after I moved to Mira, when I didn't know anybody and Coach told us to pair up. I go over more memories, practices and pranks and jokes, our days out at the bike trail, nights reading comics in his basement.

"Keep talking to me, okay?" I ask Nate out loud. "I know you have to go soon, but you don't have to leave all the way. Promise?"

I look straight into Nate's closed eyes and tap my finger to my nose. He doesn't budge.

It's too much. I have to blink a bunch because I'm starting to cry. I can't help it. I wipe at my leaking eyes with my sleeve and turn away. I need to sit down and breathe, but there are no chairs in here.

I stumble toward the door and stagger into the hall. There's a chair right outside the room. I fall into it. Head down, I start crying harder, heavy sobs like a blubbering idiot. A loud beeping sounds out, but it's not from inside Nate's room. It's coming from the nurse's station.

The nurse looks up at me at the same time I look at her. She touches something on the screens in front of her and the beeping stops. She seems a little annoyed for about a second before she notices me crying. Her expression softens.

She gets up out of her chair and comes over to me. She rests a hand on my head and pulls me close. "Oh, honey," she says. "I know it's hard. I'm so sorry."

The nurse steps back. Her voice changes a little. "But listen, those meters are really important. You shouldn't touch them, all right? If you move them like that, we won't be able to keep track of how your friend's doing. And that's our job."

She pats my hand one more time, then turns into Nate's room. I sit there rubbing tears out of my eyes and wondering about what she just said. Meters? What's she talking about? I didn't touch anything.

Behind me, she's making noises in the room. I hear her mutter, "Now how did this get all tangled?"

I stand up.

Bracing one hand on the doorframe, I peer into Nate's room again. The nurse has her back turned, and she's playing with some wires attached to one of the machines, but that isn't what I stare at. It isn't what makes my stomach flip and my heart pound and my hand start to shake.

The meter that was attached to Nate's finger—temperature and pulse—is loose, dangling off the side of his bed. Something's still hooked up, though, because a beeping starts again, from inside the room this time. Above Nate's head, the glowing 74 turns to a 75. Then a 76. 77. 78.

One of Nate's feet has snuck out from under the blanket.

Nate's elbow is bent.

Nate's head is turned toward me. His eyes flutter.

And Nate's finger?

It's touching his nose.

ACKNOWLEDGMENTS

Whether you're reading them or writing them (or maybe even if you just stare really hard at them on the shelf; I haven't tried that one yet), books always teach you the best kinds of lessons. *Dan Unmasked* showed me that friendship is a superpower, for sure, but this book also taught me lots of other things, too. Things like not all heroes wear capes, and a hero is nothing without his team.

My super team starts with my amazing agent, Alyssa Jennette. With your patience, integrity, and constant belief in this project, you created the space it needed to fly on its own. But it never would've gotten off the ground with the ending I gave it in those earliest drafts, and I'm so grateful to you for pushing me to find the right finish to this story we both love so much.

Elizabeth Lynch, my editor, quickly assumed the mantle of steady leader of this team of ours. Your passion and excitement put a roof over this book's head and gave it the perfect home. Harper Children's became *Dan Unmasked*'s not-so-secret headquarters. Your editorial guidance, your professionalism and expertise, have made this book so much more than it was when you first read it. Thanks, Elizabeth, for believing in Dan and his friends, and thanks also to the rest of the team at Harper Children's for all the hard work you put into making this book live and breathe: Chris Kwon, Craig Phillips, Shona McCarthy, Valerie Shea, Erin Wallace, and Vaishali Nayak.

Dan Unmasked's adventure wouldn't be complete without a retelling of one of its many origins: the time Emily Carpenter read one of my early flash fiction pieces, about boys and baseball, and suggested maybe I had the right voice for a full novel with those types of characters. Sometimes superpowers come in words, the right encouragement at the right time. You also read this book more than once, helping me steer it toward what it became. I can't thank you enough for our years of critique partnership and friendship.

Then there's the rest of my "Rojo" squad, a super team in and of itself: Becky Albertalli, Manda Pullen, and George

Weinstein, writers and friends who constantly prop up and encourage not just me, but other writers all over Atlanta and everywhere. Heroes, all of you, for the countless hours of support and words of encouragement over baskets of tortilla chips and the occasional margarita. Thank you also for the early reads of this book, and the smart comments that pushed it in the proper directions.

Jane Haessler, JD Jordan, and Ellie Jordan are the kinds of heroes who think nothing of opening their doors to provide a hideout, a place you can spend time rebuilding your strength enough to head out to face the lurking villains again. Thank you for inviting me and other writers into your homes to allow us to read five or ten pages at a time, for the snacks and the wine and the good times.

Much gratitude to the Forsyth County Library for forming and hosting a writers' group closer to home, one that blossomed into a huge team with many talented folks who quickly became friends and who have helped shape my stories these past few years. It's a testament to the quality of your feedback that this group has grown and grown, becoming so large I can't name everyone. The super folks who read the most of this particular book were Toni Bellon, Neil Benson, Nicole Collier Harp, Dell Isham, Justin Joseph, Leo Penha, Meg Robinson, Rich Smith, and Michelle Thompkins.

To the members of the Atlanta Writers Club's Roswell critique group: you were the first people I shared my writing with. You didn't chase me away, instead giving me the space I needed to learn and evolve. Thank you to talented writers like Gaby Anderson, Susan Ehtesham-Zadeh, Roger Johns, Kathy Nichols, Jerry Singer, Trisha Slay, and many others.

Speaking of the Forsyth County Library and the Atlanta Writers Club, thank you to the selfless volunteers who care enough about writing and reading to keep those types of groups humming along through thick and thin. People like Kim Ottensen at my local library, George Weinstein at the Atlanta Writers Club, and Scott Thompson at the Grand Central Review, who gave me my first publishing credit and has supported my work from afar for longer than seems reasonable.

Dan Unmasked was just a few chapters and a whole lot of ideas in my head the summer I traveled to the Yale Writers' Workshop and met and was inspired by people like Kirsten Bakis and Ivy Knight. That week of immersion helped set this book on the course it would eventually travel.

My parents, of course. My mom, Joyce, who never failed to ask what was happening with this book, through all the ups and downs of the publishing journey. A tireless and selfless hero who has gone from taking care of my father to my sister to my aunt to everyone else. I wouldn't have survived this long process without the perseverance I learned from you. And my dad, Al, who isn't here to see this book go out into the world, but I know is watching anyway. Love to you, both.

My sisters, Lisa and Laura, had to endure my very first stories on the way to our grandmother's, when, to ease their concern about leaving them alone, I would tell them about the parties our dogs were throwing back home while we were away; the guests a whole host of characters I conjured in my head. I think maybe there was a bulldog named Brutus. Do I have that right? As I write these stories now, I'm still just telling you guys tall tales from the back of our station wagon, no matter how far apart we might seem.

All the rest of my family, too, nieces and nephews and in-laws and aunts and uncles and grandparents and stepfathers. In the end, this book ends up being quite a bit about family. I couldn't have pulled it off if I didn't have such a great one. That goes for my friends, too. The ones I know now and the ones I knew when I was Dan's age. Because friendship is a superpower, and I don't think I would understand that without all of you teaching it to me through the years.

Finally, to my wife, Mary, the biggest, most selfless hero

of them all. You saved this book by saving me a long time ago. And the amazing thing is you keep doing it, every single day; always there for me, always supporting me, always daring me to reach for my dreams because I see you doing the very same thing. I keep checking the closet for your cape. I haven't found it yet, and maybe I never will. Because not all heroes wear capes. We know that now, right?